Y

AUTHOR MITCHELL, J	CLASS AF A
TITLE Dead Ernest	No
	01361755

DEAD
ERNEST

DEAD ERNEST

James Mitchell

HAMISH HAMILTON : LONDON

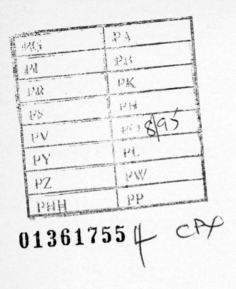

First published in Great Britain 1986
by Hamish Hamilton Ltd
Garden House 57–59 Long Acre London WC2E 9JZ

British Library Cataloguing in Publication Data

Mitchell, James, *1926–*
   Dead Ernest.
   I. Title
   823.914[F]   PR6063.I793

   ISBN 0-241-11832-8

Typeset by Tradespools Ltd
Printed in Great Britain
by Billing and Sons Ltd, Worcester

To David Lees

1

Brown's Hotel in Mayfair is a nice place to have coffee. Nice drawing room, nice waiters, nice coffee. And two entrances: one in Dover Street, one in Albemarle Street. That's the nicest thing of all. With two entrances you don't feel trapped. Maybe that's why this other geezer had chosen it – as he was entitled to do. After all he was paying for the coffee. I walked past the agents and casting directors and account directors who keep Brown's busy and into profit, and a long thin geezer shot out of a chintz covered chair like he was Marvo the human cannon ball, and said: 'Mr. Hogget?' then added 'Mr. Ronald Hogget?' as if there were fifty Hoggets there at least and he had to be careful he was talking to just the right one.

'That's me,' I said, and he sat down as fast as he'd got up. Like I'd tripped him. I sat down facing him and looked him over, but not so's he'd notice. Like I say: tall, skinny. Badly kept, expensive clothes. Dandruff. By no means the best blind date I'd ever had, but this was business after all.

'Nice of you to turn up so promptly,' he said. 'Somehow I don't think you'll regret it.' He signalled to the waiter for coffee.

'That's nice,' I said. 'What's it all about, Mr. Thomson?'

He shifted in his chair as if he didn't like it, which was funny. It was a nice chair. Comfortable. But he looked as if he wanted something in black hide that swivelled, and a desk and a row of buttons so he could push one and say, 'Fetch me the Hogget file.'

He opened his mouth to speak but just then the waiter came over and he brought his hands together and sat and watched until the waiter went away. By then I'd decided he was a solicitor – God knows why. I'd also decided that his name

1

wasn't Thomson, and that he was a crook. That he was bent I was certain of. I have to be, or I'd be out of business. Private Detection's what I do – of a special sort of kind – and I've got nothing against working for crooks. It's just I usually have to take extra precautions about getting paid when one hires me.

At last, Thomson said: 'I gather you're an expert on finding things.'

You know I am, I thought. Or you wouldn't be here. Also you've seen my photograph – or how else would you recognise me straight off? And I don't have my picture taken all that often. I'm the shy type.

'That's right,' I said. He poured coffee.

'And that you have a remarkably high success rate.'

'Right again.'

He frowned at that, as if he'd have preferred me to be modest about it, but what's the sense in being modest when you charge the fees I do?

'It is of course understood that what you are asked to do will be treated as confidential?'

'So long as it's legal.'

'Ah,' he said, and picked up a biscuit, bit into it with large yellow teeth and sprayed his trouser legs with crumbs.

'It would depend on your definition of legality,' he said at last. I waited. I wanted to know his.

'The lady whom I'm representing has mislaid two pieces of property,' said Thomson. 'She wants them back.'

'You mean they were stolen from her?'

'One was, certainly.'

'And the other?'

'It was probably – shall we say – enticed away from her. The lady wishes those two pieces of property returned. Without reference to the police.'

'Fair enough.'

'You find that acceptable?'

'Provided that she can show me that the things she lost really belonged to her. I don't find things that haven't been lost.' Well, not any more, I thought. Well, not often.

'That will not be a problem,' Thomson said.

'Then if you'll tell me what's missing, I'll tell you what it'll cost your lady friend.'

2

'I'm afraid it isn't that simple,' he said. 'The lady would very much prefer to see you herself – provided I'm satisfied you're the man for the job.'

'And are you? Satisfied, I mean?'

'My investigations show you to be resourceful, unscrupulous and cunning. Although you are not perhaps the bravest man in London.'

You've been reading my fan-mail, I thought.

'You should do admirably,' he said. 'I'll telephone the lady and tell her so. You can fly over to visit her tomorrow.'

'Fly?'

'She lives in the Republic of Ireland.'

'I'll need a retainer,' I said. 'And expenses.'

'Certainly.' He didn't like it, but he said it.

'The retainer will be five hundred pounds,' I said. 'Non-returnable.'

'Rather high, surely?'

'Depends how badly the lady wants her stuff back.'

'Very well,' said Thomson.

'You better tell her that my minimum fee if I take the job will be two thousand quid. I'll give her a better idea of what the job's worth when I know what it is. Only you better tell her I hardly ever charge the minimum.'

'I'll tell her,' he said, and looked round for the waiter. End of meeting. 'The lady is Mrs. Imogen Courtenay-Lithgoe,' he added. 'Concannon House, County Meath. Please don't write it down.'

I hadn't even reached for a notebook. He waved again for the waiter, but without success. The waiter knew a bad tipper when he saw one.

'Just one more thing,' I said. 'My retainer.'

He opened a briefcase, took out an envelope, handed it to me, and looked sad. Money was leaving him, going to me. I was causing pain. All the same I looked in the envelope and counted the notes inside it. Ten of them, at fifty pounds apiece. He really had found out all about me. 'Plus the air fare,' I said. Another envelope, with the price of a club class flight: more pain.

'That's it then,' I said, and got to my feet. Then, because the knowledge was important to me, I asked: 'Oh, by the way, would you say this job was dangerous?'

He smiled. I could see the pieces of biscuit still lodged between his teeth. 'I should describe the degree of danger as not incommensurate with the fees you charge,' he said.

I knew already that Thomson was a crook. Later I found out he was a liar as well.

*

I went to see Dave, and not only because he was the only geezer I knew who could tell me what incommensurate meant without reaching for a dictionary. He could tell me about County Meath as well, and where to find out about a bird with a name like Imogen Courtenay-Lithgoe.

Drives a mini-cab does Dave. A while back he and I both made a packet doing a job for a bent American geezer. The job went wrong but I didn't. We both came out of it with what is known as a tidy sum, only I hung on to mine and Dave didn't. What I put it down to is education. Dave went to university and I didn't, which means I still think money's important. Dave doesn't give a damn. He got through five thousand quid in three months, then went back to mini-cabbing. Before the mini-cabs he was in the paras on account of he'd studied English Literature and after that all you were fit for was teaching, and he didn't fancy it. Said he preferred duffing grown-ups.

*

So I went to the 'Mason's Arms' in Fulham, and there he was drinking a lager and reading a book. Always a book with Dave. He hardly ever opens a newspaper, all the time I've known him. I bought him another lager and a gin and tonic for myself, and told him my troubles.

'So you've got a job,' he said.

'Who knows?' I said. 'I've got a free trip to Ireland.'

He told me what incommensurate meant.

'Ta,' I said, but I didn't mean it. Sounded like it might be

4

dodgy. I didn't know the half. 'Now about this double-barrelled bird – '

'You know a bloke who can tell you anything about anybody,' Dave said.

I did, too. His name's Horace Lumley and he's worth his weight in gold, only his weight in gold it just about what he charges. I never use him till there's an expense account and the client's desperate. . . . Like I say, Dave's got no head for money.

'Or she may be on a newspaper file,' he said

'Go on,' I said.

'Like if she ever made a story or two – or maybe only one if it was big enough – they'd open up a file on her. You know – cuttings.'

'Say no more,' I said, and gave him a tenner.

'What's this for?' said Dave.

'What the coppers used to call information received,' I said. 'I'm obliged.'

'It's far too much,' said Dave.

It wasn't even ten per cent of what Lumley would have charged me.

'Take it,' I said. 'And don't spend it all on books.'

Then I made a phone call and got lucky again. Michael Copland was in. He even invited me to lunch. At 'L'Epicure', it was, in Soho. But it didn't worry him. He had an expense account.

Michael Copland isn't a mate, on account of we live in two different worlds. He works for a gossip column on one of the nationals, and he wouldn't go near Fulham, which is where Dave and I lived, even if little green men from Outer Space were landing there. On the other hand I had done him a favour. Not all that long ago either. A pop-star's girl-friend had gone missing and he put me on to find her. I found her all right. She was working on a check-out at Tesco's in Bootle. She reckoned it was the closest she could get to God. Michael had a two day exclusive with her before the rest of Fleet Street caught up, and he's still grateful.

Over the pâté he said, 'Imogen Courtenay-Lithgoe? Rings a bell. Rather a distant one, alas.' Over the Steak Aphrodite it was, 'I *know* I've heard that name.' Then with the cheese (I had profiteroles) he said, 'Dammit I'm sure I've heard of her. Let's have some coffee and we'll go and look in the library.' Coffee of course meant brandy as well and a cigar for him because I don't smoke. In the taxi to Fleet Street he said, 'You wouldn't care to tell me why, I suppose?' and I said, 'Not yet,' because I believe that people should be given hope.

And downstairs in the basement of his paper there it all was in a big, fat envelope. Her name in those days had been Imogen Klammer and she'd been married to, and separated from, a German-Swiss industrialist. Despite the separation he'd continued to support her in a manner that you or I – or anybody else in their right minds – would like to be accustomed to. Then she'd got involved with an Arab of the oil-millionaire variety. Or maybe it was billionaire. Name of Idris Majlis. And this Idris geezer had, as they say, showered her with gifts. A Roller, sable coat, diamonds, sapphires, emeralds, a brood mare and a stallion, flat in Mayfair, a castle in Spain (no kidding). And if you're wondering why then you haven't seen her picture. She was the most perfect English rose you ever saw and sexy with it. . . . only she wasn't having any. Not with this Idris geezer.

So in the end he got fed up and went round to her flat in Mayfair – the one he'd paid for – to ask for his jewellery back. Only being a bloke with a bit of common he'd got a fair idea of what she was like, so he took his bodyguard with him. So there was our heroine – all alone in her flat – when these two hulking great sons of the desert come calling – and what does she do? She shoots the bodyguard with his own gun – in the backside – then just to round off her day gives her friend Idris a belting then chases him out of the flat, which was very tactful of her as it happens, on account of he had diplomatic immunity. When the judge comes to ask her how she was able to do it she says a girl on her own has to know how to look after herself so she'd been taking karate lessons. The judge finished up congratulating her and she kept all her loot. Funny thing was Idris still kept asking her to marry him. . . . There were lots of clippings about her, and lots of photos. Ten years ago that was. She didn't look as if she knew what violence was. . . . There was a picture of her solicitor, too. That was Thomson all right – but his name wasn't Thomson of course. Even then he looked as if he'd got dandruff.

There were only three more items after that. One was a bit in a gossip column – to say she'd divorced from this Klammer geezer. Nobody seemed to know how much he'd paid her, which annoyed all the scribes no end, but the buzz was around five million Swiss francs. The thick end of two million quid, say.

Next she up and got married again, to Aylmer Courtenay-Lithgoe. Horse trainer, he was. Jumpers. He'd trained three Grand National winners. From what I gathered he'd never given her a thing – except the time of her life – until he'd killed himself going over a post and rails on a day out with the Pytchley. That was the third item. . . .

Fox-hunting's always seemed barmy to me. Cold, uncomfortable and dangerous. Silly, too. If foxes are all that much of a nuisance, why not just shoot them? A good hunter can cost thousands. How much does a bullet cost? Anyway Imogen suddenly found out what bereavement means – just like me when my old man killed my mum – and dropped out, so to speak. Didn't shoot anyone, didn't duff anyone. . . . Until she suddenly took it into her head to send for me.

2

Concannon House is – or was – enormous. Most of it's fallen down of course, but even the bit left standing's big enough to house me and all my friends. There aren't any Earls of Concannon, not any more, but while there were, they were into building. Heavily. Buildings, betting and booze were just about what destroyed the Irish aristocracy, Dave says, but by the look of what's left it must have been good while it lasted. Concannon House was mostly Georgian, a massive middle part with two wings, but dry rot got one wing and the IRA the other, and even bits of the middle were beginning to look dodgy, but even so. . . . I eased up the Volvo I'd hired in Dublin and took a closer look. (Good car, a Volvo. Shows you're serious. Sometimes a Merc can seem a bit flash.) The ruined wings had mostly been bull-dozed away and there were flowers and shrubs growing, but here and there a pillar had been left standing, or a bit of marble floor. In front was mostly lawn: smooth-shaven, elegant, expensive. Must have cost a fortune. And behind and in the distance, fields with horses. By the look of them any one of the horses cost more than the lawn.

I drove up to the house. A ten year old Rolls-Royce was parked by the door. It made the Volvo look like a peasant, and I wondered if Idris knew how nicely she was looking after it, then I went up the stairs, taking my time, on account of I wanted to see what sort of electronic stuff she had to guard the house. It was the best.

I rang the bell and a butler appeared and managed to look at me without sneering, but it was a struggle. Big geezer he was, black eyes, snub hooter, iron-grey hair cut more or less at random.

'Name of Hogget,' I said. 'I'm expected'

He looked at me again. He was comparing me with the photograph he'd been shown. 'You can come in,' he said. 'I'll do what I can.'

He didn't sound hopeful, but he let me inside.

I stood in the hall and had a look see. Painted ceiling, very nice; some real Hepplewhite and a lot of Irish copies of the same period, a Hafiz rug, the biggest I'd ever seen, and some paintings I could have done with a closer look at: what could have been a Stubbs, a Wilson, a Toulouse-Lautrec and a Van Dyck. The possible Stubbs was all horses, the possible Toulouse-Lautrec a jockey and a racehorse, the possible Van Dyck a mounted cavalier. But I didn't have a chance to get any closer on account of the drawing-room door opened before the butler could get to it and a man and a woman came out.

The man was tall, limped a bit, pushing seventy. Very elegant, but not flashing it. What they call unobtrusive. Ex-army officer written all over him. A golden labrador padded along beside him. The woman was Mrs. Imogen Courtenay-Lithgoe, no question, except she looked like only four years had gone by since the photographs I'd seen of her rather than ten. Hair really the colour of gold – not sovereigns – more like the pale kind the Swiss sometimes use for watches: eyes as blue as lapis-lazuli, straight little nose, mouth luscious and small. And a figure that came straight out of fantasy. She wore a white dress with a blue design, I remember, and her arms and face showed a tan like fino sherry, and it was Ireland in September. In that great hall it was more like February. All the same I found myself wondering how much of her was that fino sherry colour and what the rest of her would be like, then told myself it wouldn't do at all. I was there to earn.

'This feller claims he's Mr. Hogget,' the butler said.

'Berk,' she said, and I jumped. Such language from those lovely lips. Then she said it again, sort of reproving, and it dawned on me it was his name.

'Burke,' she said, 'of course it's Mr. Hogget. Why should he say it was if it wasn't?'

I knew there was an insult buried in there somewhere, but her voice was as lovely as the rest of her, low-pitched and caressing, and anyway she sort of floated up to me and offered me her hand. I took it like it was Meissen, and said 'How d'you do?' and tried not to shuffle my feet.

'I'm Imogen Courtenay-Lithgoe,' she said. 'This is my father, General Berkeley. Sir Robert Berkeley, actually.'

His daughter's file had a few pieces about him, too. M.C. as a subaltern in World War Two; mentioned in despatches in Korea, knighted on his retirement because, Michael Copeland said, there happened to be a knighthood going spare.

I tried another 'How d'you do?' but it didn't go down well.

"Got to rush I'm afraid,' said the general. 'Chap I've got to see.' He turned to Burke. 'Has Finbar got his uniform on?'

'He has, sir,' Burke said.

'Then tell him to get out to the bloody car or I'll drive the bugger myself.' He snapped his fingers at the dog. 'Not you, Sultan,' he said, and Sultan sat, looking hurt but resigned. The general nodded at me then – 'Good day to you' – and strode out. Swep' art, more like.

Mrs. Courtenay-Lithgoe said, 'Daddy's upset.'

'I thought he might be,' I said.

'We'll go into the drawing-room,' she said, and then turned to face the butler head on. 'Berk,' she said. I know it was his name, but that's the way it sounded, and anyway he sort of shimmered all over. 'Burke,' she said again, 'tell cook we'll be two for lunch.'

Then we went into the drawing-room. Big room, nice proportions. No carpet, just more Persian rugs, and a Polar bearskin in front of the fire that started me off again so I looked at the furniture instead. Robert Adam most of it, but a French ebony and ormolu commode that reminded me of one I'd found for a geezer in Austin, Texas, who'd paid 28,000 quid for it, then put it next to the central heating and cracked it. Now he really *was* a berk. Mrs. Courtenay-Lithgoe had central heating, too, but she also had humidifiers. . . . Only one picture, I noticed, but it was a Watteau.

'Whisky?' Mrs. Courtenay-Lithgoe said.

'Just a small one,' I said.

'I don't think we have any small ones,' she said, and filled me half a tumblerful.

I didn't have the nerve to ask for water or ice. She poured herself one just like mine and waved me to a chair.

10

'Mr. Whatever-he-said-his-name-was says you'll do,' she said.

'Thomson,' I said.

She ignored it. 'He's asked around. From what I hear you cut a few corners – but not with the person who hires you.'

'Not unless they cut a few corners with me,' I said.

'I won't,' she said. 'Of course everybody you work for says that. But I mean it. You'll see. Mr. What's-it says you charge high because you get results. That's O.K. too. But don't try to cheat me about money.'

I stayed quiet. I was trying my best not to think what she'd look like on that bearskin rug, and where the tan would end.

'Daddy's against it,' she said. 'That's why he was upset.'

'Why is he against it?'

She shrugged, and I wished she wouldn't. 'Honour,' she said. 'But then that's what daddy's for, so to speak. Honour. . . . Who hath it? He that died o' Wednesday.'

Dave told me later she was quoting Shakespeare: Henry IV Part One he said it was.

'And what are you for, Mrs. Courtenay-Lithgoe?' I said.

She looked at me then. I'd asked the right question. For the first time she was taking me seriously.

'Good question,' she said. 'I'm for all this.' She waved her hand. It took in not only the French commode and the Watteau, but the pictures in the hall, the rug, the horses in the paddock. 'And it costs money, Mr. Hogget. I'm for money.'

'You want me to find you some?'

'I take care of that,' she said, and grinned, not smiled. 'I don't think you have the build for my technique.' The grin vanished. 'No, Mr. Hogget. What I want you to do is find two – creatures.'

I hoped to God it wasn't kids. I hate looking for tug-of-love kids. Mind you nothing had been said about her being a mum, but in my game you never know.

'Creatures?' I said.

'A man, and a horse,' she said. 'The horse is rather important.'

So help me God that's what she said.

'Not the man?'

'Oh yes,' she said. 'He's quite important, too. As a matter of

11

fact he's my fiancé. His name is Ernest Fluck.'

I didn't laugh, but it was a damn near thing and she saw it.

'Yes, I know,' she said. 'I'll be Imogen Fluck once you find him, so he must be important, mustn't he?'

'What was the name of the horse?' I said.

'Finn MacCool,' she said. Name of an ancient Irish king, Dave says. 'Bay, just on sixteen hands, white sock on the off-fore. White blaze on the face.'

'Valuable?'

'Ah-ha,' she said. 'You've been reading the newspapers, Stallions worth millions. Kidnapped for ransom. This one's a gelding, Mr. Hogget. He may be named after a king, but he's lost his crown jewels.'

I found I was blushing. Looking like she did, she had no business talking common.

'On a good day I might get a couple of thousand for him,' she said.

'Then why was he stolen? Why is he important?'

'Because it is possible – it's by no means certain but it really is possible, – that in five or six years time he'll win the Grand National.'

'But if he does, you'll recognise him,' I said. 'You'll recognise him even if he's only entered.'

'I don't want you to analyse the situation,' she said. 'I just want you to find him.'

'Sometimes I have to do both,' I said.

'I want him back,' she said. 'It was Aylmer who spotted him. I want him back.'

I might get him back for you, I thought. I can't make him win the National. . . .

There was a piano in the corner of the room. Very pre-war it was. Fringed silk shawl and photographs in silver frames. General Berkeley being nostalgic, I thought.

'Got a photograph of Mr. Fluck?' I said.

'*Don't call him that.*' She yelled the words, then said more softly: 'I'm sorry. That's stupid. What else could you call him?' She put her hand to her hair. 'Not here,' she said. 'I don't have one here.'

'Your father doesn't approve of him?'

'Well, well,' she said. 'Intuitive as well as shrewd.'

'Why doesn't he, Mrs. Courtenay-Lithgoe?'

'Ernest is – rather vulgar,' she said. 'He doesn't ride.'

'I'm being nosey because it's the only way,' I said. 'So excuse the question. . . . Is he rich?'

'Not at all,' she said, and her voice showed no resentment. 'But it's of no importance, because I am.'

'What does he do for a living?'

'Engineer,' she said. 'I don't mean spanners and oily rags. He wears a suit and has an office. Electronics.'

'Where?'

'Wembley,' she said.

'Where did you meet him?'

'Wembley,' she said again. 'I was going to a Jumping Event there. I drove myself and I really shouldn't. – I'm a rotten driver. I nearly knocked him over. It all started from there.'

'Was he staying here when he disappeared?'

The butler came in and announced lunch.

'In five minutes,' she said, then added: 'Burke.'

Again the butler produced that shimmering effect before he left.

'I have a flat in Dublin,' she said. 'He stays there.'

'Because of your father?'

She nodded. 'Let's have some lunch,' she said.

I was glad to leave my Scotch behind. She took hers with her.

*

Lunch was game soup and grilled trout, a lot of different kinds of cheese, and chocolates. There was an Alsace Sylvaner to drink: a good one. We couldn't talk much business on account of butler Burke, but when we left the dining-room (nice Chippendale, a couple of William IV carvers, two Dutch genre pictures, 17th century – very tasty) and back to the drawing-room, I started in again. We both had coffee and she had brandy. Not me. . . .

She had no inhibitions about telling me things. Maybe it was the drink that did it. Maybe she was just built that way. What it amounted to was this: three days ago she'd driven

13

herself over to Dublin (chancing her luck again) – and when she'd got there he'd been carried off. I asked her couldn't he just have scarpered and she wouldn't hear of it and I must admit it didn't seem likely: a bird with looks like that *and* money, and him just a forty four year old electronics engineer, even if he did have his own office. I asked her if he'd packed and she said just an overnight bag, most of his stuff was still there; and that was good news for me. At least I had something to look at.

So she'd driven back to Concannon House and her father the general met her all of a tizz to say that Finn MacCool was missing, and it could only have been within the last few hours because Finbar Gleason had shod him that morning. (Gleason doubled as chauffeur and blacksmith, or more properly farrier.) The general remembered he'd also seen a loose-box towed by a Ford Granada and that they were both ones he didn't recognise, which meant they were driven by strangers. Bit later still, Burke said a bloke called Dr. Schmidt had phoned and asked for Mrs. Courtenay-Lithgoe, and Burke had said she was out and where should she call back and Schmidt said the Shelburne. Only when she did call back and Shelburne had no Dr. Schmidts: no Schmidts of any kind. And that had seemed significant, didn't I think? . . . What I thought was that Schmidt is German for Smith, and it was even worse than Thomson.

I said aloud: 'Have you told the police?'

'No,' she said. 'You and Mr. What's-his-name are the only ones, and even he doesn't know as much as you do.'

'Why haven't you told them?'

'Because I don't want publicity. I want them back.'

'On account of your father?'

'On account of me. I've had enough publicity to last a lifetime. Surely you must know that?'

I took her point.

'I'll have to talk to your butler,' I said. 'Then I'll need to see your flat in Dublin.' Nosing about among her possessions would be far easier than asking questions – if she'd let me. She didn't hesitate.

'I'll tell Burke to arrange it,' she said. 'Look at everything you want. That will save me having to explain things.

14

Explanations can be embarrassing sometimes. . . . And I've got some horses to look at anyway.'

The way she said it, that was far more important than finding Ernest Fluck, but not nearly so important as finding Finn MacCool.

*

Burke, when he came, was polite, friendly almost. Maybe it was because he'd got the idea that I'd fixed it so that Mrs. Courtenay-Lithgoe wasn't present. I took him through his story and it was just as I'd heard it told. First the phone call from this Dr. Schmidt geezer. Very heavy German accent he said. Like those comics on the telly when they're being psychiatrists or Nazis or something. That made me ask if it could have been a put on and he said it could indeed, so then I said on the other hand it might have been a *real* heavy German accent and he said by God I'd got a grip on the thing. I left it at that, and we talked about the loose-box and the Ford Granada, but not for long, because he hadn't seen either of them.

That left the horse. The general had had a cup of tea about four o'clock, then taken it into his head to put a leg over Finn MacCool, so he'd gone upstairs to change and told Burke to have the horse saddled, so Burke had phoned Finbar Gleason in the harness room, Burke being an inside man and Gleason the C.O. of the outside men. And Gleason had sent a groom to the South Paddock and the groom had come back and said the horse had gone, and Gleason had cursed him and gone to see for himself and it was true. No Finn MacCool. No gaps in the fence either, though they'd searched in every direction, even so. But no horse. I saw I'd have to see Gleason later, but in the meantime I'd better speak to the groom. But the groom and Finbar had had words and the groom had gone home in a huff, home being Kerry, if Burke's memory didn't fail him – or would it be Kildare?

I tried not to look too unhappy and asked for the key and directions to the Dublin flat, and Burke gave me both.

'Thank you, Burke,' I said.

15

This time it was me he shimmered at, but what else could I call him?

'About that name,' he said.

'What name?'

'Mine to be sure,' he said.

'Burke?'

He sighed. 'That's what *she* calls me,' he said. 'My name's O'Shaughnessy.' He paused, and I waited. Every possible move was his.

'*She* calls me Burke,' he said again, 'and I never knew why. Not for years.' He brooded a bit. 'You see I've never been out of Ireland. That's my trouble. Never felt the need. I did a bit as a boxer when I was a young man, but only so far as the Irish ABA quarter-finals. They had them in Cork that year. Fine class of a girl in Cork. Anyway I got knocked out in the second round and I gave it up. Otherwise I might have boxed for my country – travelled – learned a few things.

'Still it helped when I applied for this job. The boxing I mean. They wanted a man who could handle himself what with all them paintings. I was taken on. Two years ago. She and her father had just moved in. "Your name's Burke," says she. She could have called me Pontius Pilate the money she was offering. Double me last job.

'And from there on it was, "Burke you haven't brought the post in," or "Why is there no ice for cocktails, Burke?" Burke Burke Burke. And still the penny didn't drop. I'm not a travelled man you see. . . . Then one day a feller comes over from England with an English groom. Cockney. He told me how Berk is Cockney rhyming slang for a fool.' Burke flushed. 'It's a very rude way to call a man a fool,' he said. 'Berkshire Hunt indeed.'

'Cockney rhyming slang's like that,' I said.

He was too full of his grievance even to hear what I said. I tried again. 'Who was the Englishman?' I asked.

'Name of Sir Montague Redditch,' he said. 'Merchant banker. Came to buy his daughter a horse for the lepping.' This I'd already learned meant 'jumping'.

Suddenly he brightened. 'He tipped me a tenner,' he said. But the memory didn't linger. 'A while ago she decides to have a footman,' he said. 'We were doing a lot of entertaining

16

just then and I needed a bit more than a gaggle of women to help.'

'When was this?' I asked.

'Six months ago, maybe seven,' he said. 'Just after she'd met that fiancé of hers – And there's another thing,' he said. 'If my name's so funny, what about his? Anyway she phones the agency, and they sent this feller. Big, strapping lad. Once he got started I wasn't doing half the work I do now.'

'What happened?' I said.

'Aren't I telling you?' Burke snarled. 'Same as me. Exactly the same. "What's your name?" says she. "McGrath," says your man. "While you work here your name is Toole," says she. "It suits you." And what could he do about it? It's a fine old Irish name. Only the way she said it – she could make it seem – ' He shook his head, and I could see how he'd been a boxer, and a punchy one at that.

' "Can't you move any faster, Toole?" she would say. Or: "Toole, where on earth did you learn to do that?" . . . He didn't last the month – She's a lady with a funny sense of humour, Mr. Hogget. Very funny.'

I said I'd better be off to Dublin, and on the way there I realised how lucky I'd been. My name could have been meat and drink to her. Not that it means a pig by the way. A hogget's a lamb. All the same. . . . I reckoned she really must want me to work for her.

3

Leinster Terrace is behind Saint Stephen's Green. It's Georgian of course, but then so's half Dublin – only some of it's slums, and some of it's still as smart as the day it was built. 17, Leinster Terrace is the smart kind. Neat little bricks, sash windows, elegant fanlight, paintwork white and pillar box red, brass door knob and letter-box polished every day. I let myself in. The hall was carpeted: – nothing flash, but nothing threadbare either. Letters stacked on the hall table. Nothing for Fluck. Nothing for Courtenay-Lithgoe. I went upstairs. The one I was after was Flat C, on the first floor, so up I went. Nice door, mahogany, polished regular, and not even two deadlocks could spoil its looks. I used the keys and went in.

Concannon House is too much for me, a hundred times too much. But Flat C, 17, Leinster Terrace, would have done me a treat, only I'd have to win the Irish Sweep to afford it. Modern, fitted kitchen big enough to eat in, bedroom with canopied Regency bed and an Aubusson carpet, *and* a bathroom en suite, and the pride and joy – the living room – that ran the length of the house with an archway for a divider. Dining-room and drawing-room. Queen Anne dining-room with a Waterford crystal chandelier. Drawing-room a comfortable and elegant jumble: from George II to early Victorian. Some nice little Cotman water-colours *and* a Samuel Palmer, and a marble Apollo I'd have bet money was Graeco-Roman. Erny Fluck must have thought it was Christmas every day. . . . Wherever he was. Come on Ron, I told myself. Start earning, boy.

I began with the living-room because that's where I was, and there was Ern – or at least his photo. Tall geezer, not bad-looking. Not good-looking either. And if he hadn't got a bit of

18

a pot on him he soon would have. Of course he might have hidden depths, and I hoped he had, but he didn't look like Imogen Courtenay-Lithgoe material to me. No way. Not even if he had money, – and he hadn't, so she said. The other men in her life had all been knockouts: Klammer, Courtenay-Lithgoe, even Idris. But this geezer, he looked – well – ordinary.

More photos. A couple of Aylmer, a couple of girl-friends, the rest horses. Some with her, some without. When she was with them she was usually receiving a cup or a rosette or something. All the horses were named. That's how I found Finn MacCool. Of the two I was looking for, he was far and away the better-looking. I moved on. In the drawing-room area there was a desk with a pull-down lid. Rosewood. Early Victorian. Say six hundred quid. I opened it and looked inside. Bills. Neatly arranged. Mostly from corn chandlers, saddlers, sporting tailors, and all paid on the nail. A big one from a wine and spirit merchant, too. A whopper. I reckoned Ern or the general must shift it even more than she did. Or both. There was a diary, too. Mostly appointments. September 20th said E.F. arrives. There was no departure date. That meant he'd been there seven weeks. What sort of firm gives an employee that sort of holidays?

There was a used cheque-book there, too. Every week from the 20th September on there was an entry that read 'Cash. E.F.' Each time for a hundred quid. And she'd known it was there and she knew I would see it. The only other thing there was a list of share certificates: everything from ICI to Unit Trusts. I got out the Japanese mini-camera I always carry when I'm working, and took its picture for later, then I took a picture of Ern's picture, and then of Finn MacCool's and the client's, then I locked up the desk. Always leave the place the way you found it when you can. . . . Next I had a good feel round under the chair and sofa cushions. That brought me a lot of fluff, a piece of cork from a wine bottle and a coin about the size of a 5p piece that looked like gold only it wasn't. It was a Spanish hundred peseta piece, and at current rates of exchange it was worth maybe 45p. I kept it. I don't know why, I just did. Quick look at the books. Mostly about horses and hunting: even the novels. Surtees' 'Mr. Sponge's Sporting

Tour' – the pictures showed you what that was about. Same with 'The Experiences Of An Irish R.M.', and right next to them 'The Memoirs Of A Fox Hunting Man' by Siegfried Sassoon. . . . Lot of war books as well. Not like comics. The serious kind. More memoirs, a lot of analytical stuff, and all with the same book-plate, with 'Robert Berkeley' on it. All the books were immaculate, with three exceptions. One was a book of mathematical puzzles, one was a paperback best-seller with a tit and bum cover, and one was a hefty great brute called 'Slow Conductors: An Assessment'. This was mostly graphs, charts and mathematical formulae. All three books were grubby, greasy with use. All three bore the same signature: E. Fluck, in the neat script so many engineers use. I took photographs of that, too, and of the travel agency brochure next to it. Thomas Cook of Wembley it was. Beautiful if not specially rich people cavorting in Spain (Costa del Sol, the Balearics, Costa Blanca), or Portugal or Greece, or the Italian Riviera.

Bedroom next. Only one bed, and that a double, so they must have been cohabiting. She had the kind of nightgowns that sent my mind back to that bearskin rug: Ern reckoned that when it came to buying nightwear what was good enough for a mail-order catalogue was good enough for him. Same when it came to their other clothes. Suits and that. Hers were all Harrods or Fortnums, or Knightsbridge or Dublin boutiques. He'd gone to Marks and Sparks, and not the top of the range either. Except here and there was a nice jacket, or a dinner suit, or a bit of cashmere. All bespoke. And all with Dublin labels. There hadn't been any cheques for them. I reckon she must have used her credit card.

I went through his pockets. A comb, a nailfile, two biros, a calculator, the odd bus ticket, a lot of bits of paper with calculations on them, all of which I photographed. Nothing much else till I got to the inside pocket of the M and S suit. A brochure it was, for a gaming club up West, with an application form for membership attached. I know that club. I once helped a geezer's wife get back a necklace her husband had pledged to cover his bets there. They play high, and they like guarantors. Ern's guarantor was his ever-loving fiancée, according to the way he'd filled it in. Only he hadn't signed it, so I took its picture and put it back. The only thing left was a diary, and the only thing in it was telephone numbers. I took their picture. . . .

Undies next. Ern's were nothing to get excited about, but hers were something else. It just didn't make *sense*. I went through a pile of socks, and socks was all they were, but when I pushed them back I could feel a gap at the back of the wardrobe shelf. I tried the shelves above and below, but they fitted flush to the upright, so I eased the sock shelf forward and got my hand down the gap to where something fitted into my hand like it had been measured for it. I eased it out of the wardrobe and took a good look. It was an old fashioned Colt 38 like a miniature cannon. Naughty Erny Fluck. It was fully loaded and hadn't been used for a long time, but even so I wiped it carefully, and put it back, *exactly* as I'd found it. When it comes to guns I'm very particular. Also they scare the daylights out of me. . . .

Time for a look in the waste-bin. Very useful things, waste-bins. People chuck things in them and think they've disappeared. No way. Not with Nosey Parkers like me around. . . . Very superior class of rubbish, Mrs. Courtenay-Lithgoe's. . . . Bits of smoked salmon, empty wine bottle: Chassagne-Montrachet '79, it was: not the best year, but I couldn't see me turning it down – or Dave; what was left of a salad-vinaigrette, and not enough garlic, – not for me, anyway, but my mum was Italian; – strawberries, an empty bottle of cream, – real cosy dinner for two. Dead flowers, paper handkerchiefs, bits of brown bread – and a torn up envelope. They always tear them up. That's why I'm so good at jigsaws. Practice. Addressed to E. Fluck, Esq., at his address in Wembley. On the envelope flap there was a return address: a firm of stockbrokers in the City. No letter. Very frustrating, that was. To find out what a stockbroker, *any* stockbroker, had told E. Fluck would cost a lot of money, and maybe Imogen wouldn't want to pay.

So there it was: 'Slow Conductors: An Assessment', a Colt .38 Detective Special, application (unposted) for membership of a gambling club, and an envelope from a stockbroker, but no letter. Plus a one hundred peseta piece. So what had I got? An egg-head engineer who liked to gamble, and a doting

21

fiancée who encouraged him to do it; a nervous geezer (the .38) with an inclination to foreign travel (the travel brochure and maybe the hundred peseta piece) – if all the stuff I'd found belonged to him.

Spain's a big place, and the Italian Riviera isn't all that small. I needed a bit more than that to go on – and then suddenly I had it. At least I thought I had. Idris had given Mrs. Courtenay-Lithgoe a castle in Spain. As a place to start looking it had one enormous advantage: it was the only one I could think of. But first there were a few little things to take care of in London, and even before that I had to tell Mrs. Courtenay-Lithgoe I'd be working for her regardless of expense – her expense, that is. It seemed only fair.

By the time I got back the Roller had brought the general back from lunch, and a big, red-headed geezer in a grey suit with black buttons was giving it a going over with a chamois. Finbar Gleason in his uniform, I thought, and headed for the house, but he worked round the car as I approached and stood in my way. I moved to either side and so did he, and then I stood still. The size he was and the size I am, the next move was entirely up to him.

'The general doesn't think it's right,' said Finbar Gleason. 'What you're doing.'

I let it lie.

'His daughter's a bit upset,' he continued. 'You're taking advantage of her.'

The day I took advantage of Imogen Courtenay-Lithgoe the rivers would flow backwards, I thought. No matter how you define taking advantage. But I didn't tell him that.

'These aren't the best times for an Englishman to come snooping in Ireland,' said Finbar Gleason.

'I'll bear it in mind,' I said, and tried to move round him again, but he reached out a hand and grabbed my arm. He was strong, all right. Like the blacksmith in the poem we had to learn when I was in 4B in the Senior School;

'The muscles on his brawny arms
Stand out like iron bands.'

And his fingers nipped like pincers.

'She doesn't need to get involved,' he said. 'Why don't you

22

tell her so?'

One more nip from those fingers and I would have told him I didn't want to get involved either, but instead there was a cough from behind us, and we turned. It was Burke. Behind him, on the steps leading to the house, were Imogen Courtenay-Lithgoe and her father.

'Madam says,' Burke told me, 'that you've got to stop wasting time talking to a servant who doesn't know his place – an overweight underbrained produose who's lucky he's got a job at all – and probably won't if he goes on the way he's going.'

Finbar Gleason let go of me and eased towards Burke, who was much less impressed than I was. His fists clenched and he rose on to the balls of his feet, and he didn't back away.

'Those were her very words,' he said. 'She told me and I've said them. Show some sense, man.'

Gleason went back to polishing the car, and I followed Burke to the house. Neither the general nor his daughter were visible.

I slid a tenner from my inside pocket and when we got inside the house I shook Burke's hand and the tenner stuck to it.

'I'm obliged to you,' I said.

'I just did what I was told, sir.'

'But I liked the way you did it,' I said. 'Quick and forceful.'

'My pleasure, sir,' he said, and went into the drawing-room and announced me.

She was in the sort of riding kit called jodhpurs, and maybe one woman in a thousand looks good in that outfit, and she was the one.

'Well?' she said. Snappish she was, *and* she held a riding crop.

I made my voice soothing. 'Whatever's going on,' I said, 'I didn't start it. – But if you want to call my job off – '

'No!' This time it was a yell, the kind she would use on the hunting field. And then she spoke more softly.

'No, Mr. Hogget. I want you to go on. Will you?'

'If you want me to.'

'Well of course I – '

'Your father doesn't.'

Her fingers tightened round the riding crop and then relaxed, and when they did that *I* relaxed all over.

'My father has – ideals,' she said. 'I told you. Honour. All that.'

'What's dishonourable about finding your horse?' I said. 'Or your fiancé, come to that?'

She said, 'Forgive me, Mr. Hogget, but there's no way I can explain this without being offensive.'

'Be offensive, then,' I said. 'I can always put it on the bill.'

She didn't even hear me.

'He doesn't like my fiancé,' she said. 'And he doesn't like private detectives. He thinks that you and your methods are bound to be vulgar and offensive. Those were his exact words, Mr. Hogget.'

It seemed to be my day for hearing things verbatim, and anyway, he was right.

'He likes Finn MacCool,' I said.

'He thinks Finn MacCool is dead,' she said. 'Like Shergar.'

I remembered Shergar, the Aga Khan's Derby winner that had been taken over by a syndicate and sent to stud – then kidnapped and slaughtered. And Shergar had been worth millions.

'He could be right,' I said.

'He mustn't be,' said Imogen Courtenay-Lithgoe. And then: 'That's stupid. Of course he could be dead. But I have to know.'

'And the same goes for Mr. F – your fiancé?'

'The same goes for Ernest Fluck,' she said. 'Will you do it?'

'All right,' I said.

She sighed at that. I could name you any number of geezers who would pay good money just to watch her sigh.

'What do you do now?' she said.

'Go back to London. Ask questions,' I said. 'Then I'll come back here. Me and my assistant. . . . Then we'll see.'

'You need more money?'

'Not yet,' I said.

'If you do,' she said. 'Phone me. Whatever it is you need. Just phone.'

I shook her hand then, and she looked up into my eyes, and I knew exactly what she was doing and I hadn't a prayer.

Out in the hall the general was waiting. If he was trying to be pleasant he failed miserably. To him I was still vulgar and offensive. Always would be. All the same he did his best.

'My chap Gleason got a bit out of hand,' he said. I let it lie. 'It's because we – we have a respect for each other,' he said. 'D'you follow?'

'Yes,' I said.

'You ever in the army?' he asked.

'My father was,' I said. 'During the war.'

'What regiment?' I told him.

'Served in Italy, did he?' said the general.

'He won the Military Medal there,' I said.

'Proud of him?'

'No,' I said. 'He killed my mother.'

'Sorry,' he said. 'Sorry. Didn't mean to pry. What I was trying to establish is this. Gleason was trying to help me – you realise that?' I nodded. 'My daughter and I don't agree on this – this – '

'Snooping?' I said.

He could ignore what he didn't want to hear quite as well as his daughter.

'She's going on with it of course?' he said.

'Of course,' I said

'God damn and blast it all to hell!' he said, and stamped off up the stairs.

Burke came up, carrying my raincoat.

'Will you wear it, sir?' he asked.

'I'll carry it,' I said.

'Very good sir,' he said. 'It's a fine day still, thank God.'

It wasn't till I hung it up in the empty house in Fulham that I found the envelope in the pocket. It was the sort of envelope you keep photographs in, and photographs were what it held. Two pretty girls – a blonde and a brunette: singly or together; in a warm place far from Ireland. Sometimes they wore bikinis, sometimes summer dresses, as they laughed by a poolside, or at a barbecue, or on a yacht. I looked at the backs of the photographs. Not a bloody thing. Zippo, Zilch.

If Burke had decided to give me these pictures because I'd

bunged him a tenner, he might have thrown in a few captions as well.

*

Dave said, 'I don't think so, Ron. Thanks all the same. I haven't been on a horse for ages.'

'Can't you take a refresher course?'

'On what I earn?'

Dave's trouble is he just won't earn at all unless he has to. Lazy, is Dave, and idle with it. His idea of Shangri-La is to sit in a pub and make a lager last two hours while he reads Marcel Proust. Of course if he fancies a bird or a trip to Provence or something he has to start earning, but until then it's lager and literature. But I was ready for that.

'I'll pay,' I said. 'Or rather the client will.'

'I don't know,' he said. I put a photograph on the table.

'This is the client,' I said.

'Oh my God,' said Dave, and then: 'I sold my riding clobber.' He sounded heart-broken.

'We'll have to get you some more then,' I said.

How it would read on the expenses sheet I'd no idea, but I'd think of something. Well I'd have to. It was either that or pay for it myself.

Dave lit a cigarette by way of celebration. I don't hold with smoking, but he gets tensed up does Dave, and anyway he doesn't overdo it on account of he acts as my minder now and again. The way things are these days it's not all that more dangerous than mini-cabbing, and it pays a sight better.

I told him a few things about the client – no more than I had to because Dave's a worrier and I had a few ideas in mind that might upset him.

'A horse and a fiancé,' he said at last.

'In that order. And she would like them back in good nick.'

'What's so special about the horse?' he asked.

'I reckon it's because of her second husband,' I said. 'Aylmer Courtenay-Lithgoe.'

'What about him?'

'He bought Finn MacCool,' I said. 'Reckoned he could turn

26

him into a Grand National winner. – And she worshipped her Aylmer. She wants him to win the National for Aylmer's sake.'

'Fair enough,' said Dave. 'She loved the bloke so she wants to carry out his wishes. In Memoriam. All that. – But why would anyone steal it?'

'There you have me,' I said. He did, too, so I took out the photographs of the other birds to change the subject. Dave liked what he saw.

'Are you setting up to be a pasha or something?' he said

'Chance would be a fine thing,' I said. 'Burke the butler slipped them to me.'

'Why would he do that?'

'He must think they're important,' I said.

'How would he get hold of them?'

I shrugged. 'Maybe left by a house-guest,' I said. 'Maybe Burke overheard something he doesn't want to repeat, so he slipped me the pictures as a hint. Sort of a clue. I'm a detective after all.'

'That's a lot of maybes,' said Dave.

'It's all we've got. You recognise them?' Dave shook his head. 'Or the place where they are?'

Another headshake. 'Why not ask Burke?' he said.

'Because Burke doesn't want to talk about it. He wants to do me a favour and get the odd tenner in return, but he doesn't want anyone to say what he's done. Not even me.'

Dave looked out of the pub window. It was raining. 'I just wish I was with those birds,' he said.

'Who wouldn't?' I said. 'Take a look at the one where they're having drinks on the boat.'

Dave picked it up. 'Champagne by the look of it,' he said.

'The brunette's holding what looks like a book.'

Dave looked closer. 'More like a pamphlet of some sort,' he said.

'Good boy,' I told him, then I took out another photograph.

Photography's not a hobby with me: not really. I mean I don't go on about linear composition or social relevance or any of that, but I do *use* cameras. They're tools of the trade you might say – and far more important than guns and coshes – except for the times when you need a gun or a cosh, and then

27

I usually yell for Dave.

Anyway I'd fiddled around with the enlarger in the spare room in my house that I use as a dark-room, and I'd finally come up with something. Bit blotchy: definition lousy: – Lord Snowdon wouldn't give me the time of day, – but you could see what it was supposed to be. It was a programme with the picture of a building on the front. Weird looking building with great curving shapes above it like sails filled hard with a following wind. And under the picture was written: 'Otello': and under that: 'Giuseppe Verdi'.

'What d'you make of it?' I said.

Dave spoke at once. 'Sydney Opera House,' he said.

'That's what I thought,' I said.

'You don't sound too happy.'

'It's too far to go on a guess,' I said, and shuffled the happy snaps together. 'Go and see a man about a horse,' I said, and off he went.

4

What I did was finish my gin and tonic and put in a call to Michael Copland. It still being short of three o'clock, he was out to lunch. Langan's Brasserie this time. So I phoned him there and arranged to meet him at Fortnum and Mason's for tea. When he arrived he looked like he needed it, but then he'd just been hearing about a pop-star's current divorce, and how it all tied in with the price of cocaine.

I showed him a picture of the blonde. No bells rang. He said he preferred Imogen Courtenay-Lithgoe and I told him that wasn't the point and tried him with the brunette. That was three cherries and a fanfare, and the silver dollars cascading into the paper cup.

'You're moving in exalted circles these days, Ron,' he said.

'You know her?'

'Of course I know her.' He sounded outraged. 'It's Sabena Redditch.'

I tried to stay relaxed, and after the pop-star, Michael was too knackered to notice I wasn't.

'Redditch?' I said.

'Her father's the merchant banker. Brookes, Redditch. You must know – '

'Yeah yeah,' I said. He'd been to Concannon house, too. 'But the bird – Sabena you said? Who's she?'

'His daughter,' said Michael. 'You really haven't heard of her?'

It always baffles Michael when I don't know the people he writes about. Worries him, even. God knows why. I shook my had.

'She did all the usual,' he said. 'Nanny, expensive schools, all that. But then it's what you'd expect. It wasn't a silver

29

spoon in the mouth she was born with – hers was twenty two carats and diamond studded.'

'And then?' I said.

'Then she went to Oxford and lasted three years. Got a second what's more.'

'A what?'

'Second class honours degree,' he said. 'Only she was mad as hell she didn't get a first. That was seven or eight years ago. Since then she's kept me and the rest of the boys in work. The things she's done . . .' His voice was dreamy, almost reverent.

'What sort of things?'

He looked around the restaurant. The clientèle, eighty five per cent female, whacked into the Earl Grey and cucumber sandwiches and scones and told each other secrets at the tops of their voices, but even so Michael lowered his. 'Jumped off Tower Bridge on one of those plastic ropes that turn you into a human yo-yo,' he said. 'Flew a helicopter over Lord's Cricket Ground and landed on the pitch when England were batting. They needed three to win. They were playing Australia and she claimed she was engaged to O'Mara, their fast bowler. She certainly acted like she was engaged to him. With twenty thousand people watching. Not to mention the coverage.'

That one rang a bell all right, but I didn't let on. 'What else?'

He shrugged. 'You name it. She got into Women's Lib for a while – all that equal opportunities lark – ended up picketing a monastery. Took a nutrition course and spent six months in Africa feeding the starving. Played squash for Great Britain. Drove a bus in Milton Keynes. Owned Caramba.'

'Caramba?'

'It won the Grand National two years ago. Paid a hundred to eight. Don't you know anything?'

'Not much,' I said.

Two years ago when the National was running I'd been looking for the kidnapped wife of a millionaire. When I'd found her she'd had her head cut off.

'Is she married?'

'Divorced,' he said. 'Twice. First was a boxer. Second was a Hooray Henry Viscount. Neither lasted more than a year.

. . . Anything else?'

'I want to meet her,' I said.

'Who doesn't? . . . But are you her type, Ron?'

'I'm not divorced,' I said. 'Only separated.'

'Just my little joke,' he said, and chuckled.

'Puts it about a lot, does she?'

'No,' he said. 'She doesn't. She's a very choosy lady.'

'I still want to meet her,' I said.

'You wouldn't care to tell me why, I suppose? I mean Sabena *and* La Courtenay-Lithgoe –'

'I can't,' I said. 'Not yet. But if and when there is a story it'll be big. Very big. And you'll get first crack. Scouts' Honour.'

He brooded. 'There's a "Feed The Starving" Ball at the Dorchester on Friday,' he said. 'I could introduce you to her there if we can get you a ticket.'

'Hard to get, are they?' I said.

'Like gold-dust. But I'll try.' I knew he would, too, now there was a story in it.

'Where does she live?'

'Knightsbridge,' he said, and told me the address. 'Very handy for Harrods.'

'That's not a nice word to use in Fortnum and Mason,' I said.

*

Russell House, Carrick Street is red brick, and ugly with it, but it's expensive as well. The shiny glass doors tell you that, and the doorman who watches every visitor in – and out. And the cars in the Residents' Parking told you that as well, two Rollers, three Jaguars and a Ferrari. . . . I walked towards the block, and the doorman's eyes were on me before I'd got anywhere near, so I kept on going, on and round the corner to a telephone booth that had a phone that worked. It even contained a directory. That had to be a good sign, I thought, then: Come on, Ron. There's neither good signs nor bad signs, there's only events. And sometimes they come in sequence, and sometimes they don't.

Then just to prove it I tried looking for Sabena Redditch's

31

number and there it was. She wasn't ex-directory. So I forked out ten of Mrs. Courtenay-Lithgoe's pence and dialled the number, and got the answer-phone. 'This is Sabena Redditch speaking. . . . Out for the moment. . . . Speak when you hear the tone. . . .' See what I mean? Sequence, then no sequence. If things didn't improve I'd be relying on Michael Copland.

Not that I was ready to give in yet. Not that there was much I could do, either, except lurk for a while, moving around a bit because it was a windy sort of a day, and the wind was north-easterly. Keeping warm and not letting the doorman spot me kept me occupied for two hours and seventeen minutes. It wasn't what you would call intellectually demanding.

In the end she came round the corner where I'm strolling in an Aston-Martin and parked like a dream. There was a geezer beside her who looked mad enough to bite lumps out of the car and got out and slammed the door. She got out of the other side and he came round to her and started to speak. She didn't like what he said. The reason I knew that was that she hauled off and hit him with her clenched fist – a right hook to the gut – and I realised that when she'd been married to that boxer she'd kept her eyes open. The geezer looked a bit glassy for a moment, then managed to shamble off instead of falling down, and I further realised that the next move was up to me. Now or never. But I didn't fancy that right hook. Somehow I went over as she locked up the Aston-Martin.

'Mrs. Redditch?' I said, and that was a bad start. She'd been Mrs. Jocko Hudson, and the Viscountess Maudsley, but once she'd gone back to Redditch she was Ms.

She turned round and took her time looking at me. She looked – nice. Not a worldbeater like Imogen Courtenay-Lithgoe, but nice. About the poundage of a featherweight but a much more pleasing shape. Bold mouth, sharp little nose, big brown eyes that were clever as well – and she smelled a treat.

'What do you want?' she said.

'A ticket for the "Feed The Starving" Ball,' I said.

She didn't believe me. The look in her eyes told me that.

'You don't look like a reporter,' she said.

'I'm not,' I said.

'What are you then?'

'I'm in retail distribution,' I said, and in a way it's true. Almost everybody in the world is in retail distribution nowadays.

'Your name?'

'Hogget,' I said. 'Ronald Hogget.'

She believed that all right. Who'd make up a name like Hogget?

'And your friends call you Ron, no doubt?'

'Yes. – They – '

'Definitely not a reporter. Are you a crook, Mr. Hogget?'

'Of course I'm not a – '

'No need to sound so upset,' she said. 'So many retail distributors are.'

Then she put her hand on my arm and led me round the corner and into Russell House. The doorman was very impressed.

*

The answer-phone reeled off its messages: four in English, one in French, and a one minute silence that was me. As she listened I had a chance to look around the drawing-room. All very expensive and centrally heated, but all off the peg; no Stubbses, no Sheraton sofa-tables, no Persian rugs. Just comfort. She switched off at last, and rang a bell. A Filipino girl came in.

'Rosario,' she said, 'this is Mr. Hogget. We'd like some tea.'

'Very good, miss,' the Filipino said, and left us to it. Ms. Redditch started in at once.

'There aren't any tickets left,' she said. 'But I suppose you know that. You wouldn't want to shell out fifty pounds.'

'I've got fifty pounds,' I said.

'Lucky old you. . . . What do you want? . . . Are you a photographer? Is that it?'

'Just a hobby,' I said, but she wasn't listening. She'd come to a conclusion.

'You're a private detective,' she said.

'Well – yes,' I said, and she smiled, but the smile was for

33

herself, not me, because she'd found a correct answer.

'And you've done rather well,' she said. 'After all you've talked your way into my flat and got me talking.' The smile faded. 'But I can't think why,' she continued. 'I don't do things any more.'

'Like jump off bridges or land helicopters on cricket fields? There's nothing for a private detective in that,' I said.

She shrugged. 'Oh *that*,' she said, dismissing it. 'What I meant was I don't run around with the sort of people who snort cocaine or overwork their credit cards or get black-mailed. Not any more. . . . So why are you here?'

'It's complicated,' I said. 'And confidential.'

'I like puzzles,' she said, 'and I keep secrets.'

'I'm looking for someone.'

'Oh good. That's always been one of my favourites – the missing person.'

'This isn't a show on the telly,' I said.

'I'm reserving judgement on that,' said Sabena Redditch, and I began to feel nervous again. Rosario brought tea, and left us, and Sabena 'poured. 'It's a girl,' I said. 'About your age, maybe a little bit younger. Blonde – probably natural – grey-blue eyes, five feet four, eight and a half stone.'

'There are so many of the little dears,' she said. 'The "Feed The Starving" Bash will be full of them – not that any of them have ever starved.'

'She has a mole on her left shoulder,' I said. 'You went to the opera with her in Sydney Opera House. The opera was Verdi's *Otello.*'

Her fists clenched, and I began to get nervous. But then she opened her hands. 'My God,' she said. 'You really are a detective. How on earth did you – but that's a trade secret, I suppose?'

'Afraid so,' I said.

'But why on earth would you want to know about Heidi Pickel?' she said.

I didn't laugh. I didn't even grin. After adusting to Erny Fluck I was immune.

'Don't you think it's a funny name?' she said. 'I did. The whole of Rushcutters' Bay did. Heidi was the only one who didn't. "There was a Pickel who fought Napoleon," she used to say. Why should that be funny?'

'When did you last see her?' I said.

'I'm not sure that I want to tell you,' she said, and then the door opened and another woman came in.

This was no glamour-puss. To begin with she was old: seventy at least, and quite possibly ninety, and if she'd ever had a bath it was not within recent memory. Her clothes looked like a scarecrow's discards and her shoes didn't match – and yet she carried herself with an elegance and a sense of style that belonged to a world long gone.

'Why Poppy,' Sabena Redditch said. 'How nice of you to drop in.' Considering that Poppy had let herself in with a key, this was droll. 'Would you like a cup of tea?'

'Whisky,' said Poppy. 'A very little soda.'

Sabena went over to the drinks tray. 'How about you?' she said.

'Gin and tonic,' I said, and she made the drinks, brought them over.

'This is Mr. Ronald Hogget,' Sabena said to Poppy, who was gulping Scotch in a ladylike way. 'Poppy, Lady Tarleton.'

'How d'you do?' I said.

Poppy, Lady Tarleton nodded, went on gulping, then handed her glass to Sabena.

'You're staying?' Sabena asked.

'If I may. Just for a while.'

'Of course,' Sabena said. 'But once you've had your next one you'll have to have a bath. It's only fair to the rest of us.'

'You worry too much about baths,' Lady Tarleton said.

'And you worry too much about whisky. . . . It's up to you.'

'Oh very well.' Lady Tarleton snatched her next drink, sipped, then turned to me. 'Soon be the hunting season,' she said.

'So I believe,' I said.

'You don't hunt.' It was a statement, not a question. 'My younger brother Bobby does. Usually it's the Beaufort or the Quorn, but when we're hard up it has to be Ireland. Galway. . . . Or even Meath. Bobby doesn't mind. He says it's marvellous hunting country.'

As she told me all this her voice became lighter, younger,

35

almost a girl's. 'He's got five hunters you know,' she said, and Sabena glowered at me.

'No, I didn't know,' I said, and Sabena relaxed.

'At one time daddy said he had to make do with three, but that was before my come-out. Girls are expensive too, mummy says. But once they're married they're somebody else's expense I told her. . . . She didn't think it was awfully funny. . . . Did I say girls?'

'Yes,' I said.

'Bobby had a daughter,' she said, and then: 'But that's ridiculous. He's not even engaged.'

'You've been out of touch, Poppy darling,' Sabena said. 'He married one of the Margeson girls.'

'How exciting,' said Lady Tarleton. She finished her Scotch. 'I think I'll have a bath now,' she said. She sounded old again. Then she walked to the door, looked back at me: 'What year is it?' she asked. I told her. 'Oh dear,' she said. 'How sad.' Then she left. There was a silence.

At last Sabena said, 'She isn't *mad*, you know.'

'Of course not,' I said, and she knew I meant it.

'The past is all she's got,' she said.

'Not quite,' I said. 'She appears to have you, too.'

'She has my key,' she said, 'and the chance of a bath and a meal and a bed. She doesn't take it often.'

'What does she do?' I said. 'Dosser?'

Sabena nodded. 'There'll be half a dozen plastic bags in the hall,' she said. 'All her wordly goods.'

'She's absolutely skint?' I said. 'Broke I mean?'

'I know what skint means,' she said. 'Her husband was the last of his family. He not only died broke – he left her a mountain of debts.'

'Hadn't *she* any family?'

'She has one surviving brother,' she said. 'The famous Bobby. He's the only one who gives a damn.'

'Then why doesn't he – ?'

'He tried,' she said. 'He really did try. He and his daughter. But for some reason she just couldn't take it. . . . They live in the present, you see. She much prefers freaking out and living in the past.'

'Booze?'

36

She shrugged. 'Whatever's cheapest,' she said. 'Berkeley sends me money for her from time to time.'

'Berkeley?'

'Lieutenant General Sir Robert Berkeley.' It came as no surprise. Sabena looked at me and smiled, her eyes as alert as ever.

'You're a good listener,' she said.

'I have to be,' I told her. 'It's my living.' And then, because I really wanted to know, I asked, 'How did she get past the doorman?'

'He has his instructions,' she said. 'So you know about the doorman, too?'

'I've got eyes,' I said.

'And a still tongue. Loosen it a little, mon brave. Tell me why I'm telling you things.'

'Someone's missing,' I told her agan. 'I'm trying to find them.'

'Heidi?'

'Not that I know of,' I said. 'They just happened to have her photograph. I'm not going to harm her. Honestly.'

'You're so convincing when you say "honestly",' she said. 'Heidi and I were friends for a while. She wanted a holiday, and I went with her to Sydney. We both have friends there – only she liked it and I didn't – so she stayed on and I came home. What's it all about?'

I didn't answer. I couldn't.

'You're not going to tell me, are you?'

'I can't,' I said. 'I'm sorry. I'd better be off.'

When I was halfway on to my feet, she stood up too, and I remembered the right hook, but it wasn't like that.

'I'm sorry, too,' she said. 'Are you married?'

'Separated,' I said.

'Divorced is better,' she said. 'Believe me I know. Separated's just hanging on with one hand and pushing away with the other.'

'Tell Melanie that,' I said.

'Melanie?' She said the word as if she had tasted it and found it unpleasant, then almost at once twigged that I'd spotted it. 'Such a pretty name,' she said.

'She's a pretty girl,' I said. .

'And you're a pretty fellow, Ron Hogget,' she said, and came over and kissed me. It wasn't the ultimate in exotic experiences, but it wasn't a rush job either. I enjoyed it very much.

When she put me down, she said, 'You observed me wallop that idiot?' I nodded. 'Jack Cleverleigh,' she said. 'Of the Wiltshire Cleverleighs. He had – certain ambitions. I didn't feel inclined to help him achieve them. It's a nuisance really. He was supposed to be my escort at the "Feed The Starving" Ball. I don't suppose you'd like to take his place? – No, of course you wouldn't. That was just a gimmick to get you in here.'

I heard myself say, 'I'd like to take you very much.'

'Oh super,' she said, and kissed me again, just a peck, then backed off. 'I'll tell you something else about Lady Poppy,' she said. 'She's clairvoyant.'

'Maybe I'd better take her on as a partner,' I said. 'Could be a lot quicker than looking for clues.'

But on the way home it was something else to think about. Sabena Redditch tended to have a reason for the things she told you, and I would have bet the price of my ticket for Feed The Starving that she'd noticed – just as I had – that Lady Poppy Tarleton had taken one look at me and talked about her brother. And his daughter.

5

Stockbrokers are the sort of people I don't know an awful lot about, and Horry Lumley does, so I put Horry Lumley on to them. Cardwell, Ryecroft and Cairns, with a suite in one of those tower blocks in the City that looks as if it's floated over from Wall Street, and a lot of young men who'd been to Westminster or Rugby or Stowe. Out of my league, but meat and drink to Horry. He'd been to Eton. *And* Cambridge. Only he'd had to leave Cambridge in a hurry, having popped the college silver to cover his racing debts. Bent as a barmaid's elbow was Horry, but the best research man I knew – and Mrs. Courtenay-Lithgoe could afford the best.

Me, I was going to Wembley. That was more my style. I'd got Horry to check on him before I started – bachelor, both parents dead, only child. Now I had to see him where he lived as you might say, or rather where he *had* lived until he'd moved to Leinster Terrace, Dublin, then on to God knows where.

43, Garibaldi Avenue, the address was. Big Edwardian terrace house converted into flats. Not too bad, but it wasn't Leinster Terrace. Just a pad that was a brisk eight minutes from Magna Electronics, the place where he worked, (I timed it) and nice and handy for Mrs. Courtenay-Lithgoe to knock him down on her way to the horse-jumping.

I took my time sussing out 43, Garibaldi Avenue, and just as well I did. There's always one, in a block of flats like that. Most of the residents are off to their gainful employment by eight-thirty or nine, but there's generally one left behind, usually a woman – wife or widow – and nosy with it. And sure enough there she was. First floor, lace curtains, gleaming paintwork, and her nose against the window every time a car back-fired. She could be a nuisance. Ernie Fluck was her next

39

door neighbour. I decided to give her half an hour then go in anyway, and I got lucky. After twenty three minutes I got lucky.

She came out of the house, pushing a shopping trolley and carrying a plastic bin-liner, and dumped the bin-liner in a dustbin in the little front garden. Even the dustbin looked clean. It had 43C painted on it, in clean white paint. I crossed the road and went into 43's garden, looked in the dustbin. On the top was an empty bottle of super-market gin. . . .

I used Ernie's keys to let me in and went up to his flat. Nobody knew. Two locks on the door, but nothing I couldn't have coped with, and anyway, I had his keys. The door stuck a bit, but it was just a pile of junk mail. Offers You Dare Not Refuse, Be A Credit Card Holder, Are You Properly Insured? All that. But nothing personal. Not even a Wish You Were Here from the Costa del Sol. . . . I shut the door with my foot, and pulled on a pair of plastic gloves, and started being nosy. . . .

He was the most anonymous geezer I'd ever come across. His furniture he must have bought at auctions: it was the only way to explain why nothing matched with anything else. G Plan Danish and Oxford Street moquette and Victorian mahogany all piled in together. Clean and tidy and well kept, and with about as much character as a tailor's dummy.

The fridge-freezer was almost empty which didn't surprise me – the time he'd been away; the bed was made, radio and telly disconnected. The home-computer was disconnected too, and I looked at it wistfully, like a penniless kid looking through a sweetshop window. I don't know a thing about computers, but I sort of had the feeling there was an awful lot it could tell me if I did. . . . A shelf full of books: tit and bum thrillers, mathematics and physics and engineering, just like Leinster Terrace.

His desk was locked, but I had a Swiss Army knife with me that was sort of special. A bent locksmith I knew had adapted it for me, and it opened up the desk as quick as a key.

All very tidy inside the desk. Bills all paid, insurance all in order. No diary entries for the last seven weeks and before that it was all anonymous stuff like dentist's visits and rates to be paid. No mention of people. Not even Imogen Courtenay-

Lithgoe. I wondered if she knew, and if it bothered her, then I went on looking. Degree certificates – B.Sc. and M.Sc., both with first class honours. Imperial College, London University. I took their pictures. Maybe Dave could find someone to talk to. Then I tried the bedroom. More boring clothes in the wardrobe, and a chest of drawers with one locked drawer, so I used the Swiss Army knife again. Stacks of cardboard files, all with loose sheets of mathematical symbols. I took a few pictures then locked them up again. It was time to go.

So I nipped into the off-licence across the road and bought a bottle of gin with Mrs. Courtenay-Lithgoe's money, and tried to make myself invisible while I waited for Nosey. When she came back I gave her five minutes to get settled then went across the road and rang Ernie's bell. I didn't look up, but I'd bet money she was looking at me. When nobody answered I rang her bell instead. She answered so fast she must have run.

'Yes?'

'I'm looking for Mr. Fluck,' I said, and the door opened before I'd finished speaking. I went on up.

She was outside her door. Tall, she was, very thin, with watery eyes that didn't miss a thing, particularly the plastic bag with a bottle inside. I gave her my widest, most winning grin. It had about as much effect as throwing a cream-cake at a concrete bunker.

'He's not here,' she said.

'Well now that *is* a pity,' I said.

'I could take a message,' Nosey said, and I wondered how many she'd already taken. Her clothes were neat, clean and very worn.

'You see it would have been very much to his advantage,' I went on. 'It's so rarely one has the opportunity to pass on good news. What time will he be back?'

'He's been away a while,' Nosey said. 'If you'd give me your name – '

'It's Harkness,' I said. 'I'm from Stanford, Partridge and True. – Solicitors.'

'You'd better come in,' she said. 'It doesn't seem right – talking on the door-step.'

Her flat had about half the furniture Ernie's had, but what there was had been polished till it glowed. Pale patches on the

41

carpet showed where the rest of it had been. Most likely it was the good stuff that had gone – even the telly. Gin comes expensive when you're thirsty all the time.

'I'm Mrs. Thoburn,' she aid. 'Did you say it was good news for Mr. Fluck?'

'A legacy,' I said. 'Not a fortune, but welcome, I'd say. More than welcome.'

She sighed. It would have been welcome to her, too.

'He's not at work, then?' I asked.

'He hasn't got a job,' she said.

'But surely – ' I said.

'A man came round to see him. Said he was the managing director at Magna Electronics. Told him he was redundant. And Mr. Fluck said no he wasn't because he'd resigned.'

'Well well,' I said. 'This is a bit of a shock. Do you mind if I sit down?'

'Of course,' she said. 'I'm sorry.' Her eyes were still on the plastic bag.

'I had a bit of luck myself today,' I said. 'A chap at the office sold me a raffle-ticket. I won a bottle of gin.'

Her eyes, her whole body expressed her outrage against fate. First Fluck had a welcome legacy, and then a perfect stranger got a bottle of gin for nothing.

'Do you know where Mr. Fluck went?' I said.

'No idea,' she said. Still outraged.

'It's perhaps a little early in the day,' I said, 'but I wonder if you'd care to join me in toasting Mr. Fluck's good fortune?'

'Oh, I don't know – ' she said.

'Please.' I took out the bottle. 'I've been so looking forward to passing on the good news.'

I twisted the cap, and it came loose with a tiny metallic snap. It was like a starter's pistol to a sprinter. She was out to the kitchen and back with two glasses and a bottle of tonic in no time at all. No lemon, and certainly no ice. They take up too much room. I poured, and she looked away while I did it, terrified in case I'd gone easy with the gin, but one sip and she knew I hadn't.

'Your very good health,' I said.

She sipped again. 'And yours,' she said. She meant it.

'Tell me about Mr. Fluck,' I said.

42

'He kept himself to himself,' she said, and I gathered she didn't admire him for it.

'Not a very neighbourly man?'

'Not at all,' she said. 'A solitary, I suppose you'd call him.'

'Not married, I gather?'

'Not him.'

'Not a lady's man?'

'Gambling,' she said. 'That's what he lived for. Dogs and horses and cheap gaming clubs.'

'He went to the races?'

'Of course not,' she said. 'He went to the betting shop. Won a few times, lost a lot. But it didn't keep him away.' She sipped again. Her glass was almost empty.

'Didn't he have *any* visitors?'

'A woman came once. A blonde. Very attractive. She looked rich.'

'When was this?'

'Seven weeks ago. The last time I saw him. She'd bought him a plane ticket.'

'Where to?'

'They didn't say.' I knew that was true because it hurt her to say it. Her glass was empty, and I got up and made her a refill, casually. Just a gentleman enjoying a social drink with a lady. 'Yet he always had money,' she said. 'Odd, don't you think? Horses and dogs and roulette, yet the rent was always paid and always enough for a taxi. I – ' She hesitated, then took a swig at her gin and out it came. 'I cleaned his place for him. Charring, I suppose you'd call it. But he always paid on time. He'd got a computer.'

Her mind was darting about like a swallow, and I thought I knew why. The more things she told me, the more likely she was to get another gin.

'Did you ever see him use it?' She nodded. 'What did he do?'

'He just used it,' she said. 'I don't understand computers. – But *he* did. He used to boast about it. How clever he was. He was really rather a boastful man. Pathetic, really. He didn't have all that much to boast about.'

And you don't have anything at all, I thought. On the other hand you don't boast. And then it seemed to me that I was

43

wrong. No matter how much she drank she kept her place clean, and surely that was something to be proud of?

Her glass was empty again, and this time she filled it herself. Between the two of us a bargain had been struck and she knew it.

'And you've no idea when he'll be back?' I said.

'None at all,' she said. 'The blonde was beautiful, as I say. And rich, by the look of her. Why should he come back here?'

'For his belongings,' I said.

'They wouldn't fetch all that much,' Mrs. Thoburn said. 'Believe me I know. I've cleaned them.' She drank again, and said, 'What's he done?'

'Come into money,' I said. 'I told you.'

'Stanford, Partridge and True,' she said.

'That's right . . . Solicitors.'

'You're not a solicitor,' she said.

'What makes you say that?'

'I was married to one once,' she said. 'I must have met dozens. None of them were like you.' It sounded harsh, but her voice was much kinder than the words.

'Frank got rid of me because I like a little drink,' she said. 'But then you know that already, don't you?' She looked at the bottle. 'Raffle indeed. How did you find out? – Not that it matters. . . . Not a great deal does matter nowadays.'

'You keep your place very clean,' I said.

'Yes,' she said. 'That matters. I still have that. Are you a policeman?'

'No,' I said.

'Of course not,' she said. 'Whoever heard of a policeman who brought his own gin . . . Private?' I said nothing. 'What's he done?'

'Disappeared,' I said.

'That's a good trick,' said Mrs. Thoburn. 'I wish I could do it.'

I left her with the gin bottle. That night I had a ball to go to, so I had to hire a dress suit.

*

44

Dave thought I looked very nice, and said so.

'Not too flash?' I said. I was nervous. Hadn't had a tail-coat on since my wedding.

'Ron, boy, you look great,' he said. 'I mean it.' His voice was soothing and I began to feel less nervous. I often do when Dave's around.

He was wearing his best blue suit and carrying the peaked cap he wears when he helps out with a hire car firm that does weddings. Parked outside my door was the hire-car firm's Rolls-Royce – minus the white ribbons for once. Very dark blue with pale blue upholstery, and he'd polished it up a treat. I looked at my watch. I was starting to get nervous again. Couldn't help it.

'Relax,' he said. 'There's bags of time. Have yourself a gin and tonic.'

But I thought of Mrs. Thoburn and somehow I didn't fancy one.

'How's the riding lessons?' I asked him.

'All right,' he said. 'Bit dangerous to tell the truth. I'm out of practice.'

'You like things dangerous,' I said.

'I do when I'm paid for them.'

'You'll be paid,' I said, and spent the rest of the waiting time wondering if my tie was straight.

I'd been told to appear at seven-thirty and it was seven-thirty on the dot when Dave pulled up in Carrick Street and got out to open my door: very much the chauffeur earning his living. Nothing to show we'd been mates since the junior school – and good mates at that.

'We'll be out in an hour,' I said.

'Very good, sir. . . . After that it's straight to the Dorchester?'

'Till one-thirty,' I said. 'What will you do?'

'Go and see a chum of mine, if I may. He went to Imperial College.'

'Good man,' I said, very much the employer who pays the wages. . . .

At Sabena's there was a party, and hired servants to help Rosario, and champagne, and Sabena offered me her cheek to kiss. No sign of Lady Tarleton. I asked about her.

'She's in bed, reading,' she said. 'She doesn't like champagne.' Then she dragged me around the guests, all of whom had names like Fiona and Caroline and Roger and Nigel, and told them I was very big in retail distribution and we all drank Pol Roger till it was time to go to the Dorchester.

The Roller impressed her, and so did Dave. Once inside she sat close beside me and told me how dashing I looked in tails, but it didn't bother me because there was a dividing window between us and the driving seat, and it was closed.

'The perfect gent,' she said. 'With just the hint of a rascal underneath. How lucky I am.' She wore a red silk dress, and diamonds, and a full-length natural mink, and smelled even better than when I first met her.

'I'm the lucky one,' I said.

'Eloquent too,' she said. 'You're altogether too much, Ron Hogget.'

Then she held my hand all the way to the Dorchester.

The big room, chandeliers and jewels and couture gowns, and photographers and TV crews, and me, Ron Hogget, at the top table. The food wasn't bad either – not brilliant – well it can't be when you cook on that scale, – but not bad at all, and Sabena let me order the wine because she'd got an idea I knew something about it. So I ordered a Pauillac – Château Batailley it was, the 1970, and the sommelier began to treat me as if I might just possibly have a few brains, and even the other people at the table began to notice my existence. There was a duke and duchess, I remember, and a film-star and a record producer. They were the only ones I'd ever heard of. The rest were there just because they had money.

I even enjoyed the dancing. A lot of it was the old-fashioned kind – where you actually get to take hold of the girl, and a lot of the time the girl was Sabena. Holding on to the film-star wasn't bad either. The duchess was a cow. . . . Still, all in all it was a pretty good knees-up, even if the tombola tickets were fifty quid apiece and all I won was a bottle of Scotch. But on the other hand, as Sabena said in her speech, it all went to feed the starving, and there's nothing wrong with that.

When one-thirty came there was a bit of a wait while Sabena did the polite to all the rich and famous. One of them was a tall, chunky geezer who looked hard all over, even in a dress suit that must have cost him three hundred at least. When she came back to me, she said, 'It's very odd.'

'The muscle-man?'

'He's Theodore Pickel,' she said. 'Heidi's brother. I'd no idea he was in England.'

'What's he doing here?'

'Making money,' she said. 'It's all he ever does. But it's odd you should have a photograph of his sister, don't you think?' She took my arm. 'Let's go home.'

So we left, and Dave was outside, ready to go. As he drove off she said: 'Would you like to come in for a nightcap?'

'Love to,' I said.

'You can get rid of your chauffeur then,' she said. 'There are always taxis round here.'

So when we got there I gave Dave a wink on the sly and told him he was finished for the night, and he said 'Very good, sir,' and the Rolls floated away like a car in a dream and we went inside, to the big, anonymous drawing-room, and she poured us both a brandy, then loosened her furs, let them fall. In the dim light her arms and shoulders gleamed.

'You realise,' she said, 'that I'm making a pass at you.' I tried to speak, then found I had nothing to say. 'A very determined pass. . . . Do you like the idea?'

I got something out at last. 'Very much,' I said.

'Then it won't have to be rape,' she said, and came over to me, looked down at me. 'What on earth's the matter?' she said.

'I'm nervous,' I told her.

'*Nervous?*'

'Well of course I'm nervous,' I said. 'I mean look at you and look at me.'

'You're not going to turn out to be a snob, I hope,' she said.

'I'm a cat looking at a queen,' I said.

'No you're not,' said Sabena. 'You're a dog who's about to have his day.' She took my glass from me, put it down, drew me to my feet. 'Come on.'

She was right. It was my day all right, or rather my two a.m. till dawn, but I like to think it was hers as well. Our bodies liked each other, and our minds began to play with the idea that given time we might even love each other. Once as we lay and rested, she grabbed me by the ears, waggled my head.

'You think a lot, don't you?' she said. 'You're a bit of an intellectual.'

'It takes one to know one,' I said.

'What are you thinking?'

'I'm thinking I should get a divorce.'

Her body eased into mine. 'Yes,' she said. 'I think so, too.'

Then later: 'You're quite a ruthless person, aren't you?'

'Me?' I said. 'I'm scared to death half the time.'

'Yes,' she said. 'But you go on doing it even so. That makes you ruthless – and I'm glad. I like it.'

Her perfume still lingered; she was soft yet firm, yielding, warm. That time we both cried out together. It was the best and last.

I took a shower and she made me coffee, found some old clothes of the viscount's that were more or less my size, and a grip for my dress suit, and then it was time to go. Out the back. Tradesmen's entrance. I said it was to protect her reputation: she said I was a prude.

6

Dawn in Knightsbridge. It was like something out of an old British movie. Milk bottles on doorsteps, and a cat on the prowl through some of the most expensive real estate in Europe. Then from somebody's garden a bird started to sing, clear and pure as a flute. Then should come the violins, I thought, and me back in my tails and Sabena in her ball-gown, waltzing through the crescents and squares while a milkman and a bobby looked on and winked and smiled.

But it wasn't a milkman and a bobby who were looking on: it was a couple of blokes in track suits and balaclava helmets. Not a bad idea when you think of it. Track suits and training shoes, so if anybody asks you're out for an early morning jog, then once you're on to the target, on with the balaclava and give him a belting. *And* they'd caught me nicely. I'd cut through a mews and on to a side-street that would bring me on to the Brompton Road, and I saw about as many people as I would have done in the Kalahari Desert, and then suddenly there was this geezer in front of me. A six foot cube is what he looked like, and maybe that's an exaggeration, but then fear does exaggerate. But one thing I'm sure of – he was big. Big enough to make me look behind me, and there, sure enough, was another one, maybe not quite so tall but even wider.

The one in front came at me at a run and I started off like a wing three quarter who's got the ball and is trying to get round the biggest full-back in history. The trouble was this geezer was as fast as he was big. It didn't matter how much I doubled and swerved, he was always there, reaching out for me, and I knew, I was sure, that once he got his hands on me I was finished. So all I could do was keep on running, and wonder about the bloke behind me – until the one I was facing

49

took a flying leap, and his hands almost had me, except that I skidded to a halt and lashed out with the grip, slamming it into his face so that he yelped with the pain. But even so he still blocked me off from the corner of the street.

I risked another look behind me, and saw at once why I hadn't been attacked from the rear. Dave was heavily involved with the other geezer, and even as I watched he landed a kick on his diaphragm that sounded like a bass drum imitating a land mine going off, then following it up – as the other bloke pitched forward – by interlacing his fingers and bringing both hands down on the back of his neck.

My full-back saw it too and it caught him off balance, so just to keep the party going I belted him again with the grip, just as Dave came cruising up and hauled off and belted him one on the side of the neck. But it wasn't like a boxer's punch, not the way Dave hit. More like his arm was on a hinge that straightened out just at the moment his fist made contact. The full-back suddenly went limp, but didn't quite fall over, not until Dave belted him again, with the edge of his hand this time, a smack like one from an axe blade, just under his nose. He went down then all right. Dave turned to me then, and I swear to God he wasn't even out of breath.

'Hello Ron,' he said.

'Hello, Dave,' I said. 'Good to see you.' I meant it.

'I've got the Roller round the corner,' he said. 'Why don't I give you a lift home?'

So that is what he did. And on the way to Fulham he told me how he'd spotted these two geezers in a Ford Granada round the corner from Carrick Street, so he'd parked the Roller round another corner and come back and watched them. Stay still and watch for hours, Dave can. The patience of Job. He learned how to do it when he was in the Paras in Northern Ireland. Same with people who were watching houses looking for a target. Dave's on to that at once. If he wasn't he'd be dead. Years ago. . . . Then a copper came and started snuffling round the Roller, and Dave had to nip back and move it, and after he'd done that he'd come back just in time to save me from a belting. . . .

He drove me back to Fulham and he asked me if I was all right, and I said 'Yes', which was a lie and he knew it, but he also knew I wanted to be by myself, so we said so long, and he dropped me on the corner, and left me to get on with it. . . . As I took my clothes off I wondered if I should phone Sabena, but then I thought, Why wake her? and went to sleep instead. My day had gone on for quite long enough.

*

I was dreaming of woodpeckers. They were taking it in turns to tap the letter 'S' in morse code on my front door. Dot dot dot. Dot dot dot. Dot dot dot. Then suddenly they stopped, and a gorilla with a sledgehammer took over, and he started on the letter 'S' too, but much slower, and much louder. Boom boom boom. Boom boom boom. Boom boom boom. And then I woke up, but the gorilla was still at it, and I looked at my bedside clock. Eight thirty seven. After gin and champagne and claret and brandy I'd been allowed to sleep for two hours, and the way my head felt it wasn't even that. I put my dressing-gown on and floundered downstairs, and the banging continued Boom boom boom, Boom boom boom, until I opened the door and there he was, neat suit, clean shirt and tie, at *that* hour, CID written all over him, and suddenly I *knew*. Boom boom boom. S for Sabena.

'Mr. Hogget?' he said.

'That's me.'

'Detective Sergeant Matthews,' he said, and showed me his warrant card. 'Mind if I come in?'

'Why?' I said.

'Miss Sabena Redditch,' he said.

'What about her?'

'She's in Saint Stephen's Hospital,' he said. 'Intensive Care.'

'You'd better come in,' I said, and he followed me into the kitchen. I put the kettle on.

'I'm going to make some coffee,' I said. 'Want some?'

'Yes please,' he said. 'What I want to ask you, Mr. Hogget – '

'No sergeant,' I said. 'No asking. Not till you tell me. *What happened to her?*'

51

He took one look at me and decided it was the only way.

'About quarter to six,' he said. – Just after I'd left. – 'Her door-bell rings. Only she doesn't hear it. It's the Filipino maid who hears it.'

'Rosario,' I said.

He gave me a look as if he'd caught me out; made me admit I knew Sabena's maid's name. Idiot.

'She couldn't sleep,' he said. 'So she heard the bell and answered the buzzer. A man's voice said it was you.' He paused.

'Go on,' I said.

'So she knew you'd been with Miss Redditch – '. Another pause for me to deny all knowledge but I just stayed quiet and he went on. – 'So she pressed the buzzer to let him in and went to wake Miss Redditch, who told her to let you in. So she opened the door and two geezers in track suits and balaclavas came in and one of them clouted her one and down she went and that's all she knows.'

'Clouted her with what?'

'His fist.'

'And Sabena?'

When I used her first name he looked as if he'd scored another point, but I couldn't be bothered. There weren't any points. There was just the rotten bad luck that I decided to use the tradesmen's entrance so they didn't see me leave at the same time Dave had to shift the Roller.

'Like I say,' Matthews said, 'she's in intensive care. No chance of a statement. But the doctor reckons she'd been bashed good and proper. Should have killed her. Probably would have done – only she'd got an exceptionally hard skull.'

'She'll live then?' I said.

'They won't say,' said Matthews. 'I'm sorry. I reckon they just don't know.' For a moment he sounded human, then he changed gear and became a detective again.

'You were with her last night, Mr. Hogget?'

If Rosario couldn't sleep he'd know that anyway.

'I took her to the "Feed The Starving" Ball,' I said.

'What time did you leave the lady?'

'We went back to her place. I left about five-thirty,' I said.

'I see.' And that was all he said. I gave him full marks.

'How did you get home?'

'Tube,' I said.

'In evening dress?'

'I borrowed a change of clothes.'

'Would you recognise the ticket-seller if you saw him again?'

'I used the machine,' I said.

'Pity. . . . It would have been a help if you see what I mean.'

'I'm not lying,' I lied.

'Of course not, sir. . . . How did you go to the ball?'

'Hire-car,' I said, and he asked for a name and address and I gave it. Why not? Me and Dave had worked out our story on the way home.

'I hope you get them,' I said.

'We've got them.'

'Quick work,' I said.

He gave me a dirty look. 'We aren't claiming any credit,' he said. 'One of *them's* in intensive care and the other one's been bashed silly. Claims he's having a blackout an' all. Can't remember a thing except he and his mate went jogging. – You sure you didn't see them, sir?'

'Quite sure,' I said. 'Anyway I'm useless at violence. Always have been.'

'You're a private detective, aren't you?'

'More like an agent,' I said. 'Finding things, that's what I do.'

'What sort of things?'

'Collectors' items,' I said. 'Or missing documents, say. Or it could even be missing persons.'

'What are you working on now?'

'I'm not,' I said.

'Make good money, do you?' You must do, is what he meant. Taking out birds like Sabena Redditch.

'I do when I'm working,' I said.

'You think you could find the blokes who duffed those geezers in the track-suits?'

'There wouldn't be any money in that,' I said.

'I thought you might want to shake their hands,' he said.

'If I ever find them I will,' I told him.

53

'We'll talk again,' he said, more a threat than a promise.

'Anything I can do to help,' I said.

'You can start by telling me what happened.'

'You know as much as me,' I said.

'Not yet, but I will,' he said, and left me alone to worry about it. Only I couldn't even begin to *start* worrying about it. I was too knackered. I know it sounds awful the state Sabena was in, but I went straight back to bed and to sleep, and when you think about it it makes sense. At least when I woke up I was able to think straight.

The first thing I did when I woke up was phone Horry Lumley, but he said he hadn't got anything for me yet – with stockbrokers you need time. So I told him I would ring in now and again, and he said 'Oh ah,' and hung up. You never have to draw pictures for Horry. . . . Then I had a bath and had breakfast – it was two o'clock but I made bacon and eggs so it was breakfast – then I went over to the Mason's Arms, and there was Dave, with a glass of lager with one sip missing, and his nose in The Letters of Dorothy Osborne to Sir William Temple. I went over and shook him by the hand because I'd promised Sergeant Matthews I would, then I filled him in on the day, so to speak.

But he'd heard it all from a Detective Constable Allison who'd been more interested in me than Dave.

'Did he ask you if we were mates?' I said.

'No,' said Dave, 'and I didn't tell him.' He took another sip of lager. 'Sorry about your bird, old son. I feel better about having clobbered those two now.'

'I owe you for that,' I said. 'Thanks.'

'You going to see her?'

'They won't let me,' I said. 'She's still unconscious.'

'How about my dancing partners?'

'I didn't ask,' I said. 'Show some common.'

'Yeah,' he said. 'You're right. I was just wondering.'

And there you have him. My mate Dave. Good mind, fit as a fiddle, give you his last pound note. But when it comes to duffing blokes you'd have thought he'd been swatting flies. If I'd put a couple of blokes in hospital, never mind intensive care, I'd have been a nervous wreck. But with Dave all it amounted to was: I was just wondering. It worries me. It really does.

'Any luck on the other matter?' I asked him.

'Your friend Erny?' Another sip of lager while he sorted his ideas out. 'Yeah,' he said at last. 'Not bad.'

The nice thing about Dave is that not only has he got a few brains, he uses them. So what he'd done was ignore the two geezers he'd known at Leeds who'd finished up at Imperial College – one organic chemistry Ph.D., one M.Litt. in mediaeval French, and chatted up the bloke who was care-taker of the electronics building. And the reason for that was he and Dave had been in the Paras together. They'd even been in the Falls Road together, and there's no cement binds you together tighter than that.

So Dave had sailed up in a Roller and asked his questions and the other bloke hadn't even bothered to ask why. Dave had needed some answers so the bloke had given them. Even the present of a bottle of Scotch at the end of the evening hadn't amounted to much – just another way to say 'Thank you'. What counted was that they'd been shot at together, and I envied Dave that, even though I truly believe that being shot at is too high a price to pay for anything.

Anyway, Dave had picked up a few things about E. Fluck. Some of it was common knowledge, and some of it Dave's mate had found out by going through a few files – when it comes to extracting information Paras take a lot of beating – and what it amounted to was this: Erny Fluck was Brilliant.

From the moment he'd put his nose inside Imperial College, he'd been a runaway – but in the curiously blinkered way that some clever people have. All his brains went into electronics. For relaxation it was tit and bum thrillers and whatever pop noise the radio happened to be making; and all he ever asked of a telly was that it should be switched on.

But in his own field he was unbeatable. When I asked Dave what Fluck's own field was his mate had told him it was computers. Not making them. That was for the artisans, Fluck reckoned. Talking with them. Getting to know their little secrets. The way Dave's mate told it, when it came to chatting up computers, Erny was a cross between a psychiatrist and a con-man. None of their secrets was safe from him – and he'd scored a few triumphs even when he was a student: like

55

hacking into the computer of a merchant bank just before they had organised a new share issue of a family business that was just about to go public.

He had a girl friend at that time called Jenny Cooper. She was studying economics, and after the share issue he told her he'd known all the inside dope for days, and she'd given him a real bollocking. Apparently he could have cleaned up if she'd known. Then a few months later the government had privatised its share of a silicon processing company, and Erny had hacked on to that, too – hacking being the word for conning a computer into telling what it knows. Only this time he told his girl friend. Everything they had, they converted into ready cash. They begged, they borrowed, and maybe they stole. Whatever they did, they converted five thousand quid into nearly nine, and when it was over the girl left without taking a degree, and took off for Hong Kong, making her first killing in currency speculation. Erny didn't grieve, which surprised all his mates. He'd been mad about Jenny Cooper.

Instead, he invested his share in horses and dogs and roulette. He didn't do too badly either. It took him nearly six weeks to lose it, but when he did he got drunk and started talking and it was all very embarrassing – or it would have been if it had come out. But it didn't. Erny, it seemed, wasn't a likeable man, but he was a very gifted one, and the gift was a rare one indeed. So Erny had received a reprimand, and went back to honest brainwork, and took his B.Sc. with first class honours: then on to his M.Sc. Only when he was waiting for his M.Sc. results his girl-friend Jenny came back from Hong Kong. She'd heard a rumour that a British and a Swiss pharmaceutical company were going to merge, and shoved Erny back off the straight and narrow. He took her back without a word.

And at the end of the day the girl-friend had made a hundred grand and disappeared, but Erny stayed happy. He'd made five grand and invested it. In dogs, horses and roulette. And having lost it he got drunk and talked, and that was the end of his academic career. Nobody said anything, but Erny was out: into the hard, cold world of commerce.

Where he hadn't done too badly. Middle-range electronics firm, and Erny the star of research and development. Very well paid, too, so Dave's mate had heard. But then he had to be. Horses and dogs and roulette cost a lot of money. . . .

And that was the story of Erny, so far as Dave had managed to fit it together. And right up to date. – Until seven weeks ago, anyway. Because Erny had kept in touch with his computerising mates back at the college, or rather they'd kept in touch with him. Whenever they had a little problem they sent off for Erny – the Lone Ranger of the computer keyboard – and if ever *he* had a problem that needed the sort of equipment his firm couldn't afford, all he had to do was ask.

So he'd been in and out all the time, and after a few beers he'd bring them up to date on his life story, which was so unbelievably dull that even the geezers who were exploiting him found it hard to sit still and listen, because all he did was work and gamble – and lose, then watch the sitcoms on TV and use their equipment. . . . Until the day he met his princess: the beautiful, enchanting princess who'd promised him that one day, quite soon, she'd kiss him, and turn him from a toad into a handsome prince, and in the meantime there was money. Lashings of it, and he gambled every penny and she didn't give a damn. It seemed Erny loved her for that more than anything.

His mates of course all wondered what Erny had to do to cease being a toad, but Erny had learned a bit of sense. He stayed shtum, no matter how many drinks they bought him, so they stopped buying him any, and shortly afterwards he disappeared. And they wanted him back. They were desperate. Their computer research was in a hell of a mess. . . .

I finished my G. and T. There was work to be done. And after that I'd have to take Dave to Ireland and show him just how beautiful the princess was. Not that Dave's a toad. No way.

*

Magna Electronics is mostly a breeze-block cube in a trading estate with another smaller breeze-block cube labelled Research and Development next door. I tried the big one first. The front of the cube had a carpet, and a girl at a switch

57

board. I asked if I could speak to the Managing-Director and she said You mean Mr. Purdy and I said Is he the managing director and she said Of course he is and I said Can I see him, and she said Who was I? It looked like being one of those days, so when she asked my name I told her Harkness, then added from Stanford, Partridge and True. (Heavy pause.) The Solicitors.

It may have been the way I said it but she was on that intercom in no time flat and it was all 'Straight down the corridor, Mr. Harkness, and third door along. You can't miss it.' One side of the corridor was offices, and the other was big windows looking down on to the factory floor: clean, well-lit, air-conditioned, not a hammer in sight, not a sound to be heard. I knocked at the third door, and a voice said 'Come in,' then Mr. Purdy asked what he could do for me.

He was a tall, thin, worried-looking geezer with a desk piled high with paper, and though he said he was glad to meet me he didn't look it.

'Very kind of you to see me,' I said. 'It's about one of your employees.'

Instantly he looked better. He must have thought I'd come to serve a paper on him. Divorce? I wondered. Or debt? Or both?

'Ask away,' he said, looking more relaxed by the minute.

'Ernest Fluck,' I said, but he stayed relaxed.

'Ernest is no longer with us,' he said.

'Oh,' I said. 'Can you tell me where he's gone?' He shook his head. 'Was he fired?'

He winced at that.

'A personality clash, shall we say?' he said. 'But in fact he resigned.'

Mr. Purdy looked happy again. It had been a bit of luck – Erny's resignation. If Erny had resigned there wouldn't be any severance pay to find.

'He was in your research department.'

So far as I could gather he practically *was* the research department, but it pays to be polite.

'That is so.'

'Was he good?'

'Apart from his personality problems – excellent.'

58

'You must have been sorry to lose him,' I said.

'Up to a point,' he said, but he didn't look like he'd lost a resident genius. I wondered if Erny had stacked up enough bright ideas to keep Magna Electronics going indefinitely.

'These personality problems you speak of,' I said. 'Could you give me some idea of them?'

'May I ask the reason for your enquiry?' he said. He really did.

It was time to give him another treat.

'If you'll treat this as confidential – ' I said.

'Of course.' He was drooling.

'It's a question of investments,' I said. 'Certain irregularities.'

'Ah,' he said. You would have thought it was Christmas.

'I am making no specific charges,' I said. 'But if he could assist me with my investigation it would be – well – shall we say helpful.'

'I *see*,' he said. 'I'm sorry I can't advise you as to his whereabouts.' He was, too.

'The personality problems,' I said.

'Well,' said Purdy, 'one hesitates to speak ill of a man in his absence but really – ' He broke off to have a vision of Erny and be appalled by what he saw.

'Please continue,' I said.

'Gambling,' he said. '*Insane* gambling, and tempers and tantrums when he lost. – And he often lost. Constant requests for an advance on his salary. *And* for an increase. Plus the firm belief that he was indispensable.' He looked at me sternly. 'Nobody, Mr. Harkness – *nobody* is indispensable.'

'But he was good?'

'Oh undoubtedly,' said Purdy. 'And he knew it. The trouble was he lacked direction.'

'In what way?'

'Whenever I wanted him to work on Project A he would invariably be obsessed by Project B. Or more probably Project Fluck.'

'I beg your pardon?'

'Experiments of his own,' he said.

'Such as?'

Mr. Purdy looked stern again. 'He never told me and I

never enquired.'

'How did he get on with his colleagues?'

'Not well,' he said. 'He borrowed from them. But they thought highly of him.'

'Including his assistant?' This was a cheeky one, but worth a try.

'Charlton? He was like all the others, I should think. He found Fluck able, but unlikeable.' And what, I wondered, did Imogen Courtenay-Lithgoe think?'

7

She thought I was out of my skull, and she told me so, not
once but many times. She even came up to my room to do it.
Nice room it was, southern exposure, view of a formal garden
and a paddock with horses beyond: good, modern bed, two
fine old Dublin prints on the walls, and she comes in like the
SAS doing an embassy under siege. Wearing the jodhpurs
again she was, and I was glad she hadn't brought her whip
along as well. The trouble was Sabena Redditch. She'd got a
pretty fair covering in the dailies, including the Irish ones, and
I'd achieved a few mentions as well.

Imogen didn't like it. The way she looked at it, a detective's
business was to detect, not go grabbing publicity, and
especially not when it involved a silly bitch like Sabena
Redditch. I found myself wondering whether this might have
something to do with the fact that Sabena had owned a horse
that had won the National. Even so I let her rave for a bit
because she was the client, but in the end I couldn't take any
more and I told her to belt up. And she did, just for a moment,
then:

'*What* did you say?' she said

'I said belt up.'

'Forgive the cliché,' she said, 'but what makes you think
you can talk to me like that?'

I took out my cheque-book. 'I'll give you back your
retainer,' I said. 'My luggage is downstairs. All I have to do is
put it back in the hire-car and I'll be out of your life forever –
and you'll be out of mine.'

She looked at me long and hard. She was as bright as she
was beautiful.

'It wasn't just publicity grabbing,' she said at last.

'She was a *friend*,' I said.

'Oh dear,' she said, and then: 'Is she very ill?'

'She may die,' I said.

'I can be very stupid sometimes,' she said, 'but I want you to believe me. – I didn't read that bit. Honestly I didn't. She's not silly, either. And she's certainly not a bitch.' She gave me the bright and beautiful look again. 'Will that do?'

'Do for what?'

'Do to keep you working for me.'

'It'll do,' I said. 'Do you want a report?'

'Do you want to give one?'

'Not yet,' I said.

'Then don't.' From devil to angel, just like that. 'But – weren't you supposed to be bringing an assistant with you?'

'He's doing a chore for me in Dublin,' I said. He was, too. Picking up a gun from a contact he had there. Don't ask me how an ex-para could get his hands on any kind of weapon in Ireland. Dave had said it was *because* he was an ex-para and it was at that point that I decided I didn't need any more details.

'He'll be along,' I said.

'And he can really stick on a horse?' She should have added 'Even if he's a friend of yours', but she knew better than that.

'Certainly,' I said.

'I'll have your things sent up,' she said. She did too, with my friend Burke supplying the muscle. I gave him another tenner for old time's sake, just in case there were any photographs left I hadn't seen. Then I began to unpack. . . .

When Dave came in I was dozing in front of the fire and dreaming of Sabena. I hadn't seen her after she'd been clobbered, but I was dreaming it, and it must have showed.

'Are you all right?' said Dave.

'Only a dream,' I said. 'You find what you were looking for?' He nodded. 'That's all right then.'

'I hope so,' Dave said. 'They're armed to the teeth here.'

'Who is?'

'This big geezer in the stable-yard,' Dave said. 'Dark . . . Funny little nose . . . Heavy shoulders.'

'The chauffeur,' I said. 'Finbar Gleason. What about him?'

'Cleaning a shotgun,' said Dave. 'I reckon the stables are

secure for the time being.' He looked at his watch. 'When do I meet our hostess?'

'Any time you're ready,' I said. 'We're not changing tonight.'

He got to his feet. 'You haven't got a drink handy?'

'Of course not,' I said. 'Drinks are downstairs. Why d'you want one up here?'

'I'm nervous,' he said. 'Of her.'

'She's only a woman,' I said, but I knew it was nonsense even as I said it. Imogen Courtenay-Lithgoe was only a woman the way a tigress is only a cat. All the same I had to get him downstairs.

'Utrinque Paratus,' I said. He didn't even hear me, so I tried again. 'Utrinque Paratus . . . It's Latin . . . It's also the Paras' motto. You told me yourself . . . It means "Ready For Anything".'

'I know what it means,' said Dave. 'But I don't know if I'm ready for this.' All the same he got up and came with me when I left.

She was downstairs drinking Irish ten year old – a splash of water, no ice – but she took one look at Dave and put her glass down. Mind you, I could see her point. He's tall, is Dave, but not too tall, and lean, and hard all over. Fair hair not quite gold and big brown eyes, and always a bit of a sun-tan, God knows how. He spends most of his waking time in a mini-cab – or in the pub.

'Well well,' she said. 'So this is your partner?' I'd told her assistant, but I let it go.

'Mrs. Courtenay-Lithgoe,' I said. 'This is Mr. Baxter.'

'Imogen,' she said, 'and you are – '

'David,' said Dave. He didn't look scared any more, only shell-shocked. She moved in on him like Vikings taking a nunnery. . . . That gave me a lot of time to look at the Watteau, until General Sir Robert Berkeley came down and poured me another Irish whiskey and told me all about the Anzio bridgehead. It didn't sound the same place my father had been, but then I find it impossible to believe in anything my father ever did. Except that he killed my mother. . . . I found myself wondering if I should tell the general that I'd met his sister, and thought I'd do better to save it. I introduced him to Dave instead, and not before time. The Vikings were breaking down the last doors. . . .

We went in to dinner. Smoked salmon and saddle of lamb, and a burgundy I can still taste – and Dave putting it away like it was junk food and plastic beer. And Dave's a geezer who loves his food. And after it was over the general said 'Bridge' and I could see I was in for a terrible night, only Burke came along and saved me. I was getting very fond of Burke. Giving him Mrs. Courtenay-Lithgoe's tenners was a real pleasure. . . .

'What is it, – Burke?' said the lady of the house, and Burke got that sort of shimmering look for a second, and even Dave blinked.

'It's Phelim,' said Burke. Phelim was the head stable-lad. 'From the stables. He says Nautch Girl's foaling.'

'*Phelim* says?' She jumped to her feet. 'What about Finbar Gleason?'

'He's not there, mam.'

'*Not there?*' This time it was the general who jumped up. 'Where the hell is he?'

'Phelim doesn't know, sir.'

Father and daughter looked at each other.

'We'd better go over,' she said.

'We *have* to go over. . . . We can call the vet from the stables.' He turned to Burke. 'Tell Phelim we're coming.' Burke lumbered off.

'Can we help?' I said.

'Good heavens no,' said the general, and strode from the room.

Imogen Courtenay-Lithgoe lingered.

'You *could* see if you can find Finbar,' she said. 'We'll need him – if he's not too drunk.'

Then she was gone.

There was a sliver of moon, and we found a big torch on a table in the hall, and set out to look for Finbar. The stableyard was deserted, and even Dave couldn't pick up a sign from its cobbles. We moved off towards the paddock. The night was chilly, and the horses were under cover. From the stables there came a high-pitched whinnying sound. Nautch Girl had her problems, too. . . . The grass swished under our shoes and the dew was heavy on our feet and calves, but all the same we went on looking. Finbar Gleason couldn't have just walked off. He was too fond of his employers for that. Especially the general. . . .

Inevitably it was Dave who found him. He lay in a ditch at the edge of the paddock, under the shelter of an elm tree. But he'd never need shelter again. He'd taken one right between the eyes. Nice, neat entry wound, but the exit wasn't nearly so pretty. I could have shoved my fist into the back of his head. . . . My stomach heaved. It always does when this sort of thing comes along. I can't help it. But I didn't throw up.

'What do you make of it?' I said.

'Biggish hand gun,' said Dave. 'Low velocity. – Hence the mess in the back of his head. A magnum bullet would have kept on going and into the tree.'

'You reckon he was killed here then?'

Dave flashed the torch.

'See for yourself,' he said. 'The grass is all straight. He wasn't dragged.'

I bent over the body. Dave would have done the job for me, but there's things you have to do for yourself, so I went through Finbar Gleason's pockets. Carroll's cigarettes, matches, a plastic ball-point, three betting slips and five hundred quid in used ten pound notes. Nothing else. Dave whistled, and I wiped the haul and started to put it all back then showed a bit of sense for once and looked at the backs of the betting slips. Two of them were blank, the third said: La Torre del Sur, copied out painstakingly in block capitals. I kept that one: put the other two back.

Dave said, 'Tampering with the evidence?'

'No,' I said. 'Just keeping it out of harm's way.'

'What now?' said Dave.

'The rozzers,' I said. 'What else? He was a bloody-minded bastard, but even so – '

'I don't think you should say we found him,' said Dave.

'Why not?'

'You're in enough trouble.' I waited. 'Your girl's in intensive care.' My girl . . . I blessed him for that. 'And there's a geezer in intensive care as well. *And* another one in hospital. They could talk, Ron.'

'It's possible.' Not likely, but possible.

'And you were involved. The police can't prove that, but they know it. This isn't a good time for us to find a corpse, now is it?'

It's never a good time to find a corpse, but Dave knows that as well as I do. So I thought about my involvement – and Dave's. Dave was too much of a gent to mention *his* involvement, but he was involved right up to Grievous Bodily Harm; GBH, as we call it in the trade.

'And after all,' said Dave, 'you found what you were looking for.'

El Torre del Sur . . . Was that what I was looking for? I remembered a hundred peseta piece under a chair-cushion.

'What do you say?' said Dave.

'We looked,' I said. 'Looked all over. But we didn't find a corpse. – Maybe that was because we didn't look in the ditch –'

'Good lad,' said Dave.

'– Only I need to think about this,' I said. 'Drive around and think about it.' It was a habit I had, when there was a problem. Think and drive, Dave calls it.

'You do that,' said Dave.

'How about you?'

'I'll hang around inside and wait for the horse's midwife.'

There were only two words to say to that, so I said them.

'Good luck,' I said.

*

When I got back I at least had a list of things to do, like talk with my employer, have a word with Horry Lumley, and book a flight to Spain, probably to Malaga, but I wouldn't know about that for sure till somebody found the body and the Irish police asked questions. . . . The Garda, they were called, but whatever their name was they'd be nosy – all coppers are – and it wouldn't be five minutes after I'd been shown the door before they'd be on the phone to Detective Sergeant Matthews at New Scotland Yard. I might have had a few ideas, but I had problems, too.

66

Dave was in the drawing-room when I got back, reading a book – what else? *The Spoils of Poynton*, it was, by Henry James. Only for once he wasn't having a lager for a chaser, it was cognac. Hennessy XO. I poured one for myself and joined him. He'd changed his suit, and I would have to too. My trouser creases were ruined.

'What's up?' I said. 'Any news of the little mother?'

'The vet arrived,' said Dave. 'It was Burke told me that. There seem to be complications.'

'Finbar Gleason helping?'

'Looks like he's scarpered,' said Dave, and went back to his book. I went over to the Watteau. It had as much to tell me as any novel.

*

It was after midnight when Sir Robert and his daughter returned. The vet, it seemed, had gone home to his bed. There was nothing obstetrical about them, and I was glad of it. The foal, it seemed, showed promise.

'I'll feel better when Finbar's had a look at him,' Sir Robert said.

'But wasn't he with you?' I asked him.

'He seems to have gone off somewhere,' Sir Robert said. 'He does sometimes.'

'But where could he possibly go?' said Dave.

I would never have got away with such a question, but to a paratrooper all things are forgiven.

'Dublin,' said Sir Robert.

'To see his woman,' Imogen said. I thought: They'll know better in the morning.

But they didn't. Stable-lads were up at six, and horses exercised and turned into the paddock, and nothing was said about Finbar Gleason. After breakfast David and Imogen went riding, and Sir Robert worked at his book on Monte Cassino, and said nothing. I went for a walk as far as the pub in the village and used the telephone just in case I was overheard. On the other hand the non-appearance of Finbar Gleason bothered me so much I almost got to the point where

67

I could believe we'd imagined the corpse with the hole in its head, and Gleason had gone off to Dublin to see his woman, and that wouldn't do at all. So I walked to the village and bought a glass of porter and used the phone that they kept in a cupboard crammed with empty bottles. I fed in most of my Irish change and got Horry Lumley, hung over as usual. He must be loaded to acquire a hangover like that, the places he goes to, I thought. And then the penny dropped. It was me that was paying for it, or rather Imogen was.

'Oh, it's you,' he said.

'Cardwell, Ryecroft and Cairns,' I said. They sounded like an old-fashioned half back line.

'Stockbrokers are hell,' said Lumley.

'No progress?'

'I didn't say that.' He groaned and then there was a gulping sound. Black coffee? Prairie Oyster? 'I took a girl out last night.'

'I hope she saw you home O.K.'

'Very droll,' Horry said. 'As a matter of fact she did. She also works for Cardwell, Ryecroft and Cairns. Typist.'

'And?'

'And she's going to get what you're after. Your friend Fluck's about to buy an electronics firm, but if you want details it'll cost you extra.'

'I want details,' I said. But I didn't just want them. I had to have them.

'Take a day or two,' said Horry.

So Erny wanted to be boss, I thought, and remembered what Charlton, his former assistant, had told me. Out of the blue, so to speak.

'I'd hate to work for him.'

'Why d'you say that?' I'd asked.

'Because he never knew when to stop and he'd expect everybody else to be the same.'

'But do you think it's likely you'd work for him?'

'God, no.'

I'd pressed him. 'Then why bring it up?'

'I don't know,' Charlton had said. 'But I do know I wouldn't want to work for him. He was awful. But he was the best R and D man I've ever met.'

R and D. Research and Development. . . .

'Soon as you can,' I said, and then, to be polite, 'You're doing nicely.'

It was true enough.

'Say it with money,' he said, and then: 'I hear your girl-friend got clobbered.'

'That's right.'

'She's nice,' he said. 'Tell her I said so.'

'First chance I get,' I said. 'Have a nice hangover.' . . .

At Concannon House they were discussing Dave's performance as a horseman, or rather Imogen was relating it to her father. Dave's face seemed permanently set into what I can only describe as the 'Aw shucks' position. '– Unbelievable,' my client was saying. 'Nothing right. Not a single thing. Hands . . . Seat . . . You name it.'

'Give him time, darling,' her father said. 'He might – '

Imogen cut in on him.

'You don't understand, daddy,' she said. 'He cleared every fence I did, and he was riding Beelzebub.' Beelzebub, I'd been told, was their prize stallion, and evil with it. Sir Robert sat up as if his daughter had jabbed a pin in him, and looked at Dave. Until now the way he'd looked at Dave could best have been decribed as indulgent: now it was wary, to say the least.

'*He* rode *Beelzebub*?'

'Yes, daddy,' Imogen said. 'He rode Beelzebub when Beelzebub didn't want to be ridden.'

'Jolly good show,' said the general, and went away to fetch his best Fino sherry. Dave and I detest Fino sherry.

'You really do need to know how to ride,' my client said.

Dave made an enormous effort and got rid of 'Aw shucks.' 'I don't think so,' he said.

'Why ever not?'

'If I knew how to ride I might fall off.'

She laughed, but the laughter was friendly, enticing even, and then she turned to me.

'What do you propose to do after lunch, Mr. Hogget?' she said.

'Have a chat with you.' She started to scowl, and I added, 'Not for long. – Say twenty minutes of your valuable time.' The scowl vanished.

69

'Of course,' she said. 'Daddy will be working on his Monte Cassino book almost till dinner-time.'

She didn't look at Dave: she didn't have to. And anyway Sir Robert came back then with the dreaded Fino. . . .

She had a little sitting-room to herself on the first floor: Aubusson carpet, Louis Quinze commode and chair, second Empire chaise-longue. *She must be worth a mint.* It was a very feminine room, and I was glad there wasn't a bearskin rug about.

'You said you didn't want to make a report,' she said.

'That was yesterday. Things have changed,' I said.

'What things?'

'Finbar Gleason.'

She gestured the way people gesture at over-obtrusive wasps.

'He's got a woman in Dublin. I told you.'

'He's got a job *here*.'

'He's our chauffeur, certainly – '

'He's also your farrier. And he's a judge of horse-flesh your father respects – according to what he said last night.'

'And if he is?'

'Finn MacCool is missing, too. Did he work with Finn MacCool?'

'Of course,' she said. 'He worked with all our horses.'

'So the horse knew him well enough to obey him – do what Gleason ordered?'

She shook her head.

'He wouldn't do that,' she said. 'Not Finbar.'

'I'm not saying he did,' I said. 'All I want to know is could he have done?'

'*Could*, yes,' she said. 'But he wouldn't.'

'Who else could?'

'Daddy . . . Me . . .' she said.

'What about the servants? . . . I don't mean the house servants – but what about the stable-boys and Phelim?'

'Finn MacCool was – difficult,' she said. 'He didn't get on with the boys.'

'And Phelim?'

'Phelim least of all. But there's no point to this, Mr. Hogget. Daddy told you about the horse-box and the Ford Granada –

70

and Finbar's in Dublin. I *know* he is.'

'What's the woman's name?'

It took a bit of probing, but I got it at last.

'Anything else?' she said.

'Ernest Fluck.'

She sighed very deeply. If she does it again, I thought, I'll be whinnying like Beelzebub. 'What about him?'

It was my turn to sigh. What I was about to say might annoy her, and she'd probably start to throw things, very valuable things with hard, sharp edges.

'You hired me to find him.'

'*And* Finn MacCool.'

'And Finn MacCool,' I agreed. 'That argues that you want him back.'

'Well of course I want him back,' she said. 'He's my fiancé.'

'That's just it,' I said. 'Why is he your fiancé?'

'What the hell do you mean – *why*?'

'You're not going to like this,' I said. 'All I ask is you remember it's what you're paying me for.'

'Go ahead,' she said. 'I'll be all right.' I doubted that, but I had no choice. I went ahead. 'You are the most beautiful woman I've ever met,' I said. 'You've been courted by millionaires and princes and dashing gentleman-riders. Moreover you are very rich.'

'Is that the speech I'm supposed to dislike?' she said.

'No. It's this one. I've done a little work on Ernest Fluck – Ernest the man, so to speak. He has shocking manners and a vile temper and he's a compulsive gambler. He lost a brilliant academic career because of a mix-up with a girl who betrayed him – the only other girl in his life apart from you. And she was a crook. He has neither manners nor charm. From what people tell me it isn't so much that he lacks the ability to please – he doesn't even know that you are supposed to please. He's a sloppy eater and nearly always broke.'

I broke off there. She sat relaxed in her Louis Quinze chair, on her face a look of polite boredom as if I were reading her an especially dull Times leader, but her hands were balled into fists.

'Go on,' she said.

'That's it,' I said. 'Except for one question. Why does Mrs.

Courtenay-Lithgoe want to become Mrs. Fluck?'

She shimmered then, in the manner of her butler, Burke, but like him she regained control. 'Does it matter?' she said.

'Well of course it matters,' I said. 'It might even help me find out where to look.'

There was a pause, then she sat up very straight, like a child on its best behaviour, or a prisoner on trial.

'Ernest Fluck is a genius,' she said. 'If you talked to people who knew him, you must have been told so.'

'The word was mentioned.'

'He has absolutely no practical sense. He needs to be managed. But he can handle a computer the way Aylmer could handle a horse.' Aylmer Courtenay-Lithgoe, her last husband. For a moment she relaxed, thinking of him, then her shoulders straightened again. 'I'm a rich woman,' she said. 'You said it and it's true . . . Rich . . . ' She savoured the word as if it was Latour '61. 'You're not rich, Mr. Hogget.' It was a statement, not a question, but without malice.

'I do all right,' I said, 'but rich? – Not yet.'

'It's a wonderful feeling,' she said. 'Especially if you've been poor in your time.'

A general's daughter? Poor? She read the look on my face.

'I didn't mean starvation poor, or living in Birmingham, or something. – Though I do know somebody like that. I even try to help. . . . She refuses to be helped.' She shook her head, dismissing the thought of Poppy, Lady Tarleton, which was a hard thought to dismiss.

'What I meant,' she said, 'was that as a child and a teenager we always had only just enough to live on. To send me to school, and so on. My father has no head for business either. . . . But he did find the money to send me to Switzerland, God knows how, and there I met my first husband and became rich. Does it sound like Cinderella?'

'It does a bit,' I said.

'It wasn't in the least like Cinderella,' she said, 'but I became rich and I stayed rich. Do you know, Mr. Hogget, there's only one thing wrong with being rich?'

'You always want to be richer?'

'*Clever* Mr. Hogget,' she said. 'I don't know if every rich person feels like that – though I suspect they do. I bet you

72

Jenny Cooper does. – You discovered Jenny Cooper, I take it?'

'The bird who got him thrown out of Imperial College?'

'Last heard of in Sydney selling office space at fifty Australian dollars a square metre. She and I have a lot in common, Mr. Hogget.'

Again it was a statement, not a question, but again it required an answer.

'The need to be rich,' I said, 'and the ability to manage.'

'You also called Jenny Cooper a crook.' I let it lie. 'Come *on*, Mr. Hogget.'

'She broke a law or two.'

'So have I.' I remembered the Arab bodyguard with the bullet in his backside. 'You can't be really rich if you don't. But this time it's all going to be more or less legal. – At least I think it is.' She didn't sound all that worried, either way.

'What is?' I asked.

'A little venture that Ernest has dreamed up,' she said. 'It will make a very great deal of money – and when it does – after you've found him – some of that money will be yours.'

'Just how did you come to hear of Ernest Fluck?' I asked.

'But surely you know?' she said. 'I knocked him down with the Rolls. It was love at first sight on Ernest's part – especially after I took him out to dinner and a couple of gaming clubs.' She looked at her watch.

And that, I gathered, was all she was going to tell me. If I ever found out who gave her the idea to knock Erny down in the first place, then it wouldn't be from her. So I gouged a letter of introduction out of her, then got up and left her, politely I hoped, and without irony. Whatever was to come between her and Dave was in their own time. Nobody would be paid for it.

8

Teresa O'Byrne, her name was, and she, too, lived in a Dublin Georgian house. But it wasn't like Imogen Courtenay-Lithgoe's. This one had been a tenement even when the English still ruled Ireland. Its small elegant bricks were rotting like teeth, half the sash windows had been smashed, then boarded up, and it smelled. Dear God it smelled. Yet somehow the main door had survived, its mahogany scarred and violated by the wrong kind of paint, but even so it looked and was irreplaceable. I banged on it with my fist – the brass knocker had long since been pawned – and at last the door opened, and a horde of ragged kids swept past me, as if we were doing a TV documentary and the year was 1919. And then the door opened wider, and the year was 1985 again.

She was tall, bone-thin and irreclaimably gone on whatever it was she had to have. Heroin was my guess. She couldn't afford cocaine by the look of her, and amphetamines tended to occur a lot closer to Trinity College than where we both stood.

'Miss Teresa O'Byrne?' I said.

'She doesn't,' the tall girl said. 'Not any more . . . I do . . . But not just now. Come back in a couple of hours. Bring ten pounds.'

The price of her next fix, I thought. The fix that would replace the one she was just about to have.

'I'd like that,' I said, lying like a gentleman. 'But just at the moment I have to see Miss O'Byrne. My name is Harkness. I'm from Stanford, Partridge and True. They're a firm of solicitors. In London. Miss O'Byrne could be in for a bit of money.'

I had her then: no doubt about it.

'How much?' she said.

74

'Not a fortune,' I said. 'A few hundred after tax. All the same I should think she'd be grateful to anyone who helped her to it.'

'Joe Gallagher's,' she said. 'Second left, first right. If she's not there now she will be soon. . . . Come back when you've talked, why don't you? – And bring ten pounds.'

Joe Gallagher's was a pub – what else would it be? A pub that was like a cross between a lavatory and a non-conformist chapel, except that it wasn't so cheerful. But even so it was doing good business – with the kind of persistent, dedicated drinkers who never push it quite hard enough to qualify for the alcoholic ward, yet never lay off enough to stumble back into the real world of jobs and people and VAT. They all knew about Teresa O'Byrne and they all liked her. – A darlin' girl. A lovely girl. One of them even produced a smudgy photograph, and she didn't seem to be an eye-sore. But she hadn't been in that day – or come to think of it – the day before. Maybe not even the day before that. But three days ago was a long time. How could a man be sure?

I asked Joe Gallagher, and he was sure; didn't hesitate.

'Last Friday,' he said. 'Five days ago. I had to put her out. She hasn't been back since. A lovely girl.'

'Then why did you put her out?'

'When she's had too many she sings,' he said. 'I'm all for toleration, believe me, but you'd have to be tone-deaf to put up with Teresa O'Byrne singing.'

I went back to the house, not because I wanted to but because I had to: – I committed a felony on the beautiful, battered front door with my Swiss Army knife, then slipped inside and on to Teresa O'Byrne's room. But the door to the room wasn't locked, so it wasn't another felony – only a misdemeanour. And once inside I could see why it wasn't locked: everything worth taking was already gone. The one wardrobe was empty, and so was the chest of drawers, but I locked the door even so and went to work, just in case she'd missed something. Half a dozen Mills and Boons, with a couple of bus tickets for bookmarks, a missal from her Loving Mammy and Daddy that didn't look as if it had been used much, and two letters. One was from Finbar Gleason, and it surprised me: it was a formal declaration of love and an offer of marriage. The other was from a girl-friend who had emigrated and found work, but not happiness, in South Dakota. She thought South Dakota stank. . . . There was also a bank statement. She had a credit balance of less than twelve Irish pounds. That and a pile of dirty laundry took care of the room, so I went into what I've no doubt an estate-agent would call the kitchen area, a converted cupboard with a sink, a tiny refrigerator, a gas-ring and a pedal bin. The fridge was connected, but empty, but the pedal bin was full. I fetched a sheet of lining paper from one of the drawers and dumped the contents of the bin on it. Miss O'Byrne had drunk a lot of tea, but at least she'd used tea bags. . . . An empty baked beans tin, the end of a loaf, chocolate wrappers and some dead roses. A dozen – I counted. They must have cost at least the price of a fix for the girl two doors away. . . . Who'd sent them? Finbar Gleason? I looked very carefully, but there was no card. . . . Instead, I found a wrapper of heavy blue paper, and then another, the kind that comes with new bank notes. On one of them, very faintly in pencil, was written the figure 500. So Miss O'Byrn might have copped a thousand Irish pounds – punts they call them. Say eight hundred and fifty quid sterling. I had a sudden, urgent desire to examine Imogen Courtenay-Lithgoe's bank account, then told myself not to be a fool. Mrs. Courtenay-Lithgoe was the client. The trouble was she was the only one I could think of who could lay her hands on a thousand punts. . . .

I raked through the mess a bit further. Egg shells, and bacon rind that smelled, a margarine wrapper, and underneath it a brochure for a Spanish holiday firm stamped with the name of a travel agency in O'Connell Street. And that was the lot, but with a bit of luck it might be enough. It all depended on Mr. Harkness of Stanford, Partridge and True. . . .

Travel agents do not like solicitors, because almost the only reason they ever meet them is that the solicitor is representing a client who is about to sue the agent for selling him a lousy holiday. But that doesn't mean they won't talk to solicitors; on the contrary they're frantic to find out how much it may be going to cost them. So when I did my Harkness act I was shown into the manager's office at the double.

Mr. Kinsella was the manager, plump and anxious to please, but looking at me as if he was a rabbit and I was a stoat. When I went into my bit about the missing heiress, he was so relieved he'd got out the whiskey and glasses before I'd even finished. We toasted each other, and I sipped mine slowly. I don't like whiskey, but I had to keep him happy, because he was so relieved I wasn't suing him he'd tell me anything.

'I remember,' he said, delighted to please. 'I served her myself.' He added hastily, 'We were rather short-handed that day.' I mustn't get the impression he spent his life behind a counter.

'I understand she's on holiday in Spain. The Costa del Sol to be precise.'

'Torremolinos,' Mr. Kinsella said. 'Hotel Las Golondrinas. Rather nice, they tell me. Three Stars. Three hundred and fifty for the fortnight. Direct flight Dublin-Malaga.' He swallowed whiskey. 'Something odd. What was it?'

I swallowed whiskey, too, to show I was a mate. Suddenly he smiled.

'That's right,' he said. 'The three hundred and fifty. She paid for it ready money. All in tenners. All new. It isn't often you get ready money these days and when you do it's usually a farmer out of the bogs. And they don't go to the Costa del Sol.'

'When did she go?' I asked.

'Booked on the Friday. Flight was next day. She'll be lying in the sun now with a nice cold drink I shouldn't wonder. It'll be champagne after she talks to you. Will you go after her?'

'She's gone for a fortnight, I take it?' He nodded. 'A formal letter should suffice.' He seemed a bit disappointed at that, so I added: 'She'll have to come to London of course, when she returns.'

That cheered him. People travelling was always good news.

'Who put you on to us?'

'Oh – general enquiries,' I said. 'But I may tell you this, Mr. Kinsella. I have rarely heard a travel agency recommended so highly.'

77

I had a hell of a time declining another drink.

*

'You look like you've been busy,' said Dave

'So do you,' I said.

He was lying on my bed, coat and shoes off, smoking a cigarette. Only he'd opened the window first. Considerate geezer is Dave.

'I've been with Imogen,' he said. I said nothing. There was nothing to say. 'There's a lady who believes in getting her money's worth.'

'You don't usually have any complaints,' I said.

He sounded so sad, what else was I supposed to think? But I'd got it wrong, and I knew I had, because he blushed. Not just a flush, neither. Scarlet he was.

'I didn't mean that,' he said. 'Though as a matter of fact we did – ' His voice faded, and I let it lie. We don't interfere in each other's private lives any more, not since he had this big romance with my wife Melanie, which is why she and I were separated.

'What I mean,' said Dave, 'is she's nosey.'

'She's a woman,' I said. 'She has to be nosey.'

'About you,' said Dave. 'Are you reliable, and ought she to trust you? All that.'

'What did you tell her?'

'I told her you were my mate,' he said, 'which means I'm biassed. But I also told her I'd trusted you ever since I'd known you. And I've never had to regret it. Not once.'

'Thanks,' I said. 'Did she believe you?'

'I think so,' he said, 'because she changed the subject. She asked me how honest you were and I said that was a big one, but if she meant law-abiding I said that was what you preferred if possible.'

'True enough,' I said.

'Then she asked me if you were always honest with your clients, and I said invariably – unless they were dishonest with you.'

'So what did she say?'

78

'She said, "Oh",' said Dave. 'Then she started on about Sabena Redditch.'

'What about her?'

'How long had you known her, were you lovers, what did her parents think? The usual. I said I didn't know.'

'Did she believe you?'

'I doubt it,' said Dave. 'She talked about her husband instead . . . Aylmer.'

'What about him?'

'How she adored him,' Dave said. 'Considering where we were at the time it sounds a bit much, but it didn't bother me. She reckons I'm a nice man.'

I thought of the bloke in intensive care.

'Well so you are,' I said. I meant it.

'What I mean is – Imogen and me – it's what people used to call civilised. – What that really means is that it works while it lasts, but it probably won't last long.'

'Where was the general?'

'Out riding,' he said. 'On Beelzebub.' He grinned. 'He still can't understand why I didn't fall off. . . . Neither can I, come to that. What did you do?'

'Went to see Teresa O'Byrne.'

'Who?'

'Finbar Gleason's girl-friend. I gather his body's still missing?'

'Not a sign,' said Dave. 'I checked the paddock again myself. . . . Zilch.'

'So who moved him?'

'The geezer that shot him,' said Dave, 'whoever that was. Did you find Teresa O'Byrne?'

'She's disappeared too,' I said.

'They're all at it,' said Dave. 'A man, a woman, a horse and a corpse. You've got your work cut out this time, Ron boy.'

'Except I know where she's gone,' I said. 'How's your Spanish?'

Then I had to go and find Mrs. Courtenay-Lithgoe and make a report. I told her Teresa O'Byrne had scarpered, but I reckoned I knew where to, and Dave and me would go and look.

'I take it you don't want to tell me where it is?' she said.

'Better not,' I told her. 'That way you can't tell anybody else.'

'Did she run off with Finbar Gleason?' she said, and I felt the hair on the back of my neck rise. For the first time I realised that only Dave and I knew Gleason was dead. Just us – and his killer.

'That's something we'll check, of course,' I said.

'You make it sound as if he'd betrayed us in some way,' she said. 'But he wouldn't. I promise you. He's not very nice, but he's frightfully loyal. . . . Will you be going back to London?'

'Tomorrow,' I said.

'When you see Sabena will you give her my regards, then let me know how she is?'

'Be a pleasure,' I said.

'You dress all wrong,' she said, 'and your accent's terrible, but you really are a gentleman, Mr. Hogget. I'm obliged to you.'

*

I took a chance while Dave was buying two business class returns to Malaga and phoning the Hotel Las Golondrinas for a double-room. He'd told me his Spanish was adequate which meant it was probably better than mine. Whenever I try to speak Spanish I end up speaking Italian, because that's what my mother was. But Dave would buy the book and the tape and peg away till he got it right. A determined geezer Dave is when he has to be.

They'd put her in a private room at St. Stephen's, but nobody seemed that keen on letting me into it, not until I told the sister I was the one who'd taken her to the 'Feed The Starving' Ball.

'She's asked for you several times, Mr. Hogget,' the sister said.

'She's conscious, then?'

'Sometimes,' she said. 'She's been badly hurt – and she's in great need of support.'

'That's why I'm here,' I said.

She gave me a long, cool look, decided I meant it, and took

me to a dim, antiseptic room that was much too hot for a healthy person, but then it wasn't meant for a healthy person. There were flowers, and the sight of them hurt me, because I hadn't thought of flowers, and now it was too late, but for once I got lucky. She was asleep, and I shot over to the florist's across the road and bought half his stock, then sat and waited till she came round. She was bone-white and very thin in the gleaming white bed, a bandage the size of a turban round her head. And she looked desperately ill. This woman who had blazed with vitality now seemed very close to death. Then suddenly she was awake, and a little, a very little of the vitality returned.

'Hallo you,' she said.

'I've bought you a few flowers,' I said. They were every-where except on the bed, and I'd had to use some very unlikely objects as vases.

'I can see you have,' she said, and then: 'I've told daddy about you.'

'Oh yes?' I said.

'Don't look like that,' Sabena said. 'You'll make me laugh and I mustn't.'

'What about your father?'

'He wants to see you, that's all.'

'Why?'

'Because I like you. You'll go, won't you? The address is in the book.'

The little bit of vitality was fading fast, her eyelids closing.

'Of course I'll go,' I said.

'Too kind,' she said. 'Do you still fancy me?'

'More than ever,' I said.

'They had to shave off my hair you know. Have you ever made love to a bald person before?'

'It'll be a new experience for me,' I said.

She tried to put out her tongue at me and fell asleep instead, and because I loved her so much I panicked and rang for a nurse and the sister came. She was very patient with me. Sabena had had an operation which had gone well enough so far, but with head injuries you can never be sure so soon. . . . But falling asleep was natural, and even good. I must try not to worry. That was another way of saying I must try not to be

81

Ron Hogget.

I took a bus to the 'Mason's Arms' and had a bite with Dave: ploughman's lunch for me, large shepherd's pie for Dave. I was so upset about Sabena that I couldn't finish mine, but it wasn't wasted. Dave saw to that. The human waste disposal unit.

'Are we set?' I said.

'We fly tomorrow,' he said and gave me my ticket.

The sooner the better really, but I hated being away from Sabena, and Dave saw it straight off.

'How's your girl?' he said.

'They're not sure,' I said. 'But she doesn't look good, Dave. She doesn't look good at all.'

'These Sloane Ranger birds are tough,' he said. 'She'll be all right. You'll see.'

He didn't know a bloody thing about it, but he'd said what I wanted to hear, and I was grateful. Then he looked about him. There was nobody close enough to hear.

'What we going to do in Spain?' he said.

'Talk to a bird,' I said. 'Maybe a feller an' all.'

'Will I need a you-know-what?'

By a you-know-what he meant a Colt Python 357 magnum revolver.

'We're only going for a chat,' I said.

'Suits me,' said Dave. 'And it's a long time since I ate calamaritos.' He ate some more of my cheese instead.

'Talking of you-know-what's,' I said. 'What about the one in you-know-where?'

'Will we be going back there?'

'We will if we're successful,' I said. 'If only to collect the cheque.'

'Then we just might need a you-know-what,' he said. 'Don't worry Ron boy. Nobody else'll find it, but it's nice and handy.' He ate more cheese, then: 'There's a bit on the News about those two poor misguided fellows who got clobbered in Knightsbridge the other night,' he said.

'Oh yes?' I said.

'The one in intensive care's in a coma as well,' said Dave.

'The other one's still refused to make a statement. Any statement.'

A bit of luck for us, I thought.

'Let's hope he keeps it up,' said Dave, then he put my cheese down, and he got that look, the one that makes me nervous.

'Fuzz in the door,' he said.

It was Detective Sergeant Matthews, heading for us.

'Be nice,' I said. 'It's nice to be nice.' Then Matthews came over.

'Detective Sergeant Matthews,' I said. 'This is a surprise.'

'I doubt it,' said Matthews. 'I was looking for you, Mr. Hogget.'

'That's even more surprising,' I said. 'Oh by the way, this is my friend, Mr. Baxter. He's already spoken to Mr. – Arliss, was it?'

'Detective Constable Allison,' said Matthews, and I ordered a round of drinks to show how calm and relaxed I was. Matthews asked for a half of lager, same as Dave, which suggested he was a serious cop, but even so I managed to stay calm and relaxed, or look as if I was.

'Well what can I do for you, sergeant?' I said.

'If we could all go down to the station it might be more convenient,' Matthews said.

'For you, maybe. But it's more convenient for me here.'

'What makes you say that, sir?'

'Your nick hasn't got a licence,' I said, 'and Mr. Baxter and I have things to do.'

'May I ask what things?'

'Business,' I said.

'Something to do with Ireland, sir?'

I went through the motions of being surprised, just for the look of things. 'You have been busy,' I said.

It pleased him. 'You've been very close to a spot of bother recently, sir. Naturally we like to keep an eye on you.'

'Very decent of you,' I said. Matthews turned to Dave.

'You've been busy in Ireland, too, Mr. Baxter?' he said.

'That's right,' said Dave.

'Doing what?'

'Working for Mr. Hogget,' said Dave. Matthews got so annoyed he drank some of his lager.

'I was offered a job,' I said. 'A private and confidential job.

83

It seemed possible I might need some help – and Mr. Baxter gives me a hand from time to time. You could check on that.' – But of course he already had. 'I give you my word this spot of bother's got nothing to do with the case I'm working on – any more than I have, but it is private and it is confidential.'

In other words I was telling him I knew my rights, and if he pushed me any further, the next voice he heard would be my lawyer's. Matthews sighed.

'It's the sequence that bothers me, sir,' he said. 'You leave Miss Redditch and she's assaulted in no time. Then two blokes are assaulted right next to the road you took to the tube – and just about the time you were going there. They have to be the same two blokes who assaulted Miss Redditch. Don't you *want* to see them put away?'

'Well of course,' I said. 'But you can't possibly be saying they told you I was involved?'

'One of them can't speak and the other one won't,' Matthews said. 'I'm surprised you didn't read it in the paper.' He turned to Dave. 'In the paratroops were you, sir?'

'Quite right,' said Dave. 'Honourable discharge, what's more.'

'Do you ever wish you were back?'

'Never,' said Dave.

'Mind telling me why not?'

'I couldn't stand the violence,' said Dave.

Matthews slammed down his glass and walked out. The glass was still two thirds full.

'He suspects,' said Dave.

'He bloody knows,' I said, 'but he can't prove.'

'There could be trouble when we get back from Spain.'

'There's always trouble,' I said, and went to phone Sir Montague Redditch. He was out. Even when I told the switchboard girl who I was he was out, but she put me on to his secretary who put me on to his PA, who was very very sorry. She said so.

'I know that Sir Montague was most anxious to talk to you,' she said

'Perhaps tomorrow morning,' I said.

'Perhaps. . . . Sir Montague was called away urgently. *Most* urgently. Otherwise he'd never have left at such a time.'

'I quite understand Miss – '

'Newton,' she said. 'I shall tell Sir Montague at the first possible opportunity.'

'I'm obliged to you,' I said, and said Cheerio to Dave, now deep in Henry James once more, and took a cab to Kensington, then got out to walk round Holland Park. Most people prefer Kensington Gardens on account of Princess Margaret living there and the Round Pond and the boats and that, but when it comes to choosing a place to walk while you're thinking, give me Holland Park every time. And I had plenty to think about.

I had a corpse that had been shot dead with a revolver then disappeared, and the corpse's ex-hooker girl-friend who had suddenly come into a thousand quid and buzzed off to Spain. I had a horse that had vanished even more effectively than the corpse (at least I knew Finbar Gleason was dead) and a demented genius who might be dead and might be alive, might be kidnapped or might just be legging it because he'd realised he was out of his depth. And the reason for that was he'd figured out a way to make a fortune and other people wanted it: his fiancée for one, but there might well be others.

That brought me to the client: that beautiful carnivore who told me just enough to keep me going, but had so much more that was hidden. Then there was the fact that she'd had a photograph of Sabena and Heidi Pickel: Heidi Pickel whose brother Theodore had been at the 'Feed The Starving' Ball. And I should have asked Mrs. Courtenay-Lithgoe about the Pickel family but that would have meant talking to her about Sabena, and I couldn't bear to do that, not the way Sabena was. I thought about Sir Montague who loved his daughter and had left her, and I thought about Sydney, Australia and Torremolinos, Spain. Then I thought about phoning Horry Lumley, but I went to Bloomsbury instead, to the kind of archive library that can supply you anything from Debrett's Peerage for 1935 to the Hong Kong telephone directory, and started digging.

When they threw me out at closing time I went to another pub and another phone, and rang St. Stephen's. Miss Redditch's condition was poorly but stable, I was told. No more visitors till further notice. I went home and dined off boil in the bag kippers and a cup of tea, and switched on the telly because the silence was destroying me. A tall and over-anxious pleaser of a quiz-master was convulsed with laughter because some punter couldn't name the capital of Canada. . . . Then the door-bell rang and I switched off the box, made sure the chain was on the door before I opened it a crack. Another tall geezer, but neither anxious nor a pleaser.

'I wonder if I might come in?' Sir Robert Berkeley said. 'It might be a good idea if you and I had a talk.'

I took the chain off the door and let him in because what else could I do?

We went into the sitting-room, that had been Melanie's pride and joy. Music-centre and five-seater settee that wasn't quite leather and, for some reason known only to Melanie, a picture of a clown on one wall. The general looked about him as if he'd walked into a wigwam. I picked up my Iberia ticket to Malaga and put it in my pocket.

'Would you like a drink?' I said.

'You haven't any Irish I suppose?' he said.

All I had was Scotch, but he took it anyway, with soda, and a gin and tonic for me, then I asked what I could do for him.

'It's about my daughter,' he said. What else could it be about?

'You're working for her,' he went on. 'Looking for this awful Fluck fellow.'

'Is he awful?'

'If you'd met him you wouldn't ask that question,' the general said. 'He's ghastly.'

'How is he ghastly?'

'Vile manners, appalling accent, didn't bathe enough.' He shrugged. 'Ghastly. And he – '

'Yes?'

'He feels a need to touch people all the time.'

'Your daughter, you mean?' He flushed brick red.

'Her, of course,' he said. 'But she can handle that. She knows how to handle her men – '

He might have been a conscientious colonel assessing a promising platoon commander.

'But I'm not talking about just her. I mean *everybody*. He couldn't ask you the time of day without grabbing hold of your arm.'

86

'You mean he's queer?'

'God knows.' The question seemed almost to be without relevance. 'What I mean is he's *uncouth*. An absolute oik.'

An oik who wants to marry your daughter, I thought. But I left it unsaid.

'I suppose Imogen's told you he's a genius,' he said. 'And I've no doubt he may be. I'm no judge of such things. But Imogen's not interested in geniuses. All she likes are rich men – and gentlemen riders.' Was Dave then classed as a gentleman, I wondered.

'She seems to think there's money in Fluck,' I said.

'She told you that?' I nodded. 'Did she say how?'

'None of my business,' I said. 'My business is to find him.'

'D'you think you will?'

'There's a chance,' I said.

'I'll give you five thousand if you drop the whole thing now,' he said.

'She also wants me to find Finn MacCool,' I said.

'Yes,' he said. 'I'd like that too. Think you can?'

'About the same odds as Fluck,' I said.

'You reckon it was this feller Schmidt?' he asked. 'The Kraut who phoned from the Shelburne? D'you think he drove the Granada I saw?'

He wanted an awful lot for nothing.

'I'm sorry,' I said. 'But it's your daughter I work for.'

He didn't like it, but he took it eventually. 'Quite right,' he said. The Scotch had gone and I poured him another.

'You couldn't find Finn MacCool and not find Fluck?' he said.

'Not possibly.'

'Pity,' he said. 'All the same I'll give you five thousand if you'll drop the whole thing.'

'I'm afraid not, Sir Robert,' I said.

'Five thousand's all I can manage,' he said. 'But it'll be in cash.'

Then I got mad.

'Have you any idea how rude you are?' I said. 'Or does it just come naturally?'

His head shot up. 'What the devil do you mean?' he asked.

'I mean that what I do is work for my money,' I said, 'and

87

accepting bribes isn't work.'

He sneered, and for the first time he didn't look handsome and distinguished. He looked shifty.

'A man of honour, eh?' he said. I didn't see why not, but that wasn't the point.

'I like to finish what I start,' I said, and the sneer went. That much he could understand about me.

'I don't want you to finish this,' he said. 'It could cause my daughter great unhappiness.'

'How?' I asked.

'I'm afraid I can't tell you.' Like daughter like father.

'It isn't enough,' I said.

'I know one or two people,' he said. 'I could make life very difficult for you.'

'You couldn't make it any more difficult than it is,' I said. So Up Yours, Sir Robert.

He laughed then, a kind of snorting bark he could have learned from his labrador. 'Worth a try,' he said. 'Too bad it didn't work. My apologies.' I waited for him to go, but the time was not yet.

'I was sorry to hear about poor Sabena,' he said. 'Didn't know you were a friend of hers.' I let it lie. 'She's rather a friend of my sister,' he continued. 'Did you ever meet her? Lady Tarleton.'

I lied, trying to be tactful. 'No,' I said, and he looked relieved.

'We sold Sabena a horse – or rather my daughter did.'

'The one that won the Grand National? Caramba, wasn't it?'

'Paid a hundred to eight. I remember because I had a fiver on him. But Imogen didn't breed him. She's never had a National winner – that's why she was so upset about Finn MacCool.'

He got to his feet, and for the first time his movements were slow: he looked old. 'You're going to create trouble,' he said. 'Time was when I used to go looking for it. Not any more. Not at my age. But I can still cope with it.' He put his glass down. 'Just thought I'd mention it,' he said.

'I'll bear it in mind,' I said, and showed him to the door.

'Goodnight to you,' he said, and strode off.

I went back to the living-room and switched on the telly. The tall and over-anxious pleaser was thanking me for inviting him into my home so I switched him off and rang the hospital instead. Miss Redditch was doing as well as could be expected. She was also resting and was not to be disturbed. Rest, I had already been told, was a Good Thing, so I treated myself to another gin and tonic and phoned Concannon House and got my old friend Burke. The mistress it seemed was dining in Dublin. I left a request for her to phone me, then asked for the general. The general had gone out just after breakfast without telling anyone why or where. It was a habit he had, and very inconvenient. I went upstairs to pack for Spain.

9

Las Golondrinas means The Swallows, and there weren't any, but it was a pretty enough hotel, tucked away from what you might call the yelling and screaming end of Torremolinos. Handy for the sea and beach, with orange and lemon trees and a king-size swimming pool. No swallows as I say, but plenty of Germans and Swedes and more than enough English – and Scots and Welsh. But no Irishmen. Or women either, at least not by the pool or at the cocktail bar, or in the dining-room at mealtimes – and Ms. Teresa O'Byrne had gone on demi-pension terms. We took a walk into town and phoned from a café and asked for her, and the switchboard operator rang the room. There was no reply.

'You're sure?' I said. 'Señorita Teresa O'Byrne? Room five-oh-four?'

'Señorita O'Byrne is in room three six eight,' the switchboard operator said. So at least we knew where to start looking. But not too early. People who go to Torremolinos tend to whoop it up a bit on account of the booze being cheap, and if there's one thing I value when I do a bit of breaking and entering it's privacy.

So we sat outside a café under some orange trees and I drank coffee and Dave had a San Miguel beer and I told him how Sabena was and what had happened with the general.

'And what did Imogen say when you told her?' said Dave.

'She didn't say anything because she didn't phone,' I said, 'and when I phoned back this morning Burke said she was out. I reckon that's what he was told to say.'

'Why on earth would she do that?'

'Her father may be the sort of bloke who wanders off,' I said, 'but I have the feeling she's the sort of daughter who'd

90

know just where he wandered to.'

'Yeah,' said Dave. 'Him and all the other blokes in her life. He's skint, you know. Hasn't got a tosser.'

'How d'you know that?'

'She told me,' said Dave. 'Nice way to be skint. Live in a mansion, use of a Roller, Savile Row clothes. . . . She offered me the same deal.'

'You did get on well,' I said.

'Smashing looking bird, isn't she?'

'I never saw one to match her,' I said.

He sighed. 'Trouble is you have to do what you're told. I'm hopeless at that. Always was. The only thing I didn't like about the Paras.' He drank more beer. 'Where do you suppose your Irish bird's got to?' he said.

'I dunno,' I said. 'But I'm worried. Look what happened to her boy-friend.'

'Yeah,' said Dave. 'First he got himself killed, then he disappeared. Doing things in the wrong order, wouldn't you say? All the same – cause for alarm, old son. Definitely cause for alarm.'

We went back to our room and dozed for a while, then suddenly it was half past three in the morning and my wrist watch alarm went off. Time for a spot of burglarious entry. I took Dave along as minder, because even at half past three people were still coming in, on account of the discos and cafés were still doing business. Just as well I'd had a bit of practice on our own door earlier. Of course the other lock was different, but not all that different. We were in in eighteen seconds, just three seconds ahead of a bunch of Krauts who marched down the corridor like it was France in 1940.

Dave drew the curtain and I switched on the light. Both of us were wearing plastic gloves, the disposable kind – twelve pairs for a quid. . . . The room was a bit smaller than ours, but then she'd booked a single – cost her a few quid extra. There was a suitcase on a sort of stand by the bed and a valise on top of it. The valise was unlocked and empty: the suitcase locked and empty. There were clothes and shoes in the wardrobe and chest of drawers, a paper-back by her bedside, cigarettes in her bedside-drawer, booze in the mini-bar fridge.

I went into the bathroom. Soap and toothpaste in the

bathroom cupboard, perfume and cosmetics on a shelf by the mirror. No handbag. I went over the bathroom again, lifted the lid of the lavatory tank. Stuck to one side with a suction cup was a waterproof plastic bag. I eased it off and took a look inside. Five hundred quid's worth of Irish punts, and a Republic of Ireland passport for Teresa O'Byrne. In the space headed 'Occupation' someone had written 'Widow'. Maybe in Ireland it is an occupation. I would have to ask Mrs. Courtenay-Lithgoe.

'She can't be far,' said Dave. 'No money and no passport.'

'She might have more than one passport,' I said.

'There's new clothes in the wardrobe,' said Dave. 'The trip here cost three hundred and fifty. She had less than twelve pounds in the bank. She can't be far.'

'We'll get some kip and have a look,' I said.

'Look where?' said Dave.

'Your girl-friend's castle.'

'But why should we look there?' said Dave.

'Because I can't think of anywhere else,' I said. Also it was called La Torre del Sur.

*

The road to the Sierras is another kind of Spain to the one the package-tours go to. No jam-packed beaches and phoney bullfights and over-loud flamenco: great rolling country that goes on and on to the foothills of the mountains; dry and dusty country that is sometimes fruit trees and sometimes olive-groves and more often than not just grass and wild flowers in need of water. A huge and silent country: to see another car was an event, and even in the villages the silence persisted. It was as if the heat had burned all the noise away. . . . Poor looking villages they were, too, with unpainted houses and scraggy gardens: the major source of income the money sent home from the sons and daughters who worked as waiters and chambermaids on the coast.

Dave drove the hire-car, because he's far and away a better driver than me. It's what he does best – that and duffing blokes – or even killing them when he has to – or putting them in intensive care. He was a bit worried about Imogen.

'I can't let her keep me,' he was saying. 'You must see that, Ron.'

'Then don't let her,' I said. 'Just stay away.'

'Don't be daft,' he said. 'Have you forgotten what she looks like?'

He had a point there. . . . He drove on for a bit, not speaking. But he isn't a sulker: not Dave.

'This castle of hers,' he said at last. 'Any idea what it looks like?'

Michael Copland had done a piece about it for that gossip column of his. Originally Moorish, which was a possible reason why Idris bought it, but much restored in the early eighteenth century, which might explain why he gave it to Imogen. It wasn't often used, but it wasn't deserted either. There was farmland around, and horses – what else? There were even fighting bulls.

'So it isn't another one of your Swiss knife jobs?' Dave said.

'We go in and ask for the estate manager,' I said.

'And he lets us roam all over the place'.

'He does if he's got any sense,' I said. 'I've got a letter for him from your girl-friend.'

'You're not just a pretty face,' said Dave. 'And speaking of girl-friends – how about yours?'

'I phoned her this morning,' I said. 'When you were picking up the car.'

'How did she sound?'

'Better,' I said. 'A litle bit better.'

And that was as far as I was prepared to go. It had been one of the nicest phone-calls of my entire life, but I wasn't prepared to share it, not even with Dave. . . .

The car pressed on, and so it should. BMW it was. Cost a mint. Dave had had to go to Malaga to hire it. All the same it looked a lot better than the usual Seats and Fiats. The turn off was at a village called Alcantoro. It seemed to be doing better than most. There must have been water somewhere, because the fields were full of vegetables and every house blazed with geraniums and roses and carnations. We drove on out of the village and there it was at the top of a hill. La Torre del Sur. One surviving Moorish tower, and what looked like a half-scale model of Blenheim Palace tacked on to it. And all around were olives and fruit trees and vines, and the sort of grass that belonged more to England or Ireland than Spain, and some very superior horses to crop it. No bulls in sight, which didn't upset me, but tucked into the shade of a lemon grove a neat house of white-painted stone.

'That'll be the estate-manager's,' I said, and Dave made for it down a twisting, winding road that could have stood a bit of repair work. Then we took a blind corner and Dave stood on the brake. Facing us was a fighting bull, black and majestic, the horns white and long and nasty. It looked bigger than the car – not pawing the ground or anything; just standing there. The fact that we were in a BMW didn't impress it at all. . . . Suddenly it snorted and turned and moved off at the trot, no hurry – and I let out my breath in a long, long sigh, and I noticed that Dave did the same.

'Blimey,' he said, and we drove on to the house.

It was a maid who answered the door, and Dave asked for Mr. Mendez. We knew that was the estate-manager's name, because it said so on the letter. The maid said she'd fetch him from the stables, and after a few minutes' wait in the hall Mendez came up himself and took us into a drawing-room that was cool and comfortable and had a nice view of the mountains. He was a competent-looking geezer in a sports-shirt and jeans and riding boots, with the very faintest whiff of horse about him. He spoke far better English than either of us spoke Spanish. I gave him Imogen's letter and he read it through once, then again, then promptly invited us to lunch. After we'd accepted, he produced sherry and beer and gin and tonic and ice. That was the sort of letter it was.

'Now,' he said after he had poured. 'What can I do for you gentlemen?'

'Mrs. Courtenay-Lithgoe wants us to look over the house,' I said. 'She wants a valuation.'

'She's thinking of selling?' He looked worried.

'Not at all,' I said. 'She merely wants an updated estimate for probate purposes.' He looked puzzled. 'Her will,' I said, and the puzzlement vanished.

'Of course,' he said. 'But I hope you will be able to manage by yourselves, gentlemen. I have much business today.'

Even so he found time to eat his share of cold tortilla and roast chicken, and drink his share of wine before driving over to the castle. He opened up for us, handed me the keys and left us to get on with it. There was a lot to get on with. The place was even bigger than Concannon House. Everything was covered in dust sheets, but every floor, of wood or marble or covered in silk rugs, had been recently swept: the windows gleamed. We went from room to room. The public apartments were huge, and every room had pictures, though here and there a fade-mark on the wall showed where one had been taken down, and I wondered if Imogen had shifted the best of the collection over to Ireland. The stuff where we were wasn't all that great, except for one that might have been a Murillo.

But I wasn't there to look at pictures. Instead I pulled the covers off any piece of furniture that looked as if it might be a commode or a desk or a sofa table, anything that might have drawers. And an awful lot of them did. It was a weird hodge-podge of stuff too. French third empire, English repro, black oak Spanish antique. Hundreds of drawers, and all of them empty.

'Looks like you guessed wrong this time,' said Dave, and pulled off a dust sheet to sprawl out on a vast, overstuffed sofa and fumble for cigarettes.

I went on looking.

'I mean,' said Dave, 'just you consider what sort of a woman Teresa O'Byrne was. Girl-friend to a blacksmith, and before that what the French used to call a daughter of joy. – Though I never saw any that looked joyous.'

He got a cigarette to his mouth, produced a lighter, then swore as it slipped from his hand and went down the back of the sofa. He slid his fingers down after it, and groped around, then he looked past me to the door. 'Good afternoon,' he said.

I followed his gaze. A hard, chunky looking geezer stood in the door. He had fair hair, grey eyes and a tan that had taken years. He also carried a shotgun and his name, I remembered, was Theodore Pickel. The shotgun was open and in the crook of his arm, but it wouldn't take him more than a couple of seconds to snap it shut and start blasting.

'You appear to be looking for something' Pickel said.

'My lighter,' said Dave, and eased it out from the sofa and

used it to light his cigarette, then swung his legs down. At once the shotgun was snapped shut and held two-handed.

'No please,' said Pickel. 'Do not disturb yourself.' He turned to me. 'Did you perhaps think that your friend's lighter had found its way beneath the dust sheets and into a closed drawer?'

'No,' I said.

'Then what are you doing here?'

'If it comes to that, what are you?' I said. As an attempt at righteous indignation it was terrible.

'Perhaps I am here to apprehend two thieves,' said Pickel.

'Or perhaps you've come here to do a bit of thieving yourself,' said Dave.

I don't know how Dave does it. He didn't even sound righteously indignant, just vaguely contemptuous. Pickel's hands tightened on the shotgun. But it was me he turned back to.

'Have I seen you before?' he asked.

'No,' I said. 'What is this?'

He lifted the gun.

'*This* is a shotgun,' he said. 'A twelve-bore with two live cartridges. So listen carefully. I have no more time to waste. Tell me what you are doing here.'

I gave him the bit about wills and probate valuation. He wasn't all that keen until I told him I had a letter to prove it, and even then he made me put it down on a table and back off while he read it. Then he broke open the shotgun again.

'It seems, Mr. Hogget,' he said, 'that I owe you an apology.'

'Too true,' said Dave, and got up from the sofa. This time Pickel made no attempt to stop him. Dave walked across to me. 'My name's Baxter,' he went on. 'Any chance of you telling us who you are?'

I waited for him to say he was Dr Schmidt, but he didn't.

'My name is not important,' he said. 'I am a friend of Mrs. Courtenay-Lithgoe. I have stayed some times at Concannon House. Mrs. Courtenay-Lithgoe and the general I think I may claim to be my friends. I have a house here, too, in Andalusia, and today I took a drive to the mountains. There are hares there. And partridges, too. Then on my way back I see a car in

96

the drive. It occurred to me that Mrs. Courtenay-Lithgoe – or perhaps the general – was visiting Spain. So naturally I come to call.'

'Naturally,' said Dave.

'And I see two strangers and think at once of burglars and I have made a mistake, for which I must apologise.'

'Quite all right,' I said.

'Though I must admit you have a very odd way of making a valuation,' Pickel said. Dave chuckled, picked up a dust cover, and began to fold it up like a housewife with a bedsheet.

'All the same, that's what we are,' he said. 'It's on account of the pictures.'

'The pictures?'

I could see which way Dave was heading.

'Some of them were bought quite recently,' I said. 'Only Mrs. Courtenay-Lithgoe forgot where she put the bills of sale – '

Suddenly Dave flicked the duster like a snake flicking its tongue, straight at Pickel's eyes. He let go of the gun to cover his face and I grabbed it as it fell, passed it on to Dave.

'I don't like loaded guns,' said Dave. 'They go off.'

Pickel was saying unkind things in German, and we let him swear for a while, then when he paused for breath, Dave said, 'Do we need him any more, Ron?' I shook my head. We could have tried getting things out of him but unless we used thumb-screws all he'd probably do was sneer. It was better to let him go thinking we believed he was Schmidt.

'I'll just see him to his car then,' said Dave.

For a moment the German looked at him and I thought things were going to get physical, then he took one more look at Dave and moved off. Dave followed, holding the shotgun, and I went on searching till I heard a car drive off, and Dave came back, without the shotgun, but holding a small canvas bag.

'He's got a Merc coupé,' he said. 'I wish I had,' and dropped the canvas bag on a table.

'What's that?' I asked.

'More shot. I didn't mind giving him his gun back, but I didn't fancy letting him have the ammo as well.'

'Anything else in the car?'

'Yeah,' he said. 'A partridge, two pheasant and a hare.'

'So he was telling the truth.'

'Or some of it,' Dave said. 'Come off it, Ron. He's up to something. I can tell by your face.'

'His name's Theodore Pickel,' I said. 'Sabena spotted him at the "Feed The Starving" Ball.'

'Pickel?' he said. 'That bird in Australia – '

'Her brother,' I said.

'He's a hard one,' said Dave. 'I wonder what he came for.' He went to the sofa he'd been lying on and came back to me, with a colour photograph – the Polaroid kind that develops automatically. 'Maybe it was this,' he said.

I found I was looking at a picture of a woman in her mid-thirties sitting on a horse Dave said was a bay gelding, about sixteen hands with a white sock on the off-fore and a white blaze on the face. The woman had a kind of battered good looks I recognised at once, because I'd seen her passport photograph. It was Teresa O'Byrne.

'She doesn't look too happy on that horse,' Dave said.

'Not a lot of people were,' I said. 'He has a mind of his own – if my guess is right. He's Finn MacCool.' I looked again at the photograph. A lot of grass and sky and a horse and a woman. Not a house or a car or even a dog. 'Where d'you suppose it was taken?'

'Search me,' said Dave.

I looked at the back. Sometimes there's a place-name and a date, but not this time.

I thought about Pickel and his assorted game. He'd gone to a lot of trouble with his cover story, but that's all it was: a cover story. He'd come to the house looking for something – or somebody. The photograph – or maybe the woman herself. That made a bit more sense but not enough. The woman – and Finbar Gleason? That sounded better. Gleason and his girl-friend might well have something of Imogen's worth selling. The problem was what. The other subject of the photograph?

We went on searching the house but there was nothing at all, except another shotgun in the general's room. Dave picked it up and looked at it.

'Spanish,' he said. 'What they call an AYA. That's the

makers. Ayala y Aguirre.'

'Is it valuable?'

'Three hundred quid, I suppose.'

'Will it take the same shot you took from Pickel?'

'Course it will,' Dave said. 'It's the same gauge. Twelve bore.'

'We'd better nick it,' I said.

'*Nick* it?' Dave sounded outraged. 'It belongs to a general.'

'Just for now,' I said. 'We can always knock it off his daughter's bill if it gets damaged.' Dave looked at me long and hard.

'You know it costs you extra if I have to start blasting,' he said.

'Then I'll just have to pay the extra,' I said.

Dave checked the shotgun. Apart from a bit of dust, it was fine.

We put it in the BMW's boot and went to see Mendez, found him superintending a spraying job in an orange grove. He knew nothing about Finn MacCool, but even so I made him take us to the pasture where the horses were and name them. He didn't want to, but I had the magic letter and we went to the pasture: a stallion, and three mares with foals. No bay gelding. Then we went to the castle stables and they were empty. Mendez was getting edgy, anxious to get back to his fruit trees, but I had my anxieties too.

'Where's the best place for shooting round here?' I said.

'Shooting?'

'Pheasants, partridge, hares,' I said.

'Oh *shooting*. There is game everywhere in the mountains.'

'Is there any one place that's particularly good?'

'Sure,' he said. 'El Bosque Alto. But why – '

'Does Señora Courtenay-Lithgoe own it?'

'Of course,' he said. 'She owns everything – ' He broke off. 'Oh. – She is worried about the ones who steal the birds?'

'Poachers,' I said. 'It's her property, Mr. Mendez. She likes to know if it's being well looked after. Tell me how to get to El Bosque Alto.'

The High Wood. Seemed just the place for a wander, especially after we'd been cooped up indoors all day, and I said so. Mind you, I added sternly, it was business really. All the same if one could add a little pleasure. – And Mendez said yes indeed and almost danced up and down with impatience. Those fruit trees must really have needed a spray. . . .

Then Dave added to his woes by making friends with a golden retriever that came for a sniff round the stableyard, and asked what it's name was. It was Dorado apparently, which means the golden one and suited him fine.
He was even more snooty than the general's Sultan. Dave asked if he could take Dorado with us and give him a run because if there was one thing he really enjoyed it was taking a dog for a run. This I knew was a lie. But anyway Mendez said of course and help yourself and shot off. I turned to Dave.

'Since when have you been a dog-lover?' I said.

'Loving dogs is stupid,' said Dave. 'But no stupider than loving anything else. On the other hand – respecting them for what they can do – there's a lot of sense in that. I learned that in the Paras.'

'And what can Dorado do?'

'If I read you right,' said Dave, 'he can help us find what we're looking for.'

*

Dorado loved the car ride, and sat in the back looking as noble and beautiful as the car. Dave had left the unloaded shotgun beside him and he gave it a good sniff, but it didn't bother him. Dave reckoned he'd heard shots fired in anger before, and I was glad to hear it. It made it all the more likely that he knew his trade.

On and up we went from single track concrete road to dirt road, until at last it was no road at all, and the BMW's springs protested painfully. We had climbed maybe fifteen hundred feet higher and the snow-line was near, what breeze there was blew cool. El Bosque Alto was hardwood, chestnut mostly, but a lot of oak too, and thorn and holly. There was moss underfoot, and a lot of birds singing as if they didn't have a care in the world, but they weren't the kind of birds that got shot at, so maybe they hadn't.

100

Then the three of us got out and Dave fed a couple of cartridges into the AYA, and at once Dorado walked to his heel. According to his way of looking at things, the man with the gun was the boss. So we cruised along and the moss was great to walk on, like very hard sponges, and suddenly Dorado lunged into a thicket and there was a funny kind of clattering sound and a pheasant lumbered up into the air like an over-loaded jumbo jet. Dave watched it climb, growing quicker and surer, then the shotgun came up to his shoulder, quicker and surer than the poor bloody pheasant, and he squeezed one trigger and I saw the feathers fly, the pheasant fell like a stone, and Dorado was off in a golden streak.

'We didn't come here for the shooting,' I said.

'I know that and you know that,' said Dave. 'But Dorado doesn't. And we don't want him to start thinking we're cissies.'

Dorado came back, the pheasant limp in its soft mouth, and dropped it at my feet. It was evident who he'd cast in the rôle of servant. When I stopped and picked up the bloodied mess at my feet, I swear to God Dorado gave me a kindly nod. I carried the pheasant by the legs and wished I'd brought a game-bag, then Dorado put up a partridge and Dave bagged it and I wished it even more. Then we moved on to where the ground shelved more steeply and the trees were farther apart and Dorado began patrolling up and down, looking for hares, Dave reckoned.

Suddenly he disappeared into a thicket of briars and Dave snapped the gun shut, but no hare came out, nor did Dorado. We moved into the thicket and there was the dog, nose down, far in the thicket. Some of the briars had been torn up, others smashed with an axe, or more likely a shovel, and a lot of them were dead. The ground they'd grown on was broken and uneven, no moss – though moss grew all around it as far as I could see. We pushed on in, and the living briars tore at us, the dead ones drooped.

'I think you've guessed right,' said Dave.

'So does Dorado,' I said, and pulled at the briars, wished that I'd brought a pair of heavy duty gloves. . . . If wishes were horses, beggars would ride. . . . My father used to say that and he should know. He's been a beggar often enough.

101

. . . The churned-up ground was six feet by two or maybe a little less, and once the briars were cleared it was easy enough to shift it, even when all we had to use was our hands. The dog stayed slumped on all fours, quite motionless except for the twitching nose.

She was about eighteen inches down, the body still fresh, but even so when we exposed her Dorado sprang to his feet and howled just once, then went out of the thicket, back into the sun and howled once more. I felt the hairs on my neck rise, but somehow I kept on working alongside Dave. She wore a white T-shirt, denims and training shoes: she didn't look as if she'd been molested sexually, but she'd been assaulted all right. Somebody had knifed her, neat and clean, just below the left breast, then ripped out the knife. The bottom half of the T-shirt and the top of the jeans were soaked in her blood.

'Straight through the heart,' said Dave. 'She couldn't have gone quicker.'

'Knife?'

He nodded, peered closer at the wound.

'Sharp point, single-edged blade by the look of it. What they call a Commando knife – or maybe a hunting knife.'

'Butcher's knife maybe?'

'Doubt it,' said Dave. 'Too clumsy. The geezer who did this was a pro. He'd want something a bit more reliable. Something he was used to, probably.'

We went on digging, until the body was exposed from head to foot.

'Nothing else,' said Dave. 'We'd better cover her up, poor soul.' He reached for a handful of soil.

'No,' I said.

'But Ron,' Dave said, 'there's nothing.'

'That's what it looks like,' I said. 'But first we lift her out.'

It wasn't the pleasantest thing I ever did, not by a long shot, but we managed it, while Dorado waited and whimpered, and in the end the grave was empty.

'Now are you satisfied?' said Dave, but I'd already reached for a piece of broken briar and started poking about in the soil. After a bit some black leather showed, and then a bit more. I threw the briar away, and Dave and I used our hands and uncovered a handbag and a briefcase.

The bag was new and inside was the tag of a shop in the Calle San Miguel in Torremolinos and about fifty quid's worth of pesetas, cigarettes and matches. And that was all. No secret compartments, and the lining was new and intact. The briefcase was old, cheap-looking, and its lock was broken, smashed, so that it was no surprise to find it was empty. All the same I went through the motions of searching it. No secret compartments, nothing so exciting, but there was a torn lining, and something lodged between it and the leather exterior.

I used the Swiss Army knife to cut away the lining, then took out what lay behind it: a betting-slip, and a torn sheet of paper covered with mathematical symbols. Both had a familiar look to them, but the name on the betting-slip was the clincher.

'We've just found Erny Fluck's briefcase,' I said. 'Only it's been cleaned out. – Except for these.'

I showed Dave the papers, but he shook his head.

'No use to me,' he said. 'I don't even understand the betting slip.'

I put it back in the grave, then we put back Teresa O'Byrne's body, her handbag beside her, and covered her gently with earth. After we'd done it we stood by the grave for a moment, heads bowed. I didn't ask Dave if he said a prayer or not, but I did. Well not a prayer exactly, but just standing there, thinking.

And what I thought was it was a crying shame. I mean she'd come through her bad times from what the prossie where she lived had told me, and she'd got a bloke and he'd wanted to marry her, and now she was dead, murdered, and her body hidden away. . . . And her bloke was murdered too, and the body disappeared. A crying shame. There was no doubt they deserved something, but they didn't deserve *that*.

. . .

'Time to go,' said Dave, and we set off back to the car, and Dorado started a hare and Dave potted it just to show he wasn't losing his grip. But when Dorado brought the hare back I made Dave carry it. My hands were full of dead birds. . . . We put the bag in the BMW's boot, then I opened the rear-door and Dorado hopped in. For a minute I thought he was going to give me a tip.

This time Dave suggested I hold the shotgun for him in the front, and I said why didn't I drive, and Dave said things were dodgy enough without that. A bit strong, but Dave can't stand being driven, so I let it go. . . . On the way to the agent's house we passed the castle and I thought maybe the time had come for us to look in and put the AYA back. Dave gave me a look, and I knew he'd changed his mind.

'You said I wouldn't need a gun,' he said. 'You were wrong. I think we'd better borrow this one for a little bit longer.'

So when we got to the agent's house Dave hid the shotgun by his feet and I got out and returned Dorado to the maid. Señor Mendez was still spraying fruit trees so we drove back the way we'd come, past the pretty village and on to the lonely, winding roads.

10

The attack when it came was neat enough, and the only reason I'm here to tell it is that the geezer who made it wasn't quite a good enough shot. We were driving past the ruins of a farm which was mostly crumbling walls – the roof had fallen in long since – but there was enough cover to hide a car and a man with a rifle. Dave wasn't exactly breaking records, but the BMW's a nippy car and we both liked to see it do things and maybe that helped, too. Anyway we heard what I took to be a backfire which was stupid since there wasn't another car to be seen. Dave knew what it was right away, and his foot was already going down when the second shot came and there was a thump behind us and a wailing noise, and I knew what *that* was. A ricochet. You hear them all the time on the telly.

Dave's foot went down harder as we headed for the shelter of a bend in the road, and then there was the third shot; a double bang this time, the second bang being the off-side rear tyre blowing out. The BMW went insane and decided to go sideways, but Dave wrestled with the wheel and eased off the speed and we reached the bend in the road and got round it somehow, and finished up with the car pointing the way we'd been.

Dave was out with the shotgun and heading up the bank, leaving me to cut the engine and pull on the hand-brake, before I got out of the car too, and took shelter behind it. Better, far better, to stay where I was and leave it to Dave. Even if I'd had a gun I'd have been useless. I hate guns. . . .

Dave reached the brow of the hill and peered cautiously over, then the shotgun snapped together, he was off in a flying leap and out of sight. Almost at once there were noises: a car revving up and the sound of the shotgun being fired, once, then again, but the car noise continued, fading slowly. I went to the BMW, got out the tool kit, the spare tyre and the jack. By the time Dave came back I almost had the wheel off. He crouched down beside me and extended his hand: on it were three brass cartridges.

'Some kind of sporting rifle,' he said. '270 calibre, or maybe 300. Thereabouts. Any other damage?'

'He hit the rear bumper,' I said. 'Gouged right into it.'

Dave went to take a look.

'It's got a couple of other knocks anyway,' he said. 'I'll have a go at it in a minute.' Then he helped me with the tyre.

The spare wasn't bad, as hire-care spares go, but the one that had taken the bullet was a write-off. Tyre wall slashed through.

'You can't hand that back,' said Dave.

'Have to buy a new one,' I said. 'Nothing else for it.'

Dave sighed. 'We were lucky,' he said. 'He got bloody near.'

'You sure it was a "he"?' I asked him.

'No,' said Dave. 'I'm not. It was too far. But what woman could have done it?' I didn't answer. 'You can't mean Imogen,' he said. 'I mean why should she?'

'No reason,' I said. 'I just wondered if you'd any idea who tried to murder us.'

'None,' he said.

'What about the car?'

'Small Seat,' he said. 'Covered in dust. Beige, it was, or maybe brown. Licence plates were too far off to read.'

A small beige – or maybe brown – Seat. In Spain that narrowed the choice down to about a million.

'Did you hit him?'

'I doubt it,' said Dave. 'It was a long way for a shotgun and he was moving. – Or she was.'

We got the spare on, tightened it up, then Dave turned to me.

'About Teresa O'Byrne,' he said. 'The late lamented.' I waited. 'You going to tell the coppers about her?'

'So they can find out we're in the same hotel as her and telex London and Dublin and find out I've been looking for her *and* working for your girl-friend, who just happens to own

106

the castle? Show some common, Dave.'

'Yeah, I know,' he said. 'It's just – we saw her lying there. Nobody knows.' I didn't answer because I couldn't. It bothered me, too.

'Couldn't we phone in without giving names?' said Dave.

'How can we?' I said. 'There's our accents for a start, – *and* my name was on the letter I showed Mendez.'

'Yeah,' said Dave. 'You're right. Of course you're right. But I still feel bad about it.'

'Me too,' I said.

*

We drove back to Malaga and on our way we stopped the car outside the poorest house in the poorest village, piled the pheasant, the partridge and the hare outside, then banged on the door and drove off quick. In Malaga I bought another tyre for the BMW and left the one with the bullet hole on a rubbish dump, then we went back to the hotel bar and had a drink.

'What now?' said Dave.

'I phone my girl,' I said. 'Then I phone yours.'

He came up with me, collected the big zip-bag that had held most of his clothes, and went off again.

It was a good time to get through to London and my girl was awake and ready for a chat. This time there were no funny jokes about bald persons. Her father was with her. But even with a witness present she sounded pleased to hear me, and I could hardly believe it. I mean look who she was and look who I was – plus the fact that it was probably my fault she was in the hospital – and she would know it, being a smart one.

But all good things come to an end, and at last I was passed on to Sir Montague Redditch, who asked me how the weather was and I told him.

'You phoned me, I believe,' he said. 'Wanted to see me.'

'I still do,' I said.

'And I you. Sorry I missed you. But come and see me as soon as you can. I've left word with Miss Newton. There'll be no difficulty.' Then he hung up before I could say goodnight

107

to Sabena, and Dave came in, carrying the zip-bag. Inside it was the shotgun, plus what was left of Pickel's ammo. Then his hand went in again and came out with a hacksaw and a file.

'I've been thinking,' he said. 'You and me have gone naked into the conference chamber as the man said, and *this* isn't a proper answer.' He nodded at the AYA. 'What we need is a handgun.'

I looked at the tools. 'You going to make us one?'

'I am if you're serious about nicking the shotgun.'

'Never more so,' I said. 'You got any fifty peseta pieces?'

He emptied his pockets, and I did the same with mine. If I had another drink in an outside bar I'd have enough.

'You still don't trust the phone here?' Dave said.

'That's right.'

'But you phoned *your* girl from here.'

'That was love,' I said. 'The switchboard operator listens in and all she hears is Moon and June – but with your girl it's business.'

Dave picked up the shotgun and looked at it for a long time as if deciding what its function was, then he turned to me. He was still holding the gun.

'I trust you, Ron,' he said.

'Of course you do,' I said. 'I'm your mate . . .'

*

She said, 'I didn't tell you to go to Spain so soon.'

'You did tell me to find Finn MacCool,' I said.

'You've found him?'

'I'm getting close.'

She sighed. Even over the phone it was a sound of sheer bliss.

'What do you need to know?' she said at once.

'Did you ever meet Heidi Pickel?'

'No,' she said.

'Or her brother?'

'Theodore?' she said. 'Yes. . . . He's stayed here at the house. He's rather a good eventer.'

The last fifty peseta piece slid down the chute and into the box. Soon I'd have to ask her to call me back, but not yet.

'Is that how you met him? Because of horses?'

'His father knew mine. It was only natural he should look us up. And when he did I sold him a horse.' There had to be more, but the money ran out there, so I gave her my number and lurked in the booth till she phoned me back.

'By the way, how is your father?' I said.

'You tell me.' I stayed quiet. 'Come on, Mr. Hogget. Don't tell me he didn't come to see you.'

'He came.'

'And?'

'He tried to bribe me and he tried to threaten me.'

'But you remained true to your trust?'

I was becoming tired of sneers from her family.

'Yes I bloody did,' I said. 'Though in this job trust is a one way traffic.'

'I'm sorry,' she said at once. 'I'm rather worried about him but it's no excuse. I do see that.'

'How did you know he'd been to see me?' I asked.

'Because he'd gone all broody about you just before he disappeared. . . . How much did he offer you bribewise?'

'Five thousand,' I said.

She whistled like a man.

'He hasn't got anything like five thousand,' she said. 'And he's got nothing left to sell.'

'But surely – ' I began, but she cut in on me.

'Daddy,' she said, 'is the original bookie's friend.'

For a second I could sympathise. My daddy is the original brewer's friend.

'What about Theodore Pickel?' she said.

'Does he own a property near Alcantaro?'

'Of course not,' she said. 'He lives in Bavaria.'

'He says he's your neighbour.'

'He's lying,' she said, then there was a pause. 'Why should he lie?'

Now wasn't the time to tell it. 'I'm working on it,' I said.

'I don't like this,' she said. 'I don't like it at all. When are you coming back?'

'First chance I get,' I said.

'I may have to – ' she hesitated, then: 'Never mind, I'll tell you when I see you. Be careful, Mr. Hogget.'

It was a bit late for that, but I said I would.

'How's David?' she said.

'He's fine,' I said.

'Put him on.'

'I can't,' I said. 'He's not here. But he sends you his best.'

'Where is he?'

'Working for me,' I said. 'Just like I'm working for you.' Before she could blast me I added, 'Sabena Redditch is progressing satisfactorily.'

'Oh dear,' she said. 'I can't win with you, can I? So *boring* saying I'm sorry all the time – even though it's true. Come back soon, Mr. Hogget. Take good care.'

She hung up.

By rights I should have phoned Horry Lumley, that other Friend of the Bookmakers, but it was evening in London, too, and if Horry wasn't in Stringfellow's he'd be in Les Ambassadeurs, and if he wasn't in Les A he'd be in a gaming club. Mornings were the time for Horry. More often than not he'd be in a vile mood – hungover losers always are – but he'd be needing money, too. Horry would have to wait till morning. Now all I could do was walk back to the hotel and worry about what I *hadn't* done. I hadn't made Dave take me back to La Torre del Sur after we'd been shot at. And the reason I hadn't done it was that I was scared and that's a perfectly good reason. All the same it had been a mistake because now it was too late.

I tapped at our door and Dave let me in. He was having a lager and the place was nice and tidy. On his bedside table was a new sports bag he'd bought, the kind you sling on your shoulder to carry your football boots in, but for Dave it was the duty frees.

'Your girl sends you her best,' I said.

'That's nice,' said Dave. 'Anything else?'

'She wants us to take good care of ourselves and she's bothered about Pickel.'

'Did she tell you why?'

'He hasn't got a place here.'

'Ah,' said Dave, then: 'How did she sound – about me I

110

mean?'

'She fancies you,' I said. 'Fancies you a lot.'

I wasn't lying, and Dave knew it, and lit a cigarette to celebrate.

'Got something to show you,' he said, and he went to his bedside table, his hand scooped into the sports bag and came out holding what looked like a very crude version of an old fashioned duelling pistol, except that it had two barrels.

'That's all that's left of the general's shotgun,' he said. 'But it's enough. We'll ditch the rest of it in the morning.'

'Looks nasty,' I said.

'It *is* nasty,' said Dave. 'So's a bloke opening up on you with a rifle when you're doing seventy.'

He had a point. . . .

So in the morning Dave dumped the bits of the AYA that were surplus to requirement, and I phoned Horry Lumley, who was not happy and said so, many times.

'Why do you always phone so *early*?' he said. 'Dash it I'll have all that stuff about what's his name's share dealings any day.'

'That's nice,' I said, 'and I'm grateful. So grateful I'm going to give you another job. A thousand quid's worth.'

'A *thousand*?' He sounded better already.

'At least,' I said.

There was a very brief pause while he grabbed pencil and paper.

'Tell me what you want,' he said.

'All you can get on a Bavarian family called Pickel. Brother Theodore, sister Heidi. Father's name unknown.' I added the few scraps Sabena had given me. – 'And any possible connection with General Sir Robert Berkeley. – Go to it, Horry old man. Have a nice day.' Then I hung up. I should never have lifted the phone in the first place. He didn't dig up a thing about the Pickels that I didn't find out for myself.

*

Dave had gone broody. It was love, of course. Like he said he didn't want to be kept, but on the other hand, just look at the

111

girl. . . . And Dave's funny about love. It doesn't come easy to him. I should know. The big love of his life was my wife Melanie, and the upshot of that little lark was we both lost her. The weird thing was that we stayed mates. So long as we kept our love-lives in separate compartments there was no problem. But now we'd come across a pair of star-crossed lovers who were dead, and I had an upper-class girl-friend who couldn't wait for us to be happy as soon as she got out of hospital, and he had an upper-class girl-friend he didn't know how to handle. So he went broody as I say, and when Dave broods he looks like a fairer version of Lord Byron, except he doesn't limp.

So naturally it was no surprise to me when I got back after phoning Horry Lumley to find a note saying he'd see me at a café later, and it was equally no surprise to find him with a bird when I got there: typical Dave, that was. When in doubt play the field. Playing the field didn't count as love. . . . Amparo, this one was called. Spanish. And that surprised me a bit because Spanish girls don't usually let themselves be picked up, not even by blokes who remind them of Lord Byron. Still, everything in Spain is changing fast, and she'd had a couple of bit parts in spaghetti westerns, and that could make a lot of difference.

If she was pleased to see me she hid it well, but I didn't stay long anyway. What I wanted to do more than anything was go and lie in the sun and think. Like driving about, hot sun relaxes me, – unkind people say it dazes me – but what it really does is help me to put my mind in focus on the things I need to focus on, without other things getting in the way. Like fear. So I took my towel and my plastic bottle of Coppertone and lay by the pool in my trunks, and ignored all the pert young boobs that were pushing up around me like domes in the Kremlin. I'd gone there to think. . . . And think I did till I damn near blistered myself. But in the end I began to see the beginning of a pattern. I didn't like it, and I was pretty sure the client wouldn't either. But then the client was greedy – and with the greedy ones you never know. . . . I showered and swam then lunched in the hotel and took a nap. Fear yesterday and thinking today. I was exhausted. . . .

Dave came back at six, looking pleased with himself.

'Not bad, is she?' he said.

'Not bad at all,' I said, which was true. (But Imogen was superb.)

'Not too demanding, either,' Dave said. 'Restful you might say.'

'You been resting?'

'Her place. She's got a little studio flat on Carihuela beach. She's not a floozy, Ron.'

'I never said she was,' I said.

'She's studied theatre. Knows her Shakespeare. Funny. We did a scene from Hamlet. It sounds all wrong in Spanish. Macbeth was better.'

I said nothing because I couldn't think of anything to say.

'She's got a mate,' Dave said. 'She thinks we might make up a foursome.'

'Doing what?' I said.

'Spot of dinner somewhere nice,' he said. 'Her mate's name's Lola.'

'What's she like?'

'Haven't met her yet,' Dave said. 'But Amparo says she's lovely.'

I used a quotation. 'Well she would, wouldn't she?' I said.

'Please Ron,' he said. 'I know I shouldn't have – but I sort of promised.'

'Yeah, all right,' I said, and went back to sleep.

Dave called me at eight and I showered and dressed and was ready to go. So was Dave. Halfway to the door I called him back.

'You forgot this,' I said, and handed him the shoulder-bag.

'For heaven's sake, Ron,' he said.

'You won't go naked into the conference chamber,' I said, 'and I won't go naked into the restaurant. O.K.?'

'They're just a couple of girls after a good time,' said Dave.

'I believe you,' I said, 'but somebody knows we're in Torremolinos. – And maybe he knows where to find us an' all.' I held out the bag. 'Just to oblige your old mate.'

He took it at last. 'Yeah,' he said. 'You're right. Of course you're right. If only we could arrange our lives in compartments.'

Nowhere is far in Torremolinos and parking can be a

problem, but all the same Dave insisted on taking the BMW and of course he was right. To give a girl an idea of the class of bloke she's getting involved with a BMW can come in handy. Very handy. . . .

Double-dating like the one Dave and Amparo arranged has a kind of pattern to it: it's traditional you might say. The bird is a looker and her friend isn't. It always happens, every time. And not only that but the friend always makes it clear that she'd sooner be doing anything at all – even staying home to wash her hair – rather than be escorted by the bloke's mate. It's always been like that: it always will be like that. Only this time it wasn't. Put it this way. A darker version of Imogen, Amparo was not, but by any normal standards she was a very pretty girl, and Lola was just as pretty, maybe even prettier. They looked cool and elegant in neat summer dresses, and I was glad Dave had insisted we wear ties. For a while I even forgot about Sabena.

They were such good company, you see, that was the thing. We drank the Spanish champagne called Cordoniu, and very nice it is too, but they oohed and aahed as if it was Dom Perignon. Outside our favourite bar that was, with the moon coming up to play silver games with the orange trees. – I even managed to put that into a kind of Spanish, and got a round of applause from the girls. They were nice. Not hookers, either of them. They weren't on the batter and it's my gues they never had been. I mean you meet a girl and she tells you she's an actress only she's resting – or maybe it's a part-time model – and you know what to think straight off. But these two *were* actresses: no question. And my guess was they were big city girls. Madrid most likely, or failing that Barcelona, or maybe Seville.

So we murdered the champers and by that time it was nine-fifteen. Just about right for an early dinner, so Dave put Amparo in the front and she piloted him to a little place she knew, and I got in the back with Lola, who seemed to have pretty well-defined ideas of what the back seat of a car was for. It was a nice drive, and time sped by all too quickly as they say. . . . We went to a new development called Sol y Mar, along Bajondillo beach, past the big, expensive high rises Bernie Kornfeld had conjured up, the ones you watch from

114

the old town because when the jets come in to land it looks as if they're flying down between the buildings. . . .

But we drove on, away from the sea to a low white building with a green-tiled roof that looked as if it had been there for centuries and had in fact been erected a year ago. I know because it said so on the menu. The place was packed but Amparo had phoned to book a table and Dave handed over a thousand peseta note, and I wondered if he'd want us to pay for this one ourselves or put it on expenses.

The evening's only snag was that the car park was full, and that really was a drag because there was no street-parking permitted and the next car park was a five-minute walk away. But there wasn't any choice, so Dave shot off with the car and while he was gone I ordered more champagne and he was back in time to hear the cork pop. It was a good night. Really good. El Patio Andaluz the place was called, and it had all the trimmings:- real Andalusian food like the prawns with chilli and garlic called gambas al ajillo, and roast sucking pig, and the kind of fresh fruit and salad that isn't even a memory in England any more. . . . And with it we drank the champagne, and a red wine from Rioja; Marques de Riscal. It was a meal I'll never forget. And in between whiles there was flamenco. It's not an art form I'm mad about, though Lola and Amparo insisted they were good. Too much stamping about and yowling like the tom cat's night out for my taste, but the girls were pretty and the guitarist played like a dream, and as I say the place was packed, and that added to the atmosphere somehow. Then a girl came round selling carnations and we bought some, and Amparo threaded hers in her hair, Lola tucked hers in her bosom. I suggested coffee, but Amparo looked at her watch and said we'd get better coffee at her place. . . .

So I paid the bill and the girls disappeared to the Ladies and I said I'd walk Dave to the car. After a meal like that I needed a bit of exercise. We got outside and from a distance we could hear the sea, no louder than a sigh, and the air was clean after the restaurant fug.

'Well?' said Dave, and slung his bag on his shoulder. 'Can I pick 'em or can I pick 'em?'

'You can pick 'em,' I said, and eased my way round a Seat

115

that was parked almost between the entrance gates.

'It'll do us good to get away from business for a while,' said Dave, and I knew he was thinking of Imogen, just as I was thinking of Sabena. What I was thinking was it would do me no good at all.

'The car-park's over there,' Dave said, and pointed to where the street lights died because the street had ended, till the developers got more capital. . . . So on we slogged past the orange glow of the last street light, across hard, red earth scattered with stones. We had come so far that even the sea was silent, and in silence they jumped us.

Four of them there were, and each of them had a knife. They came at us wide apart which was no help for the shotgun, but as they ended their run they had to bunch together and as they did so Dave stepped in front of me, unzipped the bag, and the sawn-off AYA was in his hands.

He didn't hold it like a pistol, but two-handed, one hand gripped the butt, the other towards the sawn-off end of the twin-barrels. They seemed to check when they saw what he held, but they were committed now, too close to run away, and kept on coming. The leader had already begun his lunge at Dave when Dave fired and the sound split the silence like an obscenity. The leader stumbled and fell, but the bloke nearest to me continued his swerving run, and lunged with the knife. I ducked, stumbled and went down on one knee, forcing myself up again quick as he came in again. I was more terrified than ever, but at least I'd come up clutching a stone.

There was no time to look to see what Dave was up to because my bloke tried another lunge and I swerved too late, felt the knife split my shirt, bite like acid across my ribs and as it did so I swung the stone as hard as I could into his forehead, and the shotgun boomed a second time, then my bloke went down and I found myself watching the fourth man run away. He made it, too. By the time Dave had reloaded he was out of range.

Dave punched in more cartridges anyway, and glanced briefly at the men he'd shot. Even I could see that they were dead. Then he knelt beside the man I'd hit with the stone. Suddenly his glance flicked to me, and he didn't have to say it, but I asked him anyway.

'He's dead, isn't he?' I said.

He nodded. 'Your one and my two,' he said. 'Let's get out of here.'

We drove off, and nobody bothered us. It came as no surprise to me to find that Lola and Amparo weren't waiting. Dave wanted to get out and look for them because he just couldn't believe that such nice girls knew men with knives and in the end I had to let him go and find out for himself. They'd gone all right, and Dave swore himself silly, which is something he doesn't do all that often, but he'd been kicked in the vanity and it hurt. . . .

So we went to a bar in Benalmadena which is far, far away from Bajondillo beach, and watched the moon and drank brandy and worried. We had troubles, even if we had survived. The bloke who'd escaped with his life would have reported back to headquarters by now, and whoever the mastermind was would know we'd lived to fight another day, but he might also think it worth his while to tip off the police that the geezers they were looking for were sharing a double at Las Golondrinas. So the first thing we had to do was wipe off the shotgun, then ditch it, which we did down a drain. That time of year it was dry, of course, so I wrapped it in a newspaper first and dropped stones on it. Then after that we went back to the hotel and I phoned Horry Lumley.

It wasn't even midnight our time but he sounded so mad when I phoned I knew he'd been holding either four aces or a blonde. It didn't stop him using his brains though, and it made him talk fast as well, so he could get back to whatever he had his hands on.

'This is Ron,' I said.

'I might have known.'

I cut in quick, before he could start in about not having had enough time to check the Pickels. 'I've been worrying about you,' I said.

'Oh yes?' he said. Wary the only word.

'I know you haven't been well,' I said, 'but I thought if you were really ill you'd tell me. . . . Wouldn't you tell me? . . . I'm sorry to bother you, but I'm so worried I can't sleep. I mean – if you wanted me to fly home – '

'Maybe it's just as well you should know,' he said.

117

'What is it for God's sake?'

'The doctors are baffled,' he said. 'But they don't hold out much hope. Please come back, old friend.' Then he put the phone down. Hard.

That took care of any nosy night-staff, as well as giving us a reason for going. I turned to Dave. 'We're leaving,' I said.

'What time?'

'First flight we can get.'

He sighed again. 'I really fancied Amparo,' he said.

'I thought it was Imogen you fancied?'

'Well of course I do,' said Dave, 'but she's in Ireland.'

*

We were lucky. We got a morning flight and nobody tried to stop us, and the geezer who'd hired us the BMW forbore to complain about getting a new tyre. On the way home, it being a scheduled flight, we got newspapers. Dave said No thanks on account of Henry James, but I took a *Mail* and an *Express*. They both had the same story on the front page. It was about the blokes Dave had clobbered near Sabena's flat. The one remanded in custody had been sprung from Wandsworth nick. A neat job with nobody hurt except the warders' feelings. But there was more.

The one Dave had put in intensive care was dead. Only he hadn't died of what Dave had done to him, which made a nice change. The bloke had been on a life support machine in a room all by himself, and a woman in nurse's uniform had wandered in and pulled the plug and wandered out again, and that was that. . . . I showed the *Mail* to Dave and he read the story right through, then went back and read it again.

'I've been thinking,' he said. 'First Spain. Now London. I'm going to put my fee up.'

'I already have,' I said.

Dave took me back to my place, but there was nothing there except a note from Melanie to say she was skint. I reckoned that meant her mother had been shopping at Harrods again, but all the same I sent her a cheque. The way things were working out it might be the last. . . . So I phoned St.

118

Stephen's and they said I could see Sabena after lunch, so I took Dave to lunch at a place I know in St. Martin's Lane, got a cab and dropped him by a bookshop in the Charing Cross Road and went on to St. Stephen's on my tod. I didn't need a minder to see Sabena.

What I did need was a bit of privacy, because she already had a visitor. Her father again. The only reason I knew Sir Montague was pleased to meet me was because he said so. All the same he told me he was back in London for a while and he'd be pleased to hear from me at any time. He was a little shorter than me (I'm five foot nine) and beginning to run to fat and not giving a damn. His eyes were cold and grey and belonged to someone a lot leaner and a hell of a lot tougher. Suddenly he looked at his watch, then kissed his daughter underneath a bandage that was coiled like a turban, wished us Good-day and left.

'Hallo you,' she said.

'Hallo yourself.'

'Aren't you going to kiss me?'

'You sure you're up to it?' I said.

'Try me,' said Sabena and I did. When she drew away she pointed to her bedside table. There was a bottle of Dom Perignon on it, in an ice-filled bucket.

'Daddy brought it,' she said. 'I'm allowed half a glass. You cop the rest – but leave a drop for the staff-nurse. It keeps her human.'

I poured and we drank.

'I thought you were in Spain,' she said. 'Why aren't you in Spain?'

'Never mind that,' I said. 'How are you?'

'Still bald,' she said. 'But improving.'

'I love you,' I said.

'Improving by leaps and bounds,' she said, and I kissed her again. But when I went back to the champers, she went back to the agenda. She was that sort of woman.

'Why aren't you in Spain?' she said again.

'Because I finished my work there,' I said.

'What work?'

'The private and confidential work I'm not allowed to talk about,' I said.

She pulled a face at me. 'Why's daddy going to see you?' she asked.

'To find out if my intentions are honourable.'

'He's left it a bit late. . . . *Why*, darling?'

'There are things I want to ask him. . . . About Theodore Pickel.'

'What makes you think daddy would know?'

'Because he understands money just as Pickel does,' I said. 'There aren't too many like that.'

'Don't you ever stop working?' she said.

'Only when I'm making love to you.'

'When I'm out of here,' Sabena said, 'you won't work nearly so much as you used to.' Then there was a lot more stuff like that, until the staff-nurse came in and finished off the Dom Perignon and told me it was time to go and I left.

Back home then, and a message from Horry Lumley asking me to call, only when I did he was out. So just for the hell of it I called Sir Montague, and the same lady secretary answered.

'I'm so glad you called,' she said. 'Sir Montague left word he would like you to dine with him tonight at his club – if that's convenient?'

But the way she said it she knew that there was no chance at all that it wouldn't be convenient. So I asked her which club and what time and she told me, then I phoned Dave to tell him that he'd be wearing his minder's hat that evening.

'I'm worried, Ron boy,' he said, and I could feel the great gouts of gloom surging down the phone.

'Not on the phone you're not,' I said, then hung up and tried Horry Lumley again, and this time I got him.

'What was all that rhubarb last night?' he said.

'I wanted an excuse for leaving in case anybody was being nosy,' I said. It didn't make all that much sense, but Horry had lost interest anyway. He always does when there's talk he isn't being paid for.

'About our little query,' he said.

'The Cardwell, Ryecroft and Cairns one? Where your little bird nests?'

'She's Ryecroft's secretary. A dear little thing.'

'I hope not too dear,' I said.

'Ha bloody ha,' said Horry, who doesn't enjoy jokes about

how expensive he is. 'Whatever she costs she's worth it. Ryecroft handled your pal's account.'

'I'm listening.'

'You remember I told you he was after a company,' said Horry. 'A small electronics firm. Funny.'

'Not funny at all,' I said. 'Electronics was his game.'

'You don't understand,' said Horry. 'When I said a small electronics firm I meant any small electronics firm. Any one at all, so long as it was cheap and cheerful and had a decent R and D department. The punters aren't usually like that.'

'What *are* the punters usually like?' I asked him.

'They hear things. A big man in the City drops a hint – or their nephew's in the business. – Sometimes it's even what's said in their horoscope. But whatever it is it's an inside tip on a particular company. But not with your Erny.'

'Did he get one?'

'He was getting bloody near.'

'Why do you keep saying "was" all the time?'

'Because nobody at Cardwell, Ryecroft and Cairns has heard from him in four weeks,' Horry said. 'Before that he used to phone every day.'

'What was he after?'

'A little outfit called Buckland Electrics. Mostly family shares. The last Buckland in the firm died last November. They make TV components. – As well as anybody from what I hear, but not any better. The late Buckland used to fancy himself as an inventor – hence the R and D.'

'Do they pay well?'

'Six per cent in a good year. They haven't had a good year in ages.'

'So the shares are cheap?'

'Face value's a quid. You could get all you wanted at 30p. Erny had fifty one per cent lined up. He didn't need any dawn raids either. Widowed Bucklands were queueing up to sell.'

'Did Erny buy?'

'He was just about to when he disappeared. Merle says Ryecroft's livid.'

'Merle?'

'The dear little person.'

'What was Erny going to use for money?'

'His other shares.'

'How much were they worth?'

'Two grand,' said Horry.

'He'd need a bit more than that, surely?' I said.

'Just a bit. Say another hundred thousand.'

'He'd got it?'

'He said he could get it any time. Cash.'

And I knew where he'd get it from.

'Did he say why he wanted to buy Buckland Electrics?' I asked.

'Never.'

'Did anybody ask?'

'Just about everybody,' Horry said. 'As I told you, it's untypical to buy like that. Eccentric even. So they all asked, but Erny wasn't saying. . . . Is all this any use to you?'

'Not a lot,' I said.

'It's still going to cost you.'

But it wasn't costing me, it was costing Imogen: so I said 'Of course' and hung up.

11

Dave brought the Roller round about six forty-five and drove me to St. James's. A car's the worst way in the world to travel up West just before theatre time, but it's where you're safest, inside a car. Nobody can push you under moving objects: in fact you've become a moving object yourself, which means you're just that little bit harder to shoot at, and as far as I was concerned that was important. There'd been far too many corpses already, I thought – five at the last count, if you include the three Spaniards. And then I realised I was wrong. It was six. I'd forgotten the heavy on the life support machine.

Anyway Dave got me to the club bang on time and opened the door for me the way chauffeurs open doors, and I told him I'd got an idea I'd be leaving around nine-thirty and went into the club where Sir Montague was waiting in the lobby for me. If he'd seen me arrive in a chauffeur-driven Roller it hadn't impressed him. All he did was shunt me into the cocktail bar and ask me what I'd have. When I said gin and tonic he looked relieved – maybe he was expecting me to ask for a light ale. . . . It was a lousy g. and t. anyway. Then I remembered the boxer husband – Jocko Hudson. Sir Montague was entitled to be wary when he entertained his daughter's boy-friends.

He looked round the bar. It was nowhere near full, and the other geezers there weren't all that close, so he got down to business at once.

'Sabena tells me you're a recent acquaintance,' he said.

Acquaintance wasn't the word I would have chosen, but I could live with it. I had to.

'That's right,' I said.

'I looked you up,' he said. 'You're a private detective.'

'Investigator,' I said.

'What's in a name?' he said. Later Dave told me that he was quoting Shakespeare, but it still sounded rude.

'It's what the clients prefer,' I said.

He ignored it. 'You specialise in finding things,' he said, and I let it pass. It was true. 'What were you looking for when you took up with my daughter? Or can't you tell me?'

'That's right,' I said. Took up wasn't nice at all, especially coming from a man who, I was beginning to realise, I hoped would be my father-in-law. Not that he was my ideal choice. But Sabena was. He sipped dry sherry then got back to the agenda.

'You're serious, I take it?'

'Certainly,' I said. 'We both are.'

Hard to say how that went down. He didn't look exactly overjoyed, yet I got the impression that any other answer would have got me thrown out.

'You see it's tricky,' he said at last. 'Toby' – Toby was the viscount – 'Toby never worked after he'd married Sabena – but then he'd never worked before he married her either. Now where do you stand on that? Would you give up work if you married a rich wife?'

'No,' I said. I didn't even have to think about it.

'Why not?'

'I don't think I could,' I said.

He grunted. I got the impression that while it was a good answer, it wasn't necessarily the right answer.

'Sabena needs a lot of looking after,' he said. I didn't agree. What Sabena needed was other people to look after. Like Lady Poppy. . . . But our kids would be better. I kept all that to myself.

'She's been pretty wild,' Sir Montague said. He sounded, and looked, proud. 'Think you can cope with that?'

'Yes,' I said. I knew I could, too.

'There's the fact that you're married to consider.'

'Separated,' I said 'I'm going to get a divorce.'

'Naturally,' he said, and then: 'Perhaps you're thinking our chat's a little premature?'

'Well – yes,' I said

'But my daughter has already told me of her plans for you.'

He looked at me then, not at all sure whether I was good enough – or even strong enough – to cope with Sabena's plans.

'I can't stop her,' he said at last. 'Never could. Up to you, now. You won't find it an easy task.' He swigged down his sherry. 'Better eat I suppose.'

The dining room, like the bar and the lobby, was covered in polished mahogany panelling and gloomy as the inside of a brown boot. The waiters were old and very slow, and the food – country pâté, rack of lamb, and Stilton – was dreadful, but the wine, a 1966 Gruaud Larose St. Julien, was superb, and I said so. He nodded.

'The best reason for coming here,' he said. 'The food's ghastly. But then you noticed that.' It seemed I was making headway.

Over dinner we talked about British television, of which he owned a goodish chunk, and the impossibility of getting a decent steak any more unless you owned your own herd of Herefords, which he did. We touched lightly on the fact that there wasn't one decent play in the West End, though he owned a couple of theatres, nor a single newspaper that was worth the exorbitant prices that were charged for them, including the one he'd just bought. That got us as far as the Stilton, after which he ordered coffee and brandy and we got back to the agenda.

'You're working for Imogen Courtenay-Lithgoe,' he said.

Not a question: a statement.

'You're very well-informed,' I said.

'Rich men have to be.'

'Who told you?'

'Bob Berkeley. He said he was going to call on you. Try to bribe you. That's why he came to see me.'

'To borrow the bribe?'

He nodded. 'Hasn't a penny of his own.'

'Have you known him for long?'

'Berkeley? Two . . . three years would it be? I bought a horse from him. Gave it to Sabena.'

'Caramba?'

'I hope you backed him. Starting price was a hundred to eight. Won by three lengths.' He was still enjoying the memory. 'Imogen was furious, I remember.'

125

'Why was that?'

'She'd always wanted to own a National winner. Still does.'

'But you say you bought this one from her father . . . ?'

He took his time answering. At last he said, 'It was never made entirely clear whether or not it was Bob's to sell.'

This was fascinating, but almost certainly a time-waster.

'You like Sir Robert, I take it?'

He was on to that at once. 'Because I call him Bob? . . . Doesn't follow. I don't dislike him, – but I wouldn't lend him any money. Did he try to bribe you?'

'Unsuccessfully,' I said.

'Of course.' He swallowed more brandy. 'Sabena says you're interested in Heidi Pickel.'

'It's possible she could help me,' I said.

'Have you met her brother?'

'Not to say met,' I said. 'I've seen him around.'

'He's a very dangerous man,' Sir Montague said. 'All monomaniacs are. – All he ever thinks about is being rich.'

'But he *is* rich,' I said.

'Very well, then. Richer. "Do you sincerely want to be rich?" Chap called Kornfeld used to ask that. Well Pickel doesn't just want to be, he *has* to be, and he'll do anything – literally anything, that will make him more money. . . . There's a connection with Imogen somewhere. He went to see her.'

'She's a beautiful woman. Rich, too.'

'Not rich enough for Pickel. His target's a billion dollars. Minimum. Besides, she has a fiancé – Except that he's disappeared.'

I thought that Sir Montague had got a hell of a lot of information from Berkeley in return for nothing at all. I also thought it would be unwise to say so aloud.

'Are you looking for the fiancé?' Sir Montague asked. I didn't answer, and before the silence could become enbarrassing Sir Montague said, 'The reason I ask is that I understand he was a boffin of some kind.'

'Boffin?'

'Scientific experts. They can be useful, you know.' He could have been describing micro-wave ovens. 'If he's got anything – anything worthwhile – I *could* be interested.' That led to the

126

start of another silence, and again he intervened, well this side of embarrassment.

'That tough young man in the Rolls coming to collect you?'

'Nine thirty,' I said.

'Then I mustn't keep you.' He rose and held out his hand, and I took it. The hand, like the rest of Sir Montague, was pudgy, but it was strong, too.

'I think maybe Sabena has got it right for once,' he said, and nodded. I was free to go.

I could feel great surges of relief engulf me: it was as if I'd passed an impossibly difficult examination, and been told I hadn't got cancer after all, both together. . . . In the lobby I looked at my watch while the porter found my raincoat. It was 9.28. It seemed that among his many qualities Sir Montague included mind-reading.

Two minutes later Dave picked me up and drove me home. I had a lot to think about. But on the way Dave wanted a chat. He didn't ask how the dinner had gone, because if I'd wanted him to know I'd have told him. Instead we had his problems.

'Where do we go next?' he asked.

'Ireland,' I said.

'I've got to make up my mind about Imogen,' he said.

'How do you mean – make up your mind?'

'I wish I knew,' he said. 'The whole thing's ridiculous.' He slid past a 43 bus. 'And after Ireland?'

'Australia,' I said.

He flicked a look at me, incredulous. 'You mean it, don't you?' he said.

'Of course I mean it.'

'It's a long way from Ireland,' said Dave. He really would have to make his mind up about our client, I thought.

*

Back in Fulham I made a cup of instant and had a brood about my possible father-in-law. At the club I thought he approved of me, which made me four inches taller with a fifty four inch chest. But back home, being Ron Hogget, I had another idea. Maybe he was offering to sell me Sabena in return for whatever it was Erny Fluck was working on. Being so smart, he probably knew what it was already. . . .

Strictly speaking there was no need to take Dave to Ireland with me, but if I'd turned up without him I'd have lost a client. Maybe you're thinking that's not such a bad idea, since all I seemed to do was keep on finding corpses – and the wrong ones at that – but this was a case I wanted to solve, and it wasn't just the money. Apart from anything else I had to find out why everybody was so frantic to meet up with an ape like Erny Fluck. I simply had to know. It was becoming an obsession.

So I told Dave he was going and a funny thing happened. It was an early evening flight and he started drinking before lunch. Not exactly smashing it down, but steady. No lagers neither. Gin and tonics, then wine when we ate, then coffee and brandy, then more coffee and brandy. And this worried me because a) Dave never drinks like that, and b) the stupid git was supposed to be my minder, and the state he was in he couldn't mind custard. Not that he was legless. He could stand; he could even walk provided it wasn't too far, but that was about his limit. If there was to be any fighting I'd have to do it, and as I say I'm hopeless. I mean I know I killed a man, but if I'd been trying to do it he'd have killed me.

What it was of course was the woman in the case. The blonde bird answering to the name of Imogen. The more Dave talked about her the more nervous he got, and the more nervous he got the more he drank, and he never stopped talking about her. . . . Even on the plane, where he switched from brandy to Scotch. . . . When we got off I parked him with the luggage and phoned Imogen not to wait for us. We had a chore to do in Dublin. The chore was hiring a car and driving to a hamburger place that didn't sell alcohol, and stuffing Dave full of burgers to act as blotting paper, then driving him around with the windows down until he showed enough signs of life for me to head for Concannon House. . . .

Well at least Burke was glad to see me, which is more than could be said for Imogen. Or her father. Definite touch of frost in the air: a real cold-snap. The general took one look at me then disappeared to add a couple of hundred words to his book, and Imogen told me to sit and report the way an empress would tell a slave. Dave went upstairs to unpack, and I hoped he'd have the sense to lie down as well.

'So my father came to see you,' she said.

'That's right,' I said.

'And offered you money to drop the case.'

I could have told her it was money he didn't have, but it wouldn't have helped. She waded into me anyway: my lack of progress, the money I cost, my general uncouthness. I was to keep away from her father, too, and never to lend him money under any circumstances. This was droll. I'd just had a leathering because he'd offered money to me, and I said so.

'You're quite sure you didn't take it?'

'Positive,' I said. She sighed, and I watched. I couldn't help it.

'You're wondering where he got it?' I asked.

'He'd borrow it,' she said. 'He can still borrow in London.'

Not from Sir Montague Redditch, I thought, but that too was irrelevant.

'It will all be gone by now,' she said, 'wherever he got it from. And sooner or later I'll have to pay.'

She really did have lousy luck with gamblers.

Then she sighed again, and again I wished she wouldn't, or at least wear looser clothes.

'You don't give him money?' I asked.

'It's none of your bloody business, but no,' she said. 'I don't.'

'Then how did he raise his air-fare?'

'Pawned something,' she said. 'He always does.'

'Why did he want me to give up?' I asked.

'Because he hated Erny Fluck.'

'Fluck was a gambler too.'

'All the more reason to hate him,' she said. 'I was financing Erny and he knew it.'

But there had to be more than that. The general's daughter had more than enough for two, and anyway, Erny was about to make it very big indeed.

'You will find him for me?' she said.

'Depends,' I said.

'Depends on what?'

'On whether you'll pay my fare to Australia. And Dave's.'

*

129

There was a tranny in my room and I twiddled it till I got Radio Three. Pavarotti was singing 'Ah celest' Aida'. Every time my mother heard it the tears used to roll down her cheeks – and it still takes my sister that way. Doesn't make sense really. It's only a bloke going on about his bird. Still it's what we're like, us Italians. And a good cry can do you the world of good when you need one, not that I thought I did. I mean whatever his motives Sir Montague hadn't said get lost, and all his daughter had said was come hither, and I really looked as if I might be getting close to the fee I was earning. It was time I did make a few bob, and more than time the wrong people stopped getting killed. . . . Pavarotti hit the sort of top notes you think can only exist in your imagination, and I began to feel pretty good. Then the door opened and Dave came in.

I'd never seen him look like that. Never. I mean we'd been mates since my schooldays. Melanie and me had even postponed our wedding till he'd got leave from the paras so he could be best man. And even if her and him did have a bit of a ding dong later it all blew over in time. I mean we were still good mates as well as colleagues. But in all the years I'd known him I'd never seen him look like that. Dave had always had a special kind of cheerfulness about him: the sort of cheerfulness that goes with competence. He's the sort of bloke who's set himself his goals, and knows he can achieve them. Hence the cheer. But now all that had gone. He looked like the blue-print for the ultimate loser.

He was wearing a pale blue dressing gown I remember, and his hair was rumpled, – and he looked about eighteen years old. He also looked shattered.

'D'you mind if I have a word, Ron?' he said.

'Course not.' I switched off Pavarotti. 'What's happened?'

'Imogen,' he said, and stuck there.

'What about her?'

'She asked me to her room,' he said.

'So?' Again I had to wait for it, but at last he managed it.

'I think it must have been because I drank too much,' he said, and I thought Oh my God no. Don't tell me. But this time he kept on going. 'It was the first time in my life I –' He swallowed. 'I couldn't do either of us any good.'

'Leave it, Dave,' I said. But he didn't even hear me.

'She's got a nickname for me, now,' he said. 'I'm Finn MacCool. And we both know why, don't we Ron?'

I knew, all right. The horse we were looking for was a gelding.

'Relax,' I said. 'Don't worry. You'll be all right tomorrow.'

'Not for her I won't,' he said.

'Course you will.'

'You don't understand,' said Ron. 'This is a very special kind of bird. Very beautiful – and very cruel.'

'Like a golden eagle,' I said.

'A golden eagle that enjoys its work,' he said. 'Also she deals in absolutes. Either you're perfect – or you're a failure. And if you fail you can never get back to perfection. . . . Once a failure always a failure. . . . With another bird I could be a stallion all night, but with her I'd always be Finn MacCool. . . . Got anything to drink?'

'Of course not,' I said. 'This is a private house.'

'I've had far too much already anyway,' Dave said.

'Why?' I said. 'Surely you knew what effect it would have?'

'I'd have been far better off with Amparo', he said. 'The worst *she* could have done was kill me.'

'Maybe you do need a drink,' I said. 'Shall I sneak downstairs and get you one?' But he settled for a cigarette, and when he'd finished it he went back to his room and I turned on the radio, but Verdi was over. Now it was Mozart – *Il Seraglio*. I turned it off. I can't stand Mozart; he makes you think. But even so, when I lay down to sleep, I was thinking anyway.

131

12

Sabena was home. That was the big news when I got back and I went round to see her as soon as I heard, stopping off at Harrods for red roses and champagne and caviar. She was mad about caviar. . . . Rosario let me in and she was in the drawing room, lying on a couch, dressed in a kaftan and still with a bandage round her head. She looked like an odalisque by Delacroix and I said so.

'Well of course,' she said. 'Only odalisques get roses and caviar and Roederer Cristal.' She kissed me as she always did. Never once did she try to hide the passion in her kisses.

'What does the doctor say?' I asked her.

'That I'm a lucky lady – but then I know that. Everything's healing, everything's fine, he says. Quite soon I shall cease to be bald.'

'That still bothers you?'

'It would bother any woman,' she said. 'For a woman in love it's absolute bloody murder.' Then Rosario came in with the ice bucket. Thank God.

'Daddy says you're by no means as stupid as he'd been led to believe.'

'My goodness,' I said, 'that's praise indeed.'

'It is for him,' she said. 'It's the best thing he's said about any of my boy-friends.' The way she said it made me think of serried ranks, like the Foot Guards at Trooping the Colour. I changed the subject.

'He knows about Lady Tarleton's brother,' I said.

'He bought Caramba from him.' She looked at me, frowning. 'Does Imogen ever talk about Caramba?'

'Never,' I said.

'She was livid when daddy bought him and livid when I

132

sold him. There was no pleasing her.'

'Why did you sell him?'

'I'd gone off racing, so I sold him to a good home.' Another frown, more intense this time. 'You're not detecting again, I hope? Working for dear, sweet Imogen?'

'Just nosy,' I said. Rosario came in again with a plate of water biscuits with caviar smeared on them, very thick. I decided I'd give her something nice for Christmas. I owed her a lot. Then she asked if she could go to the pictures, and Sabena said it was fine. Mr. Hogget had learned to open doors all by himself. I prepared for battle, but she waited till the door had closed.

'I'm getting at you,' she said.

'So I notice. – Any particular reason?'

'You over there in Ireland with darling Imogen – and me back here in London, bald as a coot.'

'*Me*?' I said. 'With *Imogen*?'

Again, the hard, cold stare, but it softened at last.

'No,' she said. 'You're not that good an actor.'

'I wouldn't want to be,' I said, 'and anyway – why should she pick on me?'

'Why should I?' said Sabena. 'But I did.'

'I'm lucky,' I said. 'Lucky as a bloke who wins the big one on the Pools every week. . . . Who needs her?'

'You are absolutely scrumptious,' she said, 'to say a thing like that.'

'I mean it,' I said.

'And I love you for it.' She savoured it. 'Imogen Courtenay-Lithgoe. Who needs her? I mean *look* at her. You've spent absolute days with her.'

'I've seen her in action.'

'She has *got* a gentleman-friend, you mean?'

'My mate Dave,' I said.

'Pour champagne,' she said, 'then bring the drinks and the bikkies over here.'

I did so, and we sipped and ate.

'It's an aphrodisiac,' she said.

'Which one?'

'The caviar. It will make us randy.'

'I'll catch up with you when you're better.'

133

'You'll catch up with me in twenty minutes,' she said, 'if you don't mind me keeping the head-dress on. All part of the odalisque service.'

I thought of Dave, and went easy on the champagne.

I was a lot more nervous than she was, which wasn't difficult because she wasn't nervous at all, trusting me and helping me even as she made it plain that I was helping her, and when we'd done I'd never felt better – or happier – and we were dressed and in the drawing room only just in time for Rosario's return from the cinema. We sat and talked, lazy and content, and champagne and caviar drifted on into sandwiches and red wine, and at last I asked her about Lady Tarleton.

'She was in here the other day,' Sabena said. 'She asked about you.'

'Well I never,' I said. 'What did she say?'

'I'll give you her exact words,' said Sabena. 'She said: "It's strange. I mean I'm sure he didn't do it to us deliberately. It must be one of those – ironies of fate, I believe they're called." I told her you hadn't done anything to us and she said "Then it can't have happened yet." So I asked her what hadn't happened and she said she hadn't the faintest idea. That's Poppy all over. Never the complete picture. Never. . . . But you aren't going to do anything to us, surely?'

'I've done quite enough to you for one day,' I said, 'and I have no aspirations of any kind towards Lady Tarleton.'

'Pig,' she said. 'But I'm serious. She could have meant her brother as well.'

'All he wants me to do is go away,' I said. 'And all I want to do is oblige him – as soon as I get paid.'

'All the same she meant it,' she said. 'And she *knew* it, if you see what I mean. Knew it would happen some time.'

'Whatever it is,' I said.

'Just don't hurt me,' she said. 'I don't think I could bear it, and I'm very easily hurt, believe it or not.' Then in the same breath: 'Did you mind my doing it with my headgear on?'

'I loved you doing it with your headgear on.'

'Then you'd better come again tomorrow – If you're still here.' I looked at her, surprised. 'It seems I can always tell when you're itching to be off,' she said. 'You go all furtive. It'll be the bane of our marriage. Where are you going?'

'Australia,' I said.

'Then I hope you won't hurt Heidi too much, either. She's even more vulnerable than I am.' She yawned. 'I'm not mad at you, my darling. Please don't think it. Just a teeny bit knackered. – I can't think why.'

I kissed her and said I'd go, but she wouldn't hear of it, not without my minder, so I phoned Dave and he came round in the mini-cab and got out to ring the doorbell, and Sabena peeped from behind the curtain.

'Imogen always did like the pretty ones,' she said. 'Has she been nasty to him?'

I knew it would be our secret. 'Yes,' I said

She studied him more closely. 'I hope she doesn't regret it. – No. That's a lie. I hope she does regret it.'

Then she kissed me goodbye. It took a long time.

*

There was a bloke in Australia House who owed me a favour, and I'd got on to him before we went to Spain, but even so we had to wait for our visas for a day or two. Nowadays it's not all that easy to get into Australia. Maybe they're worried they'll run out of room. Still it gave me time to ring Horry Lumley again. He greeted me warmly.

'Funny,' I said. 'You sounded like you were glad it was me.'

'I am glad it was you,' he said. 'You pay so promptly. What can I do for you?'

He listened while I told him.

'You disappoint me, Ron,' he said. 'Infallible systems, indeed. I never knew you were a gambling man.'

'Never was and never will be,' I said, but I was lying. I was gambling with my life, and Dave's, but I didn't want to tell Horry that and Horry wouldn't want to know.

When I hung up I thought to myself that a) Horry was getting greedy and b) either Dave or I could have found out

135

what I was after, but on the other hand we'd have been spotted, maybe even recognised. With Horry that could never happen. So I tried not to think I might die and went about my business: buying lunch for a Cambridge physicist I'd once found a piece of Staffordshire pottery for – he had a hundred and forty three pieces at the time, but he couldn't rest till I'd made it a hundred and forty four; seeing my solicitor about making a new will and getting a divorce – what you might call making the worst and best of it. And seeing my sister.

My sister lives in Putney: quiet, nice part, near the river. She's married to an assistant bank manager called Sydney Muspratt, which makes her Anna Maria Muspratt. The Anna Maria is because it was my mother's name, her being Italian. Very like my mother is Anna Maria; a little taller and thinner, but very like. When she saw me she at once began to scold me because I hadn't come at a proper meal time: lunch, or dinner, or even breakfast, but I wanted to see her before the kids finished at school and while Sydney was still at the bank, so I'd insisted on tea, which was two kinds of sandwiches and three kinds of cake. She had a biscuit.

I asked her the things I had to, including how my father was, but she hadn't seen him since I had, which meant the old git must have had a good win at the dogs. He only ever sees either of us when he needs money for the boozer. Still, no news was good news. Then she asked me about Melanie, and I said I was going for a divorce if I could work it.

'You got somebody else in mind, Ron?'

'Could be,' I said.

'Sabena Redditch?' she said, and before I could ask her how she knew she told me she'd seen pictures of us at the 'Feed The Starving' Ball in every paper that ran a gossip column. She only took two, but her mates had shown her all the others. Thrilled to bits they were. So was she, which surprised me.

'You don't think she's a bit above me?' I said.

'I think Melanie was a bit below you,' she said. She and Melanie never did get on.

'You don't mind then?'

'I just want you to be happy,' she said, and looked around her drawing-room with its over-stuffed furniture and cocktail cabinet and pictures of elephants and purple-faced Chinese ladies. 'Same as I am.'

*

I've done my whack of long-distance flying, and Australia's about as far as you can go, if you don't count New Zealand, so I took my precautions. There's only one, really. Never arrive there and get off the plane and go straight to work. The jet lag is murder. So Dave and me – we had round the world tickets, business class, and you should have heard madam scream when she found out how much they cost – Dave and me stopped over in Hong Kong on the leg out. Stop over meant get off the plane and into the hotel and go straight to bed, and wake up when you had to and wonder what time it was. We were in the Peninsula, Kowloon, where they send a Rolls Royce in the hotel's colours to meet you, which Dave enjoyed very much because he'd never been a passenger in a Roller before, only the driver.

Of course when we woke up we felt terrible, which was only natural, but at least we were in the same time zone we were heading for, more or less, so we did some shopping and went off to Aberdeen to eat in a floating restaurant, then went back and forwards on a Star ferry just to enjoy the view. Hong Kong to Kowloon, back to Hong Kong, and then Kowloon again. No reason except it was marvellous to watch the lights of the land, sense the black water, see the junks and power boats and cargo ships gleam in the moonlight. There were peaks all around us and water beneath us, and I got a feeling of enormous strength, but enormous peace, too, peace as strong as war. It wouldn't last; it couldn't, but at least it was there and we were part of it. Then we got off and joined the crowds by the shopping complex and it was gone.

When we prepared for bed that night Dave asked if things would be rough in Sydney and I said more than likely and did he mind?

'Not a lot,' he said. 'It's what I'm here for. Only I haven't got a gun, remember.'

'Everything comes to him who waits,' I said.

'Not if he waits too long,' said Dave, so I told him not to

worry. I was doing the worrying for both of us. So like I say, the peace of the harbour hadn't lasted very long. The only nice thing was I could still remember it.

*

Sydney at first seemed to have no peace to offer. Planes were stacked over the airport, customs and immigration officials glowered in a way that even their New York counterparts might envy, and traffic snarled up even more than it usually did because the buses were on strike. But we rented a car – a Holden – at the airport, so we dodged the taxi queue. On the credit side the Harbour Bridge and the Opera House looked just like their pictures, and the season was Spring instead of Autumn and the sun was warm. We went to our hotel that overlooked the harbour, and Dave took a lager out of the mini-bar, and I took a tonic and mixed it with my duty-free gin, and we looked down at another great port, sunlit this time, the yachts on the water buzzing about like insects.

'They've got ferries, too,' said Dave. 'Nice.'

Better than nice, I thought, but not yet. This wasn't the time to start feeling at peace. They say that corpses are at peace, too. . . .

Dave went off for a shower and I looked through the telephone book for the place Sabena had told me about. Mario's. It was there all right, but all I got was a recording machine that told me the place didn't open till nine and wouldn't get going till ten, but I could leave a message if I wanted to. I didn't. I sat and wished the phone would ring instead, and it did, and a voice said was I a mate of someone I better not mention, then we fenced about a bit till each of us was sure of the other, then I mentioned my modest requirements.

'A thousand dollars,' the voice said. 'American.'

That was steep, but I was in a hurry. Besides, I'd been paid in Yankee dollars for my last job.

'How soon?' I said.

'Half an hour,' said the voice. 'No bill bigger than a hundred.' Then he hung up because there was nothing more to say.

Then Dave came out of the shower and I told him he had a present coming, then showered and changed in time for a knock on the door. Dave opened it, and a geezer came in carrying a parcel.

'You're the joker who ordered the books?'

'That's me,' I said. 'One set of books. C.O.D.'

I took out the wad of greenbacks: five hundreds, nine fifties, two twenties and a ten. His eyes looked like they were on stalks and his hand shot out.

'We'll just check the goods first,' I said.

Dave came over and opened the parcel. Inside was a Colt Python 357 magnum revolver, twenty rounds of ammunition, and webbing harness and holster.

'Give him the money,' he said, and fed bullets into the magnum as I handed it over. The geezer took it and prepared to leave, but Dave waved the magnum – he was too much of a gentleman to point – and said, 'Better check it', which the other bloke did, but he was a bit nervous and it took him three times to get it right, and by the time he had Dave had checked the gun out. It must have been O.K. because he said, 'Mustn't keep you,' and the geezer was gone so fast it was like switching off a light.

I said, 'The gun's O.K. then?'

'Better than a sawed-off shotgun,' he said. 'This place we're going – do we have to wear coats? I mean what with taxi drivers wearing shorts – '

'It said formal wear on the tape,' I said. 'That means coats.'

'Just as well,' said Dave. 'This thing could make us look conspicuous.'

Then he put on his harness and we dressed and ate fish in a restaurant and drank white wine – you can always get good fish and wine in Sydney – then dawdled over coffee till half-past nine, and then we took a cab to Mario's, which is near King's Cross but not of it. Sydney's King's Cross is a kind of Soho gone sour, but nearby is O.K. Risqué but upmarket. Just the sort of place to start looking for Heidi Pickel.

Mario's was a disco: cute and expensive, the kind that caters for the well-heeled the world over. The décor looked as if it might have been designed by Hockney when he wasn't concentrating, and the lighting was clever, inventive and easy on the eyesight. The waiters were pretty boys dressed for the most part in roller skates and boxers' trunks, like all the other disco waiters that year, and the DJ made jokes in French and Italian as well as English. He wasn't all that funny in any of them. . . . We hadn't reserved, the maître told us severely, so we'd have to make do with a table at the back. It was what we wanted anyway, but I gave him a big tip even so, then I ordered a bottle of wine. A cutie called Noel brought it over. I knew his name was Noel because it was embroidered on his shorts. Dave sipped, and stared at what he called the beautiful antipodean people. And indeed, some of them were beautiful, and a lot of the beautiful were gay. Men and women alike were either sun-tanned and lean or else sun-tanned and fat. Hardly any in-betweens. With girls I prefer in-betweens. So does Dave.

'Who in the hell told you to come here?' he yelled above the music.

'Sabena,' I said. '*She* used to come here. With Heidi Pickel.'

Dave grunted. I'd given him a good reason, but he didn't have to like it.

'What do we do?' he said. 'Sit here for the next three or four weeks on the off-chance she might look in?'

'We wait a while,' I said. 'Then we ask questions. Nicely. Politely. In the meantime we drink our nice wine and maybe dance a little.'

Dave looked at me appalled. 'Dance with each other?' he said.

'Just dance,' I said. 'Do our own thing. . . . You know.'

'Oh God,' said Dave, but when the time came he got up and did his thing, and very graceful he looked.

After an hour the wine was well down in the bottle, and Dave was complaining that the webbing harness was beginning to chafe, so we headed for the foyer. The maître was ready with the bill and I added more money. Too much, and we both knew it.

'Leaving so early, sir?' he said. 'I hope you weren't disappointed?'

'Not in the least,' I said, 'but we were hoping to meet a friend of ours here. . . . It's rather important – so we'd better look elsewhere.'

A good maître hates to see money leave his place before closing time. This one said, 'If you care to give me his name, sir – I can check if he has a reservation for tonight.'

'It isn't a him,' I said. 'Her name's Heidi Pickel.' His face didn't even flicker.

'Pickel?' he said. He made it sound as if it was a name he heard every day.

'Maybe I've got a picture of her,' I said. We both knew damn well I had, but I went through my pockets anyway, and came up at last with one of Heidi by herself. He looked at it, and I looked at him.

'I do remember her,' he said. 'She used to come here a lot last year – sometimes with another young lady. Dark-haired. Very attractive.' (I felt glad I'd over-tipped him so much.) 'Then the other young lady stopped coming – round about November that would be. English, she was. This one – ' he nodded at the photograph – 'is foreign. Then this one stopped coming, too. . . . About April.'

'Any idea why?'

'She wasn't all that well, she said. She didn't look well, come to that.' It seemed as if he chose the words carefully.

'Did she come here with anybody else – apart from the dark girl?'

'Oh yes,' the maître said.

'Who?'

The tap turned off. 'I'm sorry, I forget,' he said. 'Excuse me.'

He tried to walk away, and found he couldn't on account of Dave who was standing bang in front of him.

'I want you to promise me something,' said Dave.

'Sir?' The voice was icily polite, but the worry was beginning to show even then.

'I want you to promise me you'll take extra good care of yourself,' Dave said. 'I've just had a premonition you might not be all that well, either.'

The maître took another look at Dave, and didn't like what he saw.

He said at once, 'I seem to think there was a man came in with her a few times, but I can't remember his face.' I took out a hundred dollar bill.

'Do you have an address where they could be reached? Or even a telephone number?' I said. 'It really is extremely urgent.' I added a fifty, made them rustle.

'A yacht,' he said. 'They were going to a party on a yacht one time. Called the "Lucky Me".'

I gave him the fifty. 'Where was it moored?'

'Rushcutters' Bay.' I gave him the hundred, but Dave reached over and twitched it from his hand.

'Promise me you'll take care,' he said, 'and not endanger your health by gossiping.'

'I promise,' the maître said, and Dave gave him back the hundred and we left.

*

According to the marina the 'Lucky Me' was cruising, not due back for a couple of days.

'The "Lucky Me"?' I said. 'You're sure? The sixty foot ketch, white with orange trim?'

'Not unless she's had an accident,' said the voice. ' "Lucky Me's" a hundred foot power-boat. Twin diesels. Who are you anyway'

'Lloyd's of London,' I said and hung up.

Dave said, 'What do we do now?'

'Sleep,' I said, 'and try to dream up an idea.'

Dave took off the harness and gun and put it in his suitcase.

'Aren't you going to keep it under your pillow?'

'You can put it under yours if you like,' said Dave. 'But I like my head where it is. On top of my neck.'

*

It took me a while to get to sleep, but I woke up fast enough. We had a visitor.

The reason I knew was he had switched on the light and was pointing a gun at me. I flicked a look at Dave. He was unconscious. Being a detective I deduced that he had belted

142

Dave one – probably with the automatic he was carrying – before he turned his attention to me. The knowledge did nothing at all to make me feel better.

'Get out of bed,' said the geezer, and I did what he told me. Besides the gun he was a good two stone heavier than me. 'Now put your hands on your head.' I did that too. Like when you were in the infants' school being naughty. But it didn't feel like that. In the infants' school the teacher didn't wear a stocking mask for a start. . . .

The geezer backed away from me and switched on the television, switching channels till he found an old war movie that was good and loud.

'You know why I did that?'

I shook my head.

'It's so nobody will hear if you start yelling.' I waited. 'Now why should you yell?'

'I've no idea,' I said. It came out a croak, but at least I said it.

'Course you have,' he said. 'You'll be yelling because you won't co-operate and I'll be forced into making you co-operate, and it'll hurt you, sport. My oath it will.'

'Co-operate about what?' Another croak.

'About what you're doing here.' He lifted the automatic. 'Maybe you'll start off being brave but you'll tell me sooner or later. No worries.' He moved a little closer. 'What you doing here, sport?'

'We came here to find a girl,' I said.

'What girl?'

'A girl called Heidi Pickel,' I said.

'Who sent you?'

'Her brother Theodore,' I said. 'He's worried about her.'

He hit me with the gun's muzzle, slamming it against my head with nicely controlled force. I went down like a pin in a bowling alley, and I went down flat. At once he began to kick me, not hard enough to break ribs, but hard enough even so. And I got the message without him telling me. The kicking would go on till I got back on my feet. So I got up. It hurt, and it took time, but I did it.

'You see what happens when you lie?' he said.

'I'm not lying – '

143

He swung the pistol again and I ducked, so he hit me in the belly with his fist instead, then tripped me as I pitched forward. As soon as I fell the leathering started again. Through the pain I could hear the sound track of the movie. It was one I'd seen on late night TV not long before. 'Bataan Victory' it was called. All about U.S. marines and Japs killing each other more than forty years ago. The movie had got to one of its quiet bits, but there would be more uproar shortly. His right shoe rebuked me for dawdling and I scrambled upright once more.

'Maybe you're queer,' my tormentor said. 'Maybe you're one of those jokers who likes being beaten.'

'I hate it,' I said.

He chuckled. 'You'll hate it some more soon.'

He glanced at the TV screen. The marines were loading their weapons, waiting for the death or glory rush of the Japanese soldiers. Soon the bangs would start up again, and I couldn't take another bashing. I sagged forward.

'Don't pass out on me,' the geezer said. 'It'll hurt you all the more when I bring you round.'

'Please,' I said. 'I can't help it.'

He swung the gun back.

'Listen,' I said. 'I can prove it. I've got a letter.'

That worried him. He had me pegged for a liar, but if I had a letter that made things complicated. I wished to God I did have a letter.

'Get it,' he said. The Japs charged: the marines blasted them.

I went over to Dave's suitcase – walking there was like being stretched on the rack – opened the case and took out the magnum and shot the geezer: the real gun booming like artillery against the movie's sound effects.

I hit him in the arm that held the pistol and he dropped it. That doesn't mean I aimed for the arm that held the pistol, I just pointed and fired and hoped that some part of the geezer in the stocking mask would get in the way, and it did. The shot slammed him against the door and he sort of rested against it and looked at me, waited to see if I was going to fire again. When he was sure I wasn't, he did something I could never have done, not in a million years. 'I'll be seeing you

144

sport,' he said, and walked out on me. He even closed the door after him. Moving like a drunk I went over to the door myself, and shot the bolt home. Locks seemed to be unreliable.

Next thing was to feel better – that might take a week or two. In the meantime I lurched over to the bathroom and got under the shower, running it cold, then hot, then cold again. Then I put on a robe and used a towel and ice-cubes from the mini-bar to make a cold compress, and pressed it where it hurt most, then turned off the telly and went to take a look at Dave. His eyes were just starting to flicker.

'What happened?' he said, then he turned his head and groaned. I gave him the compress, and lurched off and made another. When I got back Dave was sitting up, his compress pressed to his head, and sniffing.

'I've been coshed,' he said. '*And* there's been shooting here.'

I told him what had happened. He didn't enjoy it. When I'd finished he said: 'It's just what I've been saying, Ron. First Imogen, and now this. I've had it, Ron.'

I needed that kind of talk like a rabbi needs a pork sandwich. It wasn't self-pity I wanted to hear: it was vows of vengeance.

'He took you by surprise,' I said.

'But he shouldn't have,' said Dave. 'I've been *trained* not to be taken by surprise.'

'Maybe he was trained too,' I said.

Dave thought about the idea: began to like it.

'Could be,' he said. 'They've got an SAS mob here. Maybe he trained in that.'

The one group that Dave would admit to be better than the paras was the SAS. But then as he said, any other para would say the same.

'Yeah,' he said again. 'Could be. I mean look at the way he walked out on you I mean – a bullet in the arm and he still figured out the odds just right. He certainly *sounds* SAS.' He seemed enthusiastic, even admiring, which was good news for me. Dave's adrenalin was beginning to flow again. He looked at his watch, and I sighed. It was twenty to three.

'I bet you're thinking what I'm thinking,' he said.

He was right. The only link between our visitor and us was the maître at Mario's, and Mario's didn't close till three. Dave

145

looked at my face. I wasn't exactly registering the aggressive spirit and the will to win.

'Up to you, Ron,' he said, 'but it's the only chance we've got. We may not have it tomorrow.'

Slowly, because my bruises still hurt, I began to put on my clothes.

13

Holdens are a subsidiary of General Motors, and they tend to make the kind of cars Australians like, big and thirsty and a soft-sprung ride. A lot easier to coax an unwilling guest into one of them than a Mini Metro. This time I drove. Dave was still far and away the better driver, but he was also far and away better at coaxing in unwilling guests. So I drove. In my pocket was the Browning Hi-Power automatic I'd made the other geezer drop when I shot him, but that didn't worry me. I'd made Dave take the magazine out before we started. . . .

When we got to the club it was a minute to three and a couple of motor-bike police were already in attendance. Not to prevent any uproar. I didn't think that for a minute. They were there to make sure that the rich and famous got into their cars and taxis without molestation. But anyway I kept on going, left and left again. (It's relaxing driving in Australia. They use the same side of the road as we do.) After the second left we found plastic sacks full of garbage on either side of a door, and a mini-bus already waiting. I kept on going another fifty yards, slid into a patch of shadow and cut the lights.

'That'll be the group's transport,' I said. 'They won't be long.'

And how right I was. Musicians never linger once they're no longer being paid. They were into the bus and away in three minutes flat, and I backed the Holden down to a nearer patch of shadow and the real wait began, till out they began to come, first a trickle, then a flood: chefs and washers-up and the pretty waiters who looked overdressed without their boxer shorts on show. And then at last, the maître. He was all by himself, which I considered a good thing, but not Dave. The way Dave was feeling by then it was a cause for regret. The

147

maître by himself meant one less geezer he could knock unconscious.

Anyway the maître came out by himself, and if he looked our way he didn't see us. Dave was in the back, and he eased off the catch of the offside door, then squeezed my shoulder, which was the signal to move. I moved. I doubt if a Holden has ever moved so fast in reverse before or since. We shot backwards down the lane, and Dave let the door swing open, then scooped in the maître before he'd gone three strides. Then I stood on the brake, Dave swung his door to, and I put the Holden into forward and drove off, smooth and steady. Nothing to earn the coppers' ill-will.

In the back David was showing the horrified maître a piece of American technology, a Colt Python 357 revolver with the four-inch barrel and chequered walnut butt. The maître found it so fascinating he was unable to speak for a while, which was as well. We had a lot of driving to do. We needed privacy. In a city like Sydney there isn't all that much until you're well out of town, and then there's nothing else, thousands of miles of it. So I kept on driving from the city to the suburbs, skyscrapers all finished, neat little houses just beginning. Neither Dave nor I spoke. We'd plotted the route on the maps in the Holden's glove compartment. All I had to do was watch for the signs and try not to think about how much my body ached. Inevitably it was the maître who cracked first.

'Where are you taking me?' he said.

'That's the wrong question,' said Dave. 'You should say why are you taking me.'

The maître was silent again. The neat little houses became less thick on the ground. Scrubland began to appear, between houses that were only half finished. There was the first eucalyptus, then more and more, then a good road that ran beside the ocean, and then a rutted track that led inland to nowhere. We took the rutted track, until at last I saw a stretch of hard-baked, empty earth, and turned off the car from the road and into nowhere. The thin grey light of the false dawn was beginning to appear, and as I pulled on the handbrake there came the sound of a dreadful, laughing scream, like a raving maniac being tickled beyond endurance. But I hadn't been to all those Aussie movies for nothing. That was a kookaburra, bang on cue. Dave turned to the maître.

'You have the advantage of us,' he said. 'You know our names. What's yours?'

'None of your business,' the maître said. Dave sighed, as if the whole thing bored him to distraction, then stuck the three middle fingers of his left hand into the other's gut, in what he tells me is called a spear-strike. The other bloke made a noise like a damp paper-bag bursting, and slumped forward, which made it easier for Dave to go through his pockets, which he did. First thing was his wallet, which Dave flicked over to me. Besides that there was a lighter, and cigarettes, keys, loose change, and a little book full of names and addresses that looked as if it might come in useful, comb and nail file and sunglasses and a driving licence, and that was about it.

'According to his licence he's Bruno Cardena,' said Dave. I grunted. I was still going through his wallet. Money. A hell of a lot of money, including bribes he'd had from me. I took that back for a start. Then there were half-a-dozen credit cards, though why he bothered with all that ready cash I had no idea. And that was all, except for the zipped up compartment I'd saved till last. In that one were a number of small transparent envelopes, each with its carefully measured dose of powder.

'You want to say anything?' I asked in Italian.

He said a lot. The accent was Australian, the words pure Sicilian. None of it was relevant.

'He's all yours,' I said to Dave, and Dave smiled at Bruno Cardena. It was a smile that frightened even me.

'You and me are going to get out of the car and have a fight,' he said, 'and I am going to win. And when you're conscious we're going to have another fight. And another. And another. Smashing way to start the day, eh Bruno?'

'I – ' Cardena seemed to be having trouble talking. 'I don't like fighting.'

'You should have thought of that,' said Dave, and handed me the magnum, pushed Cardena out of the car, and went out after him in a flying dive. I sat and watched in the car's headlights. Two Gun Hogget.

It wasn't much of a fight. One-sided. No drama. No conflict. Dave dished it out and Cardena took it. In fact

149

Dave's only worry was not to put him out too soon. And it was a worry. He was still mad at being taken by surprise. It made him hit hard. As for me – I was mad because my bruises still ached and it was partly Cardena's fault. All the same I hoped it wouldn't last too long. Then Cardena indicated that he'd had enough by fainting, but Dave knew a cure for that, too. It wasn't very nice, but it worked.

When Dave hauled him up to his feet I got out of the car and walked over to them. I had a featured part, after all: Mr. Nice Guy. When Dave hauled off to hit Cardena again, I reached out and grabbed his arm.

'Wait,' I said.

He gave me a look that was supposed to be disgusted, but it went further than that. It looked more like raging hate, and I wondered if he was mad at me because I'd got away from the Stocking Mask Sadist without his help. But that wasn't the time to analyse our relationship.

'Wait,' I said again.

'Why should I?' said Dave. 'Mr. Cardena's tough. He likes a good fight, don't you, Mr. Cardena?'

He hit him again, using the arm I wasn't holding, and down Cardena went. I went over and helped him up, whispering as I did so:

'I want to help you, honestly I do,' I said. 'But if he starts again I won't be able to stop him. He'll kill you. Believe me I know. But if you – co-operate, I'll get you out of this.'

'You promise?'

A stupid question, but he'd taken a hell of a hiding.

'Honour bright,' I said.

'Why don't you kiss him goodbye and let me get back to work?' said Dave.

'No,' I said, all pure and forgiving. 'Mr. Cardena wants to co-operate.'

Dave came over to us; stuck his face close to Cardena's.

'You better mean it,' he said. 'Otherwise we go into our routine again.'

'Please,' I said. 'Give him a chance,' and I offered Cardena one of his cigarettes and lit it with his lighter. Even so we sat him on the ground smack in the glare of the headlights. We ourselves stayed in the shadow.

150

'How did you know where to find us?' I asked.

'You got the doorman to park your car,' said Cardena, and drew on his cigarette as if the firing squad was taking aim.

'Answer the question,' said Dave.

'He spotted it for a rental car,' said Cardena, 'so I rang the bloke who works at the airport. He remembered you. Told me where you lived.'

'That wasn't very nice of him,' I said, and Dave snorted. 'It's a breach of confidence in fact. *Why* did he tell you?'

'He – owed me a favour,' Cardena said.

'What favour?'

I kept my voice gentle, but I already knew the answer, and hated him for it. Cardena was silent.

'*What favour?*' said Dave, and reached out in the darkness, slapped his face open-handed, left then right. 'Smack? Snow? Shit? Was that it?'

Cardena whimpered, then gabbled into speech before more blows came.

'I – I used to help him out sometimes,' Cardena said.

'*Help him out?*' Dave's arm reached out again, but this time I grabbed it and hung on, and Cardena scrabbled in the dirt for his cigarette.

'The man at the rental agency knew where you were staying,' he said at last. 'So naturally he told me.'

'Oh naturally,' said Dave. 'And who did you tell?'

Cardena hesitated so long that I thought I'd have to let Dave loose again. The fact that Cardena pushed heroin made it a little easier to bear. Even so I tried again, making my voice regretful, reproachful even.

'I can't help you if you won't help us,' I said, and as I did so, Dave's hand reached out again.

Cardena yelled at once: 'I don't know his name. Honest. Sometimes he calls himself Smith. Sometimes it's Brown. Or Robinson. He seems to think it's funny. All I know is he's a Pom.'

'Describe him,' said Dave, and Cardena gave us a terrified but accurate description of Erny Fluck.

'Where did you meet him?' I said.

'At the club.'

'Not last night you didn't.' Again I used my regretful,

you're-forcing-me-to-hand-you-over-to-my-partner voice.

'I phoned him,' he said.

'And the number?'

'It's in my book,' he said. 'Under Smith.' And so it was. And an address, too.

'Why did he come to you?' Dave asked. 'Was he on the needle, too?'

'God, no.' Cardena was amazed, and it had to be genuine. He was no actor. 'He was the one who came to see Heidi Pickel.'

He seemed to be in the mood to tell things. I encouraged him.

'Why did you send us after the "Lucky Me"?' I said. No answer. The mood had worn off.

'You fancy another fight?' said Dave.

'No I don't – ' said Cardena.

'Well then?' A silence that stank of fear because Cardena knew he was going to be hurt, and of worse fear even than that.

I said, 'You got it wrong,' didn't you? You thought my friend and I would be known to the people on the "Lucky Me", then you thought it over and decided you were wrong and phoned your friend Smith.' More silence. More stink.

'That's another thing we've got to talk about,' said Dave. 'The geezer you had sent round to our hotel. . . . He isn't very well.'

'What – ' Cardena said. 'What – ?' He couldn't finish it.

'He played silly buggers with a gun and it went off. Now suppose that happened to you?'

'It will if I talk any more.'

'And likewise if you don't.'

I hated all three of us: the two clean-cut sadists and the friendly neighbourhood pusher. Besides, Dave was on the wrong tack.

'Is Heidi Pickel on the yacht?' I said. Dave counted aloud to ten then hit him, but his heart wasn't in it.

'I tell you what,' I said to him, 'you're scared because of someone on the "Lucky Me". Right?' He nodded. 'But it's away at sea till tomorrow. By the time it docks you could be miles away.' He began to look a little less terrified. 'If we let you go.' Back came the fear. He even gave me the kind of look they call reproachful. That was because I'd conned him into thinking I was the nice guy. Finding out I wasn't hurt his feelings, but it also bewildered him, which was what I was after.

'Answer us and we'll let you go,' I said. 'Now – is Heidi Pickel on the yacht?'

'Yes,' he said.

'What's her relationship with this Smith geezer – are they lovers?'

'Of course not,' Cardena said. 'He wouldn't ever – ' That silence again.

'Who wouldn't?' said Dave. *Who?*'

'Smith,' Cardena said at last. 'She wasn't his type.'

He was lying, but I pressed on before Dave could interrupt.

'Why did they meet, then?'

'I always thought it was business.'

'You reckon he had money?'

'He must have. Mario's isn't cheap.'

'What about Heidi Pickel?'

'Loaded,' said Cardena, and I believed him. Whatever his shortcomings as a human being, Cardena was a good maître. He would react to money the way a hound reacts to aniseed.

'Was Miss Pickel on her own?' He nodded. 'All the time?'

'Yes,' he said. Another lie, but one that didn't bother me.

'If we let you go,' I said, 'will you stay in New South Wales?'

'My oath no,' he said. 'I won't even stay in Australia. It isn't big enough.'

He watched as I went back to the Holden, switched off its lights. The real dawn was coming up in those tender pastel colours that never last, and already the heat was beginning. I came back and gave Dave his magnum, and he took off his coat, let Cardena gawp at the webbing holster, then put up the gun. In the quiet the kookaburra had another fit of hysterics, then packed it in. The outback silence was now absolute, until Dave suddenly clawed the gun from its holster and put a bullet between Cardena's feet. Cardena screamed.

Dave said, 'Be missing by tomorrow, old son, because next time I see you I'll shoot higher up.'

153

He got in the car, and I tossed Cardena's wallet, lighter and cigarettes into the bush. When he went after them I got in beside Dave and he switched on the motor. Cardena grabbed up his stuff and raced to catch up with us, running beside Dave.

'Wait,' he yelled. 'Wait. What about me?'

'Who needs you?' said Dave, and stood on the accelerator.

*

On the way back to Sydney, I leaned back and closed my eyes. Dave thought I was dozing, but I wasn't. I was thinking – about him, among other things. Like I say, Dave's nice. Good mate, birds' delight, *and* a scholar. Never reads a paper when he can get his hands on a book. That's Dave. Good-looking but not too much, drinks only beer and wine. He smokes, that's true, which is the one thing I can't stand, but he doesn't overdo it. He daren't. On account of having to be fit.

I say 'having to be' because of his obsession with judo and kung-fu and all that. On the dojo mat three times a week, and the other days work-outs and jogging and weight training. Not to mention his visits to the pistol club to keep his eye in. It's all target pistols at the club of course, but what he uses when he's minding me is always a Colt Python .357 magnum when he can get it, on account of that's the gun he took off an IRA Provo in Ulster when he was in the Paras. Took it off him after he'd killed him. He has that streak in him, and he told me once it was just as well I hired him as a minder from time to time, otherwise he might have started robbing banks. A real Jekyll and Hyde is Dave. Of course it's Dr. Jekyll who's my mate, but it's Mr. Hyde I want with me when I'm working. Every time. I began to think of other things, till Dave gave me a nudge and woke me.

'We'll soon be home,' he said. I tried to get back to being a thinker.

'Erny Fluck knows we're there,' I said. 'Also I shot somebody. – Could be tricky going back.'

'There wasn't any blood in the corridor,' said Dave. 'I looked.'

154

'And if Erny wants to give us to the cops – he can tell them about our car. I'd like to risk going back.'

'Suits me,' said Dave. 'I'm knackered.'

But when we did get back the receptionist asked us if we wouldn't mind waiting to have a word with the manager, and I kept worrying about the magnum under Dave's arm. It still had five bullets in it. The manager when he came was looking grave indeed. There had been a complaint he said. About noise. A very serious complaint. There was a notice in every room asking guests to turn down the volume after midnight. The volume? we asked. Of the television,' he said. We promised that never again would we play the television loud, but he still looked stern.

*

When we got back to our room we were whacked, but even so Dave looked around for the bullet I'd put through our visitor. It couldn't possibly have stayed in his arm, he reckoned, not with the velocity it had. And he was right. It had gone on into one of a set of books on a shelf: one of Dave's: 'The Idiot' by Dostoyevsky. It was a paper-back, a thick one, and the bullet had gone right through it. Dave gouged it out and gave it to me as a souvenir. It had messed up his reading, but he didn't bear a grudge. . . . We went to bed for a kip. Dave still didn't put the magnum under his pillow, but he didn't shut it up in a case, either.

But nobody shot at us: nobody so much as phoned. We got sandwiches from room service and sat on the balcony and tried to figure out what to do. Dave reckoned that if Fluck wasn't coming to us, we should go to Fluck, and I agreed with him, but first off I wanted a look at the 'Lucky Me'. It bothered me. So we found a sports shop and bought Dave a pair of binoculars, and I took my camera with the telefoto lens, and we drove to the marina at Rushcutters' Bay. Of course it was private, but you can't fence off the Pacific Ocean, and anyway there was a sort of promenade beside the marina that was stacked with people, and about half of them had cameras and a quarter had binos. We blended nicely.

155

The 'Lucky Me' was in, but only just by the look of her. Some geezer was still busy tying her up as we strolled past. We kept on going till we reached a kind of guard-rail, then we leaned on it and Dave started bird-watching and I pretended to take a few pictures. The sailor on the 'Lucky Me' finished his tying up job and rigged an awning on deck and disappeared, then after a bit two other people came up from below and lay down under the awning. They were Theodore and Heidi Pickel. He wore a pair of faded blue shorts and nothing more. His body was thick-waisted, but hard all over, but for once his face looked gentle. He was talking to his sister.

She wore a pair of long, lightweight trousers and a top. Her face was tanned, like her brother's, but there was no health in it. She looked miserable, and her brother's gentleness was wasted on her. I took their pictures. . . . Time dragged a bit, and Dave wanted to move on, but I'd said we'd stay and just as well I did. The Pickels had visitors – two fellers. One of them was Erny Fluck without doubt, but an Erny transformed. Lacoste sports shirt, natty shorts, Adidas trainers. The feller with him was six foot, big shoulders, cautious eyes, and a long-sleeved shirt.

'He looks a hard one,' said Dave.

'You should know,' I said.

You don't have to draw pictures for Dave.

'You mean he's the one who duffed me last night?' he said. I had to grab his arm to hold him back. He took another look through the binos.

'You sure?' he said.

But stocking mask or not, I was sure. 'Look at his arm,' I said. 'See how stiff it is.'

We stayed on watching, then Pickel said something to his sister and she went below. After that it was strictly business.

'Wish I could lip-read,' I said, but there were no prizes for guessing. The agenda was Dave and me, and what Bruno Cardena was up to.

'What now?' said Dave.

'We wait,' I said. But it wasn't for long. Suddenly Erny got up and got ready to go. He looked neither happy nor sad: just a working man who'd been told what his next job was.

Dave and me put away our gear and picked up the Holden,

156

then waited by the Marina car-park till Erny came out in a brand new gold coloured XJS Jaguar. Doing all right, was Erny. Dave was driving the Holden, which was just as well. It was a very tricky job. To begin with the Sydney traffic was even heavier than usual, on account of the bus strike. Dave settled for two cars back, and we followed Erny into the city and out again, and then we lost him.

It wasn't Dave's fault. It was the stupid berk who suddenly felt the urge to cross the road without looking first. Dave slapped on all the anchors and missed him by a whisker, but by the time he'd stopped swearing, we'd lost the Jaguar.

'I'm sorry, Ron,' said Dave. I took out Cardena's address book.

'Not to worry,' I said. '234, Reynolds Street. Flat 3.'

We took the Sydney street-map from the door-pouch, squinted a bit, and set off again.

14

Reynolds Street was nice. Inland, for a change, the top of a sizeable hill; all big, expensive houses with a lot of space between them, and the spaces all filled with grass and trees and shrubs, and the shrubs all in flower. Very nice. . . . We drove round a curve that took us past number 234. Outside it were parked a Cadillac, a BMW and the Jaguar.

'No Roller,' I said.

'No class,' said Dave, but he was wrong there. It was a very handsome house.

We parked farther down the street, and enjoyed its peace. No city noises here, only the distant hum of a lawn-mower some minion was paid to push. Then suddenly there came again the sound of a kookaburra's crazy laughter: our factory hooter. Time to get back to work.

Dave checked the harness of his magnum, and I took the Browning from my pocket, stuck it into my trousers' waistband. Not that I was worried: it still wasn't loaded. Then we took another look at the house. Same as the one we'd parked beside, by the look of it: a mansion block designed as flats, with a front door that would stand up to dynamite.

'I don't think this is a Swiss knife job,' said Dave

'No way,' I said. 'We'll try to bluff our way into one of the other flats.'

'I think I've got a better idea,' said Dave, 'if your knife can open up the Jag.'

Of course the Swiss knife did that no trouble at all, once we were sure we didn't have an audience, then Dave reached inside, opened up the bonnet and got busy for a minute. Suddenly the Jag's horn started to blast, and went on blasting, and he shut up the bonnet, and ducked for cover behind a magnolia. The Jag's horn went on and on and on.

'Now what?' I said.

'We take what the Good Lord sends,' said Dave.

What He sent was Erny's minder, (who turned out to be the one who'd been lifted from Wandsworth prison back home) and Erny Fluck, running out at the gallop to see who was molesting their Jaguar, then cursing it because it wouldn't stop roaring. Dave and me slipped into the house and took the stairs to flat 3, and on the way up Dave produced his magnum and I had the Swiss knife ready for the front door, but we didn't need it. The men of the house had left it ajar, and in we went.

It wasn't Concannon House or even Leinster Terrace, but it was a whole lot better than 43, Garibaldi Avenue, Wembley. The kind of modern that means comfort, and the kind of comfort that means money. And in the midst of it all, at the window, a short rather tubby lady, wearing a gown she really ought not have given in to.

'Miss Jenny Cooper?' I said, and she turned to face us, spinning like a top. I was the one who'd spoken, but it was Dave she looked at, or rather his Colt Python .357 magnum.

Like I say, a tubby little lady, Jennifer Cooper, but not a stupid one, by no means. Dark, shrewd eyes, chin small but determined, nose as beaked and combative as a falcon's bill.

'Who said you can come walking in here?' she said.

She was listening hard, but the Jaguar still bellowed.

'This does,' said Dave, and waved the magnum. 'Keep her covered, Ron.'

I took out the Browning automatic and pointed it at her. Now she had two guns to worry about, and if mine was useless she wasn't to know. The Jaguar suddenly became silent.

Dave moved behind the flat's front door and said, 'Now it's entirely up to you. If you want to die just make a noise. Any noise. Stay silent and you'll live a bit longer.'

She looked into the magnum's barrel as if it were the mouth of the Mersey tunnel. 'I don't want to die,' she said. The clever ones never do.

So we waited while Erny and his merry man used the lift because it seemed Erny wasn't into exercise – and anyway we'd left it for them. Then in they came, Erny leading, making noises about the way cars were shovelled together nowadays, at what I hoped was the top of his voice, which somehow managed to be whining and aggressive at the same time. I'd moved back out of his line of sight so he couldn't see me, but two strides into the room and he knew there was trouble, and so did his minder. The trouble was, two strides was too far. Even so, the minder was pretty good. He'd already started to turn when Dave hit him, and down he went. Erny swivelled round and looked at Dave and was appalled, but he had more sense than to start anything.

I said, 'Mr. Fluck – you've no idea how glad I am to see you.'

'You don't act like it,' said Fluck. 'Who are you anyway?'

He still looked appalled, but at least he was making the right noises. Nothing the general or Imogen had said had suggested he had guts.

'My name's Hogget,' I said. 'Ron Hogget. I'm a private detective – and this is my associate, Mr. Baxter.'

'Couple of tearaways,' said Erny. 'You bust in here and assault poor Joe – '

Jenny Cooper found her voice. 'Erny,' she said. 'Sweetheart,' cooing a warning for all she was worth. But Erny was off on a righteous indignation trip. He wouldn't listen.

'If it's robbery you're after I'm telling you now there's nothing here,' he said, 'and if you don't leave at once I'll see you both put in gaol.'

'Poor Joe knows a lot about gaols,' I said. 'He's just been lifted out of one.'

The righteous indignation died: wariness took its place.

'There *was* a misunderstanding,' Erny said. 'More like a miscarriage of justice really. We couldn't let poor Joe – '

'Erny!' Jenny Cooper screamed again, and this time it got to him. He shut up.

'Nice try,' I said to her, 'but you're too late.' I turned to Dave. 'Tell them.'

'There wasn't any miscarriage of justice,' Dave said. 'Joe here had a mate, and the two of them assaulted Mr. Hogget.'

'How do you know?' Jenny Cooper said.

'Because I assaulted them,' said Dave.

Erny made a spluttering noise.

'You put Alec in intensive care?' he said.

'That's right,' said Dave. 'Just like Alec did with Mr. Hogget's fiancée.'

I was watching Jenny Cooper. The fact that Sabena was my fiancée, (even though she wasn't: not yet anyway –) meant big trouble and she knew it.

'You could have killed him,' she said.

'But he didn't,' I told her. 'It was you who did that, Miss Cooper.'

Reluctantly, Joe decided that it was time to return to the real world, and groaned aloud. Immediately Dave squatted by him, put up the magnum and went through his pockets. No gun. Just a cosh and a flick knife, and a wad of Australian banknotes so thick it was almost an offensive weapon in itself. Dave moved them out of harm's way, then began to slap Joe's face left and right, over and over. Joe groaned again, and his eyes opened at last, he found he was looking at Dave.

'Jesus,' he said.

'We can't go on meeting like this,' said Dave. 'Up on your feet.'

He got on to his own, and produced the magnum. Somehow Joe scrambled to his feet.

'Don't say anything,' Jenny Cooper said. 'Leave the talking to us.'

I said, 'We've been having a bit of a chat about you, Joe. You and your mate, Alec. Did you know Alec was dead?'

Joe looked at Jenny Cooper.

'He knows,' she said.

'And does he know who killed him?'

Again the look. 'Of course he doesn't,' she said.

I said to Joe, 'Why don't you go and sit on her knee? Like all the other dummies?'

He flushed at that. Probably he was a male chauvinist, most heavies are. But he still kept his mouth shut.

'Alec a mate of yours?' I asked him, and again Jenny Cooper opened her mouth, But I yelled at her 'Belt up!' and swung the gun on her, and she said nothing.

Dave said, 'It's your turn, my son. Let's be hearing from you.' Joe mumbled something. 'Louder,' said Dave.

'He wasn't a mate,' Joe said. 'We just hired out for a job.'

'Duffing me,' I said, and Joe said nothing, because what was there for him to say?

'And duffing Miss Sabena Redditch,' said Dave, 'who is Mr. Hogget's fiancée.'

That got to him almost as fast as it had to his ventriloquist, and like her he knew it was bad news.

'We were after this gentleman,' Joe said, nodding at me. – One of the few times in my life I'd been called a gentleman and it was by a heavy who tried to cripple me. – 'We thought he was still with her. We didn't mean to hurt her, – honest – only she put up a fight and Alec belted her.'

'Maybe that's true and maybe it isn't, but it won't worry Alec,' I said. 'He's gone to his reward.'

Joe looked baffled.

'Dead,' said Dave. Enlightenment didn't make Joe any happier. 'And you know who killed him, don't you?' I said. 'It was your spokesperson here. Miss Cooper.'

Erny spoke up then.

'She isn't Miss Cooper,' he said. 'She's Mrs. Fluck.' He even sounded happy about it.

*

I'd drawn what I believe is called a bow at a venture, but it twanged all right. Maybe it was because I'd sounded so certain about it, and I *was* certain, because who else could it have been? But whatever the reason they believed I could prove it, and you could almost see the two quick minds working away: extradition, intent to murder, aiding and abetting, the whole shmeer, while Joe just stood around and waited to be told what was going to happen to him.

Then Erny took a look at his Jenny, and it was the sort of look that's a dead giveaway, no matter how clever you are. No doubt about it, Erny Fluck adored his missus, and I wondered what Imogen would make of that.

Erny said, 'It needn't come to that surely?'

'Why needn't it?' I said.

'There's enough for everybody,' Erny Fluck said.

'And who's everybody?'

162

'You and Mrs. Fluck and me. A piece for your friend. A little piece for Joe here.'

'And a big fat slice for Theo,' Jenny Fluck said.

'Theo?'

She shrugged. 'Herr Theodore Pickel, if you want to be formal.'

'What about Mrs. Courtenay-Lithgoe?' I said.

'Oh *her*,' said Jenny.

'Who needs her?' said her loving Erny. 'Silly bitch.'

I risked a look at Dave: if ever there was a man who looked as if he couldn't believe what he was hearing. . . .

'Mind you, she had her uses,' said Erny, in the voice of one determined to be fair. 'She helped us to get started on – '

'Just a minute, Erny,' his wife said. 'No need to give anything more for nothing.' She turned to me. 'Just how much *do* you know, Mr. Hogget?'

It was Dave who answered her.

'You asked the wrong question, Mrs. Fluck. The only question you should ask is "What do you want to know?" Only ask politely.'

She snorted. 'Just because you've got a gun.'

'Just because I'll use a gun,' said Dave. 'Not that I need one. Ask Joe here.'

'Jesus,' said Joe, sounding like a born-again Christian.

'Mind you maybe I will,' said Dave to Mrs. Fluck. 'I put one in Erny here, say in the shoulder. That wouldn't kill him but it would hurt a bit. But let's say you're tough. Just because Erny's hurting a bit doesn't mean *you'll* talk. O.K. So I put one in his elbow. Now that would *really* hurt. Probably be permanent damage an' all. But you're brave, you can take it, even if Erny can't. So what are we left with? Only your love-life, Mrs. Fluck, because Erny here won't have any, not when I've finished with him.' He swung the gun on Erny, who was the kind of bilious green colour they used to paint my junior school 'Any time you're ready, Mrs. Fluck,' he said.

He can't mean it, I thought, not my mate Dave. And then: Can he? Mrs. Fluck was in no doubt.

'Ask your questions,' she said to me. 'Please.'

'You knew about Dave and me,' I said. 'How?'

'We had an idea there'd be somebody,' she said, 'on

163

account of that stupid horse of hers. Whoever stole it didn't know her. She'd kill to get it back. So Erny asked his computer.' She made it sound like asking his Aunty Mabel, and maybe it was to Erny. 'It told him you'd be the most likely, on account of your reputation for finding things.'

'So you had me followed and set Joe and Alec on me.'

'We didn't think they'd turn out to be *quite* so useless,' said Jenny.

' 'ere,' said Joe.

Dave reached out and thumped him, left-handed, just hard enough to hurt.

'We stay silent,' he said. 'We know our place.' Then to Joe: 'What do we stay?'

'Silent,' said Joe.

'And what do we know?'

'Our place,' said Joe.

'Good lad,' said Dave, then to me: 'Sorry about that, Ron. It won't happen again.'

I know it must sound like infantile cruelty: a nasty little boy pulling the wings off flies, but it was meant for Mrs. Fluck much more than for Joe, and it was having its effect. She gabbled into speech at once.

'We under-rated you,' she said. 'We never thought you'd make Spain, never mind Australia.'

A hundred peseta piece, I thought. A brochure and a Moorish castle, an Irish butler with a heart of gold and a passion for ten pound notes. Add it all up and it made me a genius.

'What we're after,' she said, 'is – '

'Low conductors.' I interrupted her. If I was supposed to be so ruddy clever it was up to me to show it.

'Do you know what they are?'

I hadn't the faintest, but my Cambridge scientist friend had.

'It's a system for storing electricity at very low temperatures so you can keep it for when it's needed,' I said, 'or it would be if anybody could make it work. Only it takes more energy to produce the sub-zero temperatures you need for storage than the amount you can store.' At least that was what the Cambridge wonder had told me.

'Quite right,' she said, 'or it used to be till Erny found a way round it.'

'I didn't know your husband was an expert on low conductors.'

'He's not,' she said. 'My husband is a thief – perhaps the most cunning thief who's ever lived. Or perhaps he's more of an electronic Fagin. He can teach a computer to steal from other computers.'

This time it was she who gave him the adoring look, but he sent it right back to her.

'The information's all there,' he said. 'Only it's scattered about all over the place. – Massachussetts, California, Dresden, Cambridge, Hamburg, Kiev, Toulouse.'

East and West, they all came alike to Erny.

'You're forgetting Nagasaki,' said Mrs. F.

'So I am, dear,' he said.

Even with a gun on them they sounded like a Darby and Joan club.

'Get on with it,' said Dave.

'Before the computer nobody could ever have stolen the stuff,' said Erny, 'but before the computer nobody could have made the calculations anyway.'

'Never mind the philosophical paradoxes. Get on,' said Dave.

The two looked at him, then away: aware now that Dave was not just a sadist but an educated one.

'We needed finance,' Jenny said. 'I'd made a bit here, but not nearly enough. Then Erny got to hear about that Imogen.'

'How?' I said, getting it in quick, – not wishing to start Dave off again.

'Her father,' Jenny said.

'Sir Robert Berkeley,' said Erny. 'The bookies' friend.'

Coming from him that was bitter, but I let it pass.

'He was interested in a computer betting system Erny was working on,' Jenny said. 'Erny needed capital and advertised in "The Sporting Times" and Sir Robert replied by return.' This I already knew about. I'd had a cable from Horry.

'Only he didn't have any money,' Erny said. 'He *never* has any money. Imogen sees to that. All the same we met up – Ascot it was. He gave me a nice little tickle – Shropshire Lad –

165

40 to 1 – I had a quid on him. Each way. . . . And we got to talking. . . . About computers and low conductors and that.'

'And the next thing we know,' Jenny said, 'is that Imogen bumps into him. Quite literally. . . . Just fancy that. You could have knocked me down with a Rolls Royce.'

'You got what you wanted,' I said.

'We thought we did,' said Erny. 'Bit tight with her money is our Imogen. *Very* tight.'

'So?'

'So she wanted to know how much she could make and I told her.'

'How much?'

'Thick end of a billion,' he said. 'Six hundred million easy.'

I looked at him awe-struck. He said it like he meant it.

'Only it meant capital outlay to start with,' said Jenny. 'Say three hundred and fifty thousand.'

I thought of factories and machinery and equipment. 'As little as that?' I said.

'Oh we aren't going to make the stuff,' said Jenny. 'Just develop it, then sell the idea to Exxon or Shell or maybe even BP.'

'Sell electricity to an oil company?' I said.

'Well of course,' said Jenny. 'Oil's a tough enough game as it is, without getting that kind of competition.'

'Electicity's more efficient than oil,' Erny said. 'It's far less dangerous than atomic power, and it's clean – ' I held up my hand.

'Save it,' I said. 'I can't afford it anyway. . . . So you tried to put the bite on Imogen for three hundred and fifty grand?'

'She wanted to spread the load a bit,' said Erny. 'She didn't fancy the risk on her own.'

'Theodore?'

He nodded. 'It seemed they knew each other quite well – and he's even richer than she is. She cut him in for half. Then she had another idea.' He looked at Jenny.

'I'm listening,' I said.

'Marriage,' said Erny. 'Her and me. I didn't fancy that.' He looked at Jenny again.

'I can quite see why,' I said, but I didn't dare look at Dave.

'Yes. . . . Well. Then Theodore saw me on the quiet and

said why did we need Imogen, and I quite saw his point. I mean if he was willing to put up all the development money –'

'Quite so,' I said. 'So you scarpered.'

'You've seen Imogen,' he said. 'Wouldn't you have scarpered?'

'You came here?' He nodded. 'Straight away?'

'Too right,' he said. At least he'd begun to learn the language.

'What about Finn MacCool?' I said, and he looked puzzled.

'What about him?' he said. 'It'll be years before he's ready for the National. He's only been over the hurdles so far. Whoever stole him hadn't done his homework.'

I left it. 'What about Finbar Gleason?' I said.

'The chauffeur who doubles as farrier? I don't like him,' said Erny.

That made two of us, but duty comes first.

'*Didn't* like him,' I said.

'He's dead?'

'Shot,' I said. 'Revolver. Low velocity. Blew a hole in him the size of a saucer.' Jenny gulped, and Erny looked reproachful.

'I came straight here,' he said. 'Jenny and I got married. I know nothing about Gleason. Maybe it was the IRA.'

'Did Pickel know him?'

'Theodore? . . . I suppose he must have. I mean he's stayed with Imogen and I presume Gleason would chauffeur him – just as he did for me. But why would Theodore kill Gleason?'

Information received, I thought, for cash on the nail, and then friend Finbar gets a bit too greedy – and bang!

'Do you know a woman called Teresa O'Byrne?' I said.

The phone rang. In that atmosphere it made a noise like a burglar alarm. Jenny and Erny and I jumped a foot apiece, but Dave didn't bat an eyelid, Joe looked no more bewildered than he'd done before. Professionals. I said to Jenny, 'You take it,' and to Dave, 'Keep your gun on Erny in case she decides to be brave,' then followed her to the phone, which had an extra ear-piece.

'Keep it simple,' I told her. 'Dave means what he says.' Then I picked up the ear-piece and listened.

167

'Yes?' Jenny said.

'This is Heidi,' the phone said. Its voice was young, shrill, near demented, with just a hint of Teutonic accent.

'Yes, Heidi?'

'Bruno Cardena is missing,' Heidi said.

'Missing?'

'I've phoned his number twenty times. There's no answer.'

'He must have gone out,' said Jenny.

'Not at this time,' Heidi said. 'He knows I always phone at this time. I've run out.'

'Is it bad?' Jenny said.

'Not yet,' said Heidi. 'Soon it will be terrible. Is Erny there?'

Jenny looked at me and I nodded.

'He's here,' she said.

'He's keeping some stuff for me,' Heidi said. 'I'm coming for it now.'

'I don't know,' Jenny said.

'I must,' the phone screamed.

I covered the mouthpiece.

'Tell her it's O.K.' I said, and let go.

'Oh very well,' said Jenny. 'But just this once. Does Theo know?'

'Of course not,' Heidi said. 'If he knew he would kill us all. I'll be with you in twenty minutes.'

Jenny hung up, and turned on Erny, snarling.

'And just what do you think you're doing,' she said, 'hiding smack for that silly little bitch?' Then she turned on me. 'She means it, you know. Theo *would* kill us.'

'Belt up,' I said. 'I'm trying to think.' Sometimes it takes a lot of doing, because next it was Joe's turn.

'When you say Theo,' he said, 'do you mean Mr. Pickel?'

'Who else?' said Jenny.

'I want to be tied up,' said Joe, then added: 'and locked away. It isn't a lot to ask, now is it, sir?'

I was fascinated. 'Why do you want to be tied up and locked away?' I said.

'Because that way Mr. Pickel will know I didn't have anything to do with it.'

'Anything to do with what?'

'Anything to do with *any*thing,' said Joe.

'You mean you're scared of him?'

'Terrified,' he said.

And that from a heavy whose only stock-in-trade was guts.

I took him away and found some plastic clothes-line, tied him up tight and locked him in a cupboard, and when I'd finished he said 'Thank you', and meant it. Back in the living-room the party looked a bit dull, so I ordered a round of drinks that came out as a lager for Dave, Scotch and water for Erny, and two gin and tonics, for me and Mrs. F. We were on maybe our second sip when the doorbell rang, but we all knew what to do. Dave put the magnum on Erny, Erny turned green again, Mrs. Fluck went to the door and let Heidi in, and I waited.

15

She was bone thin, thin like somebody with anorexia nervosa, but then they always are. Food doesn't interest them, their body fat burns away just to keep them going. Naked she'd have looked like a Belsen victim: even with the trousers and shirt, – sleeves buttoned at the wrist, – you could tell she was all skin and bone. Nothing else. And yet the remains of her prettiness still lingered: the memory of the Heidi who'd been on holiday with Sabena was still there, like a face reflected in a clouded mirror.

Jenny shut the door behind them and pushed Heidi gently into the room. 'Hallo Heidi,' Erny said, and Dave said 'Hallo there', and I said 'Hi'. But her eyes, that looked huge in her tiny, shrunken face, could look only at the gun Dave held. She was in a bad enough way, but she still knew what a gun was.

'What – ' she said, then stuck.

I made my voice as soothing and gentle as I could.

'It's all right,' I said. 'Nothing serious. Dave was just showing his gun to Erny here.' I looked at Dave.

'That's right,' he said. 'Erny was very interested. Weren't you, Erny?'

'Very,' said Erny. 'Oh very.'

'I'll just put it away,' said Dave, and the gun disappeared beneath his jacket. 'After all I can always get it out again if Erny wants another look. . . . Or anybody else come to that.'

'See,' I said to Heidi. 'All friends together. Oh by the way – I'm Ron Hogget and this is my mate Dave Baxter. Would you like a drink?'

'Of course not,' she said. 'I want a fix. I told Jenny.' Then all in the same breath: 'Ron Hogget. My brother said something about you.'

Erny and Jenny tried not to look interested, but I didn't bother.

'What did he say?'

'I forget,' said Heidi, 'but I know he doesn't like you.'

This was bad news for the Flucks. After all they were trying to put a deal together with me and Heidi's brother.

'I want my fix now,' said Heidi. She was polite, but quite firm. The small talk was over. Now it was time for the nitty-gritty.

And indeed she did want her fix. Her eyes were wandering all over the place, her fingers and hands were restless, and her nose ran like a tap. 'I want my fix,' she said again. This time her voice held an edge of shrillness.

I turned to Erny. 'Get it,' I said, and even Dave looked reproving, but there was no other way to keep her quiet except to belt her, and he wouldn't want to do that either. And even if he did, even a slap might kill her, the state she was in. Erny took another look at me and saw I meant it, then went to the IBM computer that dominated the room. Beside it was a plastic box that contained a great pile of computer software. Erny flipped deftly through it and came out with a little transparent plastic envelope.

'Oh very ingenious,' said Mrs. F. But Heidi was looking at it like a pilgrim looking at a piece of the True Cross. She grabbed it before Erny could change his mind.

I tried to keep my voice gentle, soothing.

'I'm sorry, love,' I said, 'But I'll have to ask you to use it here.'

She shrugged. 'Why not?' she said. 'You have yourselves another drink.' You go to your church, her voice was saying.
. . .

Then she opened her bag and took out a syringe. At least she had an unopened pack of sterilised needles. . . . All four of us, the electronic Fagin, the tubby lady conperson, the two private detectives who killed people from time to time, all four of us looked away as she rolled up her left shirtsleeve, as if it were the prelude to an obscenity. Then came the small, sly sounds: the tearing of the plastic envelope, the mixing of water from the bar, the screwing together of the hypo. And then the sigh as the needle went in, the clatter of the hypo when she put it down. When at last I looked at her she was buttoning her shirt, and already her hands were competent, she no longer sniffed, her eyes blazed with that false awareness that heroin gives.

Erny suggested another drink, and I told him to get on with it. It wasn't a social ritual, it was a need. So Erny poured and Heidi smiled her 'I told you so' smile, that said as plain as daylight we were all sinners together.

'Well now,' she said, 'now we're all comfortable – what shall we talk about?' She turned to me. 'Weren't you asking about my brother?'

'Weren't you saying he didn't like me?' I said.

'He doesn't like a lot of people. That's because he suspects they're after his money. Usually he's right.'

'He likes you,' I said.

'Well of course,' she said. 'I'm his sister.'

'And Erny,'I said. 'He likes Erny.'

'Because Erny's going to *make* him money, not take it away,' she said.

'He wouldn't like Erny if he knew he kept the white stuff here for you,' I said, and Erny got indignant and started to stand up. Dave rammed him back into his chair.

'Oh dear,' Heidi Pickel said, 'life can be so *awfully* compli-cated', then she closed her eyes and went to sleep. So help me God she went to sleep.

Erny Fluck said, 'Now what?'

His wife said, 'What do you mean, now what? We go on with our negotiations. Nothing's altered.'

I said, 'Everything's altered', and this time I had their attention. Oh boy, did I.

At last Erny said, 'I'm not quite with you, old man.'

'Of course you are,' I said. 'You're ahead of me.'

'All the same,' said Mrs. F. 'If you wouldn't mind spelling it out – '

'We didn't have a very good hand,' I said. 'Couple of high cards. No more. Pickel had all the court cards. But not now. Now we've got ourselves a queen.' I looked to where Heidi was snoring softly. 'Maybe an ace.'

'Oh no,' said Jenny.

'Dear God, no,' said her spouse.

'Show some sense,' I said. 'Do you think you can keep it a secret that you hid heroin for his sister?'

'Who would tell him?' said Erny.

'She would,' I said. 'For one.'

'For a clever man,' Jenny Fluck said to her spouse, 'you're an idiot. Why on earth did you do it?'

'I thought it would give us a hold on her,' Erny said, and from that moment I wrote him off: a) because of the implications of what he'd said, and b) because he couldn't even do it right. Dave stirred softly in his chair, and I knew he was with me.

'Let's get back to the beginning,' I said.

'You mean our offer,' said Mrs. F.

'I mean my client's offer,' I said. 'Mrs. Courtenay-Lithgoe's offer. The one she made your husband.'

'Made is right,' said Erny

'You mean she didn't pay?'

'Expenses certainly. Nothing out of the way.' I thought of bills for clothes, the food and drink, the gambling debts. It would have been out of the way if I'd been paying.

'Nothing else?' I said, and Dave produced the Colt Python again.

'Twenty thousand,' Erny said. 'Enough to get us started and that's all. Then not another penny till she'd had a word with Theodore.'

'And so?'

'So *I* had a word with Theodore. As I said, it seemed that we didn't need Imogen. And so – I departed.'

'To Australia?'

'As you see.'

'Why Australia, Erny?'

'Because Jenny's here. I joined her so that we could marry.'

'The word in England is that you'd split.'

Jenny smiled. 'We worked very hard to create that illusion,' she said.

But not quite hard enough. Erny always took you back and never worried when you left. . . .

'And that's the only reason you came to Australia?' I asked.

Erny said, 'What other reason could there be?'

'A reason Theodore Pickel gave you,' I said, and looked to

173

where Heidi was snoring in a refined sort of way. 'To keep an eye on his sister and see she didn't get into trouble.'

'That's ridiculous,' said Erny. 'Theodore knows she's on drugs.'

'I bet he knows who her pusher is too,' I said. 'Bruno Cardena – who has strict orders to keep her in limits. Only Bruno's out of the game now.'

'You're sure?' Erny said.

'Certain.'

'But how can you be?'

'Show some sense,' said his wife. 'Mr. Hogget and his friend put him out.' She turned to face me. 'What a clever bastard you are to be sure.'

'All part of the service,' I said.

'Maybe,' said Mrs. Fluck, 'but what's it got to do with that stupid cow, Imogen?' A realist was Mrs. Fluck.

'The point is,' I said, 'that I was hired to find Mrs. Courtenay-Lithgoe's fiancé, and now I've found him.'

'Were you supposed to return him as well?'

'It wasn't in the contract,' I said. 'And anyway what would be the point? He may be her fiancé – but he's your husband.'

'So what do you do? Just ring up and say you've found him?'

'It's what I'm supposed to do,' I said.

It was a treat to watch her think. Her first thought was 'Oh what the hell? What difference does it make?' But her second thought was of course there's a difference. Imogen scorned will go beserk. Then came the third thought. This bloody little creep (i.e. me, Ron Hogget) knows far too much anyway, and how do we fit that piece into the puzzle? She decided not to try.

'We've made you a good offer,' she said. 'Why don't we stay with that?'

'Oh yes,' I said. 'The deal with Exxon or Shell, or maybe even B.P. Six hundred million wasn't it? And what do we get? Two per cent for me, say, and one per cent for Dave? One point two million and six hundred thousand re – what's the word?'

'Respectively,' said Dave.

'I know it sounds a lot,' said Erny.

'It is a lot,' said Dave.

'Not when you consider the wonderful property we're selling,' said Erny, as full of boyish enthusiasm as a vacuum cleaner salesman.

'How much up front?' I said.

'That's really up to – ' Erny's voice faltered.

'Up to Theodore Pickel,' I said. 'It's your problem. Why don't you ask your computer to solve it for you?'

'Don't think it couldn't,' said Erny.

Dave said, 'You mean it fires a gun as well?'

Jenny said, 'Let's be rational about this.' I waved my hand, inviting her to be rational.

'We know we've got a winner,' she said.

'How do we know?' said Dave.

'Because Mrs. Courtenay-Lithgoe and Mr. Pickel have checked us out.' She had a point. 'Now because we can get a better deal and also because of personal reasons – ' she fluttered her eyelashes at Erny – 'we decided we'd go with Mr. Pickel.' She looked at Heidi. 'On the other hand because of certain complications we may not be able to remain with Mr. Pickel. That means we'll have to go back to Mrs. Courtenay-Lithgoe.' Erny began to rumble, but she cut in strongly. 'We have to, Erny. It's too late to find another source of money. – Well Mr. Hogget?'

'I was just wondering,' I said, 'if you'd heard about the Irishwoman in Andalucia.'

Mrs. Fluck snorted. 'I was being serious,' she said.

The telephone rang.

'Same drill as before,' I said, and Dave's gun appeared as Heidi continued to snore and Mrs. F. picked up the phone and I used the extension ear-piece.

'Let me speak to my sister,' said Thedore Pickel. Mrs. Fluck looked at me, and for once she seemed flustered.

'Don't bother to lie,' Pickel said. 'She's with you all right. She took her car. You're the only ones she knows who live a car-ride away. You've been giving her that filth.'

I put my fingers to my lips, but Pickel didn't want any silence.

'Answer me, woman,' he said, and I made miming gestures. Jenny got them right.

175

'Yes, she's here,' she said. 'No we didn't give her any dope. Where would we get dope?'

A good question, but it took a lot of nerve to ask it.

'Let me speak to her,' Pickel said.

'What I did give her was a sleeping tablet,' said Jenny. 'She was very – upset. Now she's fast asleep.'

'Don't touch her,' said Pickel. 'I'll send someone over to collect her.'

'We'll be here.'

'I hope so,' Pickel said. 'We have things to talk about.' Then he hung up. It didn't sound as if they'd be very nice, the things they had to talk about. Jenny Fluck put down the phone and spoke to me.

'We have to get out of here, Erny and I,' she said. 'Any price you want but we have to get out of here.'

'Why the rush?' I said.

'Theodore's mad because of Heidi. When he's mad he – does things. He can be sorry later, but what's the use of that?'

I thought for a moment.

'Please,' she said. 'Just name your price.'

'You can go,' I said. 'It won't cost you a cent. – But you go empty-handed.'

'Meaning what?'

'Meaning just as you are,' I said. 'No suitcases, no briefcases – and no Heidi.'

'Oh God,' she said.

'Take it or leave it.'

But she was already on her way to the door, with Erny running a very good second.

I sent Dave to see them off, then went to cut Joe loose, and told him to scarper. At first he wasn't too keen, but then I told him Dave would be back any minute and he was off like a fox with the Beaufort Hunt behind him. Then I went through the flat and gutted it of every scrap of information I could find: floppy discs, paper, cassettes, and in the middle of it Dave came back and helped me.

'Nice car that Jag,' he said.

'Very nice.' I found a hold-all that would just about hold what we'd collected.

176

'Even had a telephone,' said Dave. I froze. 'It's all right, I broke it for them. You know how clumsy I can be.' A good mate, Dave. Got a weird sense of humour though, sometimes.

He opened a drawer that was mostly Erny's shirts, but underneath them it was all Aussie twenty dollar bills, and underneath *them* six little plastic envelopes full of dream dust. A real caring friend was our Erny. . . . The phone rang again, just as Heidi yawned and stretched and picked it up.

'Hello?' she said. I streaked across and took it from her. Theodore Pickel was talking German.

'We'll do better if we speak English, Mr. Pickel,' I said. There was a tiny pause while he switched languages.

'Mr. Hogget?' he said. 'But I think it was my sister who answered?'

'It was,' I said. 'She's here with us. Quite safe.'

'You had better be telling the truth.'

'Don't start that,' I said. 'We're the ones who've got her.'

I know it sounds brave, but my heart was in my mouth. The thing was I daren't let him take the initiative. He would in time of course: he had the money, and I'd no doubt the men, too: but he mustn't take it yet.

'Who do you mean by "we", Mr. Hogget? Your assistant Baxter, and my friends the Flucks?'

'Just Dave,' I said. 'Your friends the Flucks have left.'

Just saying the words made me want to giggle, but he wasn't in a giggling mood.

'They were foolish to speak with you and not tell me,' he said.

'It wasn't their idea.'

'Ah,' he said. 'And who put you on to them? Cardena?'

'That's right.'

'Where is Cardena?'

'Search me,' I said. 'If he's alive he should be on his way to Singapore or Djakarta or somewhere. But he may not be. Alive I mean.'

'Then at least you may have done one thing I approve of.' But it sounded as if there were an awful lot on the debit side. Suddenly the control snapped.

'Let me talk to my sister.' His voice was a yell.

'No point,' I said. 'You know she's here.' I took a look at

177

her. She was lying back in an untidy sprawl, humming a pop-tune that had been a hit four years before. Whether she knew we were talking about her I had no idea.

'I want her back,' he yelled.

'Of course,' I said.

'So tell me the price.'

'All the notes Fluck gave you on low conductors – paper, discs, cassettes. The lot.' He thought for a moment. 'How can you possibly trust me to give you all?' he said. Coming from him it was a good question.

'Fluck gave me a list', I said, and oh how I wished it was true.

'Very well,' he said. 'I will send someone. He will be with you in an hour. A tall fair man driving a blue Mercedes.'

'We'll be here,' I said, and hung up. I'm not a bad liar when I put my mind to it. 'Time to go,' I said to Dave, who'd been on the spare ear-phone.

'I was hoping it might be,' he said. 'I didn't much fancy waiting around for Mr. Pickel's tall, fair man in a Merc. Not to mention the busload of goons who'll come along to hold our hands.'

'If that's all they hold,' I said, and started ramming stuff into the canvas grip. Dave joined in.

'What about the filthy Aussie lucre?' he said.

'Spoils of war,' I told him. 'Pack it.' So he did, and I pocketed the little plastic envelopes. Dave gave me one of his looks: one of the sad ones.

'Only if we have to,' I said. 'But she won't be any use to us if she gets the screaming ab-dads.'

'Yes, I know,' said Dave. 'I just wish I'd never seen what this stuff can do. Even in the Paras.'

'Only if we have to,' I said again, and Dave chewed on it a bit and said, 'I hope that bastard Cardena hasn't made it.'

And that isn't like Dave. It really isn't. Using language, I mean.

I went over to Heidi: 'How about a nice car-ride?' I said.

'Have you got any more smack?'

'Of course,' I said.

'I'll do anything you like,' said Heidi, and I've never felt sadder.

178

So we loaded up the Holden and cruised around for a bit, taking the Sydney road. It was early afternoon and the sun shone and the roads were empty, but man is born to trouble as the sparks fly upwards. Ahead of us police lights flashed, and on the hard shoulder where it had been towed, was a gold-coloured XJS Jaguar. Beside it, rolled up in bandages like mummies, two bodies waited for an ambulance that would be no use to them at all. A cop waved us on. He didn't have to wave twice.

'What now?' said Dave.

'We change our car,' I said.

'But why?' said Dave. He liked the Holden.

'Because Pickel's not only bloody good he's thorough with it,' I said. So we found a hire-car centre and swopped the Holden for a big Ford Dave said wasn't as good, but it would do, and drove on to a hamburger joint. 'I'm not hungry,' I said.

'How could you be?' said Dave. 'This isn't a banquet, Ron. It's fuel.'

So Dave and I ate burgers and even Heidi managed half a tubful of ice-cream. For her that really was a banquet. I picked up a golf cap that advertised the burger-joint and put it on her head. She at once looked like a sloppy, rather scholarly boy, which was good. What her brother was after was two blokes and a girl.

It was time for the tall, fair man and his Merc.

Dave drove us back to the late Erny's flat and we parked discreetly. In no time at all the Mercedes came along, and the tall, fair geezer, who just happened to have three mates with him. The tall, fair geezer got out, carrying a canvas sports grip like the one Dave used to use for his sawn-off shotgun, and his mates came round him like a wall. We gave them a couple of minutes then got out to follow, and I asked Heidi to wait in the car. She looked bright and alert and cheerful, but I knew she'd wait no matter how she was feeling. I was the one with the smack.

Dave loaded the Browning for me, and we got out and went up the stairs. I had Erny's spare keys but I didn't need them. They'd opened the place up without bothering to be elegant about it, and were going through it like methodical and very

179

quiet monkeys. . . . I waited for Dave's signal because on a caper like this he's the one in charge, and he'd eased through the gap and dotted the nearest one with the magnum's barrel while I was still making my big entrance. The fair geezer who was going through Erny's shirt drawer, the one where the money used to be, came round in a swirl and his hand had a gun in it before he straightened. All picturesque stuff, but Dave shot him anyway, more in sorrow than in anger. While he was doing it I nipped over to the Flucks' bedroom, and showed the seekers there the Browning. It impressed them enough for them to stay still while Dave fetched the plastic clothes line and tied them together, then we went back to the fair geezer. He was nursing his right shoulder, which had a hole in it. Dave stooped and picked up his gun, a Smith and Wesson 38.

'You think you're so clever,' the fair geezer said.

'We make a living,' I told him.

'Fishbait is what you'll make when Mr. Pickel catches up with you.'

I picked up the sportsbag. It was pleasingly full of what I hoped were Erny's records.

'You go back to the car,' Dave said. 'I'd better take care of this joker. He's too vocal.'

'You stupid bastards,' the fair geezer said. 'Can't you get it into your heads? Mr. Pickel wants his sister back.'

He said it as if it were the only thing in the world that mattered. Dave took out the fair geezer's handkerchief and wadded it into a gag.

'He even offered you a fair trade,' said the fair geezer, and I wanted to ask him why that made the day so remarkable, but then Dave shoved the gag in and I couldn't. I went out with the records instead.

16

The bloke in the Ford had gone to a lot of trouble to make himself inconspicuous, himself in the background and shadow, Heidi in the foreground and sunlight, all that, but I recognised him at once, even so, even if he'd worn a stocking mask the last time we met, when he'd belted Dave unconscious while he slept, and given me a pistol whipping. Last time he'd carried a Browning automatic, and now he had another one just like it.

'Gudday,' he said. It's a thing Australians do say, but the Browning was more sincere than the greeting.

'Put the grip on the front passenger seat,' he said, and I did just that. This was a bloke who had walked out on me after I'd shot him. Even Dave would have found him a handful.

'Get in and drive.' he said.

I got in. 'Where to?' I said.

'To take this poor little girl back to her brother,' he said.

'So he can cure her of her habit?' I said.

I was hoping for some kind of reaction from Heidi so that I could play for time. I got rather more.

The other bloke leaned forward to belt me one with the gun – an old gag of ours – and as he did so Heidi opened her handbag and said, 'I need a cigarette.' Despite the pain I felt this surprised me. I'd never seen her smoke. But her hand went into the bag and came out with a Llama 32 revolver and she shot him. The little gun made a sound about as loud as a pencil snapping, but even so she shot him better than I had.

'Well I'll be – ' he said, but we never did know what he would be. He slumped forward in the seat, and I felt for a pulse. There wasn't one.

'He's dead,' I said.

181

'Please don't expect me to weep,' she said. 'I know some of the things he's done for Theodore. It was clever of you to remind me that Theo can stop my drugs.'

I looked at her: she looked relaxed, friendly, and quite mad.

'I don't think you need the gun any more,' I said, but she didn't agree. She pointed it at me.

'The rest of the dope Erny was keeping for me,' she said. 'I want it.' I gave it to her, no arguments.

'What now?' I said.

'I'm leaving,' she said. I looked for the car she'd told us she'd come in; a Honda four-door. It was still there.

'You want me to get it for you?' I asked.

'I'm not leaving in that,' she said. 'I'm taking the Mercedes.'

'Won't that make you a bit conspicuous?'

'Why should it?' she said. 'It's mine. The Honda's just an old tin can of Theo's he lets me use when I'm a good girl. Look, Mr. Hogget – Theo doesn't have all the money in our family. Nearly a half of it is mine. That's why he lets me use the smack – so I'll keep quiet while he spends it for me.'

'But I thought you said – ' She waved her little gun and I was silent. 'Don't interrupt,' she said. 'I've been thinking. It's not something you do a lot of when you're on the stuff. I used to think all the time. Me and my friend Sabena.'

'Sabena Redditch?' I said. 'I – '

'*Don't interrrupt*. I shan't tell you again,' she said. She sounded more like her brother than I'd thought possible. 'I've been thinking about you and your friend. You must be quite the nicest people I've met in ages. And you are both violent and dangerous criminals. And yet you are both infinitely nicer than my brother – or this Neanderthal here. – With every possible respect, Mr. Hogget, I should not be quite so pathetically grateful for your company.

'So I have made a decision. I am going away from here, and in my own time and in my own way I am going to be cured of this habit of mine. Do you believe that?'

'Yes,' I said, and I did. It wasn't just the gun. 'But isn't that what your brother wants, too?'

'My brother wants me cured just enough so that I can appear in public and sign certain documents. Once I have

182

done that I will have no money at all, and then I can go back to my habit again, if my dear, kind brother will give me the price of a fix.' She put away the gun at last, held out her hand. 'Goodbye, Mr. Hogget. It was good of you to listen to me.'

I took it, and she smiled.

'Do you need money?' I said. 'I've got plenty.'

'I know,' she said. 'I saw you steal it.'

'Steal?' I said. 'It isn't as simple as that.'

'Stealing's always simple,' she said. 'And anyway it was probably Theo's money. You've earned it.'

'Thanks,' I said. 'About Sabena Redditch?'

'You know her?'

'Very well,' I said. 'Why don't you call her? She'll help you.'

'I must help myself,' she said. 'But one day when I'm better – *if* I am better, I will call her. Please tell her so. Goodbye.'

Then she squeezed my hand and went over to the Merc, turned the key in the dashboard and was gone.

Dave appeared beside me, making about as much noise as grass does growing. 'Busy busy,' he said.

'She did it,' I said. 'I was too scared.'

'Tell me later,' he said. 'We need the car. Where'll we put him?'

I remembered she'd said the Honda belonged to her brother, so we put the corpse in that, then drove into Sydney and checked out of our hotel and into the Airport Hilton. We ordered drinks, and I ordered a meal that was neither sandwiches nor hamburgers, and after a lot of counting on fingers we decided that it would be about five thirty a.m. in Ireland, and a good time to phone Imogen. But first I asked Dave to go to the desk and get us the first flight home he could manage. Any class, any direction, so long as it was home.

'I don't get to speak to my girl?'

'You can if you want to,' I said. 'You think you're up to it yet?'

He brooded a bit, then lit a cigarette. 'It'll keep,' he said, then left me with the phone.

She was not pleased and said so, loud and clear, but I just kept on saying I'd found her fiancé, and then at last she shut up and listened. The fact that he was dead didn't go too well, but the fact that I'd got his effects eased the pangs.

'How did he die?' she said.

'Car crash,' I told her. 'Him and his wife.' There just wasn't time to go into the Pickel question, nor did I want to. The word wife set her off again, and again I had to remind her of the deceased's collected works to bring back joy.

'When will you be back?' she said.

'First chance we get,' I told her. 'Any word from Spain?'

'Nothing,' she said. 'Why do you ask?'

'Just wondered.'

'Nothing at all,' she said, 'except that Mendez rang to tell me I'm supplying the bulls for a corrida in Malaga on Sunday. Ring me as soon as you get in.' Then she hung up, and I sat and felt relieved that no-one from Spain had asked about me and Dave, and then I began to worry without knowing why. Then I thought I'd phone Sabena, but it was half past five a.m. in London too and she needed her rest, so I switched on the telly and it was the news, and the news was all about a golden XJS Jaguar that was a wreck, and they had pictures to prove it. The police were not prepared to make a statement at this stage, but parts of the car had been sent for tests. . . . Then Dave arrived and so did our meal. Dave wanted to know if Imogen had mentioned him.

'She sends her love,' I said, which was a lie. She hadn't even mentioned his name. Dave said the first two available seats home were first class on British Airways so I took them, and serve the rotten bitch right.

Just before the flight call I rang the marina at Rushcutters' Bay and persuaded somebody to give me the number of the 'Lucky Me', then I called it and asked for Theodore Pickel, who had certain plans for me, and began to outline them.

'Never mind that crap,' I said. 'I've had a chat with your sister, and she's told me all about her and you, so you just lay off her, because if you don't I'll pin Erny and Jenny's murder on you if it's the last thing I do.'

Pickel said, 'Where are you?'

'Don't raise your hopes,' I said. 'I'm at the airport.'

'Very wise, I'm sure,' he said. 'Tell Imogen she'll be hearing from me.'

I hung up, and found my hands were trembling, so I put

them in my pockets. Dave looked at me, approving, admiring even. 'You sound as if you meant that Ron,' he said.

'I hope I did,' I said. Then we said farewell to Sydney, Australia without ever having seen Bondi Beach.

*

I was forty thousand feet up in the air, half-way between Singapore and Bahrein, eating caviar and drinking champagne when it hit me. – Mendez had been wearing riding boots at the castle, when every riding horse listed was out to pasture, Mendez, I was all but certain, was on Pickel's payroll and Pickel said Imogen would be hearing from him. I swigged at the champers and added another one. Imogen's ranch was providing the bulls for Sunday's corrida. We had to get to Malaga in a hurry, I thought, and looked at Dave, who was having a kip, which was just as well. He'd be getting plenty of exercise later if I was right.

At Bahrein I went to the BA desk and told them my problem, but the magic bit of plastic solved it. Someone would meet us at Heathrow, they said, and somebody did, with tickets to Malaga. Baggage could have been a problem too, but it came through all right on the carousel. Not Erny's notes of course – the grip they were in never left my hand.

The time was eight in the morning, so it was O.K. to phone Sabena. More than O.K. when I got through to her, though it got a bit sad when she heard I was off to Spain again.

'Don't you ever come home to your women?' she said.

'Just you wait,' I said.

'What the hell do you think I've been doing? By the time we see each other my hair will be down to my ankles.'

'It's nearly over,' I said. 'I promise.' Then I told her about Heidi.

'I hope she phones,' she said.

Then I took advantage of her good nature and asked a favour. She said she'd turn her father loose on it – her father had money invested everywhere. *Anything* to get me back home. Then there was love talk till our flight was called, and Dave and I were travelling in style again, and I had two and a half hours to worry about how stupid I'd look it I was wrong.

The favour I'd asked for was a fast car, and Sir Montague had managed that all right. Waiting for us was the most enormous Porsche I'd ever seen, the one that does a hundred and fifty plus, and Dave took one look at it and promptly forgot how miserable he was because he was missing Imogen. Once behind the wheel of that Porsche he wasn't missing anything. The only sad one was its owner, an elegant young Spaniard who kept stroking the Porsche's white bodywork as if it was his favourite dog that was about to be put down. Sir Montague must have had enormous clout to persuade him to hand it over, and even though Dave and I kept telling him we'd be careful he didn't believe it, and neither did we.

The drive to La Torre del Sur is something I don't remember all that clearly. In the first place I was jet-lagged and in the second place we were going too fast for me to see anything. Most of the time I kept looking at the bullfight tickets the Porsche's owner had given me, and hoping to God we wouldn't have to use them. Sombre they were, right next to the barrera. Any closer and we'd have been sitting next to the bull. I hoped to God we didn't have to go, and Dave drove on, rock steady. But that's Dave for you. The kind of feller who can postpone his fatigue until there's time to enjoy it properly.

We got there sooner than I'd have believed possible. There wasn't time to work out a plan, but then we didn't need a plan: just a straight 'yes' or 'no'. When we drove up to Mendez' front door there was a beige Seat parked outside, so maybe he was going to the bulls at Malaga, too. We knocked, and Mendez let us in himself. He said he'd given his maid time off to go to mass. He was surprised to see us, but not unduly worried, not until Dave hit him. But that one blow was all it took, and then I put the question and the answer was yes, so we had to go to the bullfight after all.

First we ripped out all the telephone wires – though I doubt if Mendez would have wanted to tell anybody what he'd done – but it was a habit, almost a reflex action, – and got back to Malaga even faster than we'd left it, so fast there was time for a snack at a café near the bullring. I thought I wasn't hungry, then found I was ravenous. Dave even ordered the steak sandwich, but I could never be that nonchalant. Then he lit a cigarette and we went off to the corrida.

If you like the bulls you won't need me to describe them for you – you'll know all about them already – and if you don't, nothing that I or Hemingway or anybody else can tell you will make you like them. Still, there it was: the brash and cheerful music, the rented leather cushions, the blokes selling beer. And out there in the middle the labourers watering and raking over the sand, making sure it was firm underfoot.

And then the business with the president and the horseman who looked as if his riding clothes had been designed by Velasquez, and the keys. And then the grand parade. . . .

There were three matadors as usual that day and they came on with a lot of swagger, wearing their suits of lights and their ceremonial capes. Behind them came their entourage: cape men and banderilleros, the blokes who plant the darts in the bulls' hides – some say to make them lively, and others to weaken them even more, and last of all the picadors, two big and mean-looking geezers with the flat hats and spears, the villains in every corrida. One of them rode a grey, a typical picador's horse, an elderly, clapped-out looking specimen that looked as if its last owner had been Don Quixote.

The other was a bay gelding, sixteen hands, white sock on the off-fore. It looked far too good for a picador's horse, and a lot of the crowd were saying so.

What Dave said was 'Jesus' and as I say he doesn't use language often. 'I'd never have believed it,' he went on. 'Even after Mendez – ' He broke off for a while, then he said, 'What are we going to do, Ron?'

But there he had me. I'd made my deductions and pushed my luck, and that was me finished. The rest was entirely up to him.

As it happened Dave had plenty of time to make up his mind. With the first two bulls, the grey did all the work, as the bulls tended to stick to that part of the ring. The grey was blindfolded so that he couldn't see the bull, but he knew it was there all right. The poor brute was sweating with terror. There was a lot of yelling and applause, I remember, so the killings must have been good, but I can't remember a thing about it. I wasn't even *seeing* it. All I could do was worry about which side of the ring the next bull would favour.

Our luck ran out with number three of the seis hermosos torros – seis, supplied by Señora Imogen Courtenay-Lithgoe. The number three matador – who is also the number six if he survives that long – is the star attraction, and so, if it can be arranged, are the number three and six bulls. Number three was well up to standard: black all over and with a wicked sweep of horns, he looked about the size of a rhinoceros and came on like a train. The cape men and even the matador were wary, and it looked as if he was going to do as little as possible before he brought the picador on to slow him up with the spear in the neck muscles, but the crowd were on to that one and whistled and yelled a warning. So the matador did a bit more, and twice the bull nearly got him, – he was moving like a projectile – and the crowd relented and the picador came on, riding a bay gelding, sixteen hands, white sock on the off-fore.

'Oh Jesus,' Dave said again.

Usually the matador, or one of the cape men, tries to lure the bull towards the picador, but this one didn't need any luring. Without any warning, as soon as horse and rider appeared, it put its head down and went roaring in. The picador wasn't ready for it: it's against all the rules. On the ranches where the bulls are reared they grow accustomed to horsemen. It's the man on foot who's the enemy. . . . That's the theory of it, anyway. But it didn't apply to this bull. This bull hated everybody – and so he charged without warning.

Dave reckoned the picador hadn't got his feet settled in the stirrups. Whether he had or not, when the charge began the horse reared up, swirling, its blindfold slipped free and the bull thundered past where the horse's belly had just been and smacked into the barrier, and at the same time the picador was flung out of the saddle like a stone from a sling. The bay sidled away, sticking close to the barrier, and the matadors and cape men clustered round the picador, who was unconscious. The bull looked around for a target, and decided on the horse, just as it reached the spot below which Dave and I were sitting, but this time it turned to face its target and pawed the ground for a change before it charged.

This time Dave said, 'Oh God,' then vaulted over the barrera and into the bay's saddle, like a man going through his front door into his home, as the bull went into its projectile act.

Dave coaxed the bay on to its hind legs and the bull swept by like before, missing the pair of them by inches, then Dave made the horse swerve away and took it at a canter to the other end of the arena. The crowd went mad.

That bull was a trier, I'll give him that. The matadors and cape men came up to him, but he scattered them like chaff and had another go at the horseman – it seemed like he hated horsemen – and this time Dave lost him by sheer speed, and the crowd loved it even more as the bull stood sulking in the evening sunlight. Then the barrera door behind the bull opened, and Dave thought it was time to go. He slapped the bay with his heels, and it charged the bull sideways, sailed over him in a flowing leap and disappeared through the barrier door that slammed shut just as the bull took off after them yet again.

By that time everybody in the crowd was on their feet yelling like maniacs, and I found I was too. Then I realised I couldn't just stand there and shout 'Encore' or whatever it was. Dave needed me. I hurried round to the door that said 'Private. No Entry', and went through. In a sort of stableyard behind the arena Dave stood stroking the horse's muzzle while he was being yelled at by assorted Spaniards who seemed to include the manager of the bull ring and a captain of police. I finally got through because I was yelling even louder than they were, and words like 'stolen thoroughbred' and 'Grand National' and 'La Doña Courtenay-Lithgoe' began to explode among them like bombs.

At last they began to listen as I finally got it through to them that Dave was not an espontaneo – which is the word they have for enthusiastic amateur bullfighters inspired by the heat of the moment – but the heroic saviour of Finn MacCool, a valuable animal which could very possibly win thousands and thousands of pounds, and the loss of which would annoy La Doña Courtenay-Lithgoe very much indeed. To make things easier for them I said Dave wasn't after publicity in Spain, and he looked a bit cheesed off by this until I told them he'd get quite enough publicity in the U.K. and Ireland, and then he started agreeing with me.

In the end the captain of police and I decided that I could leave at once, and Dave would follow as soon as he could charter a plane to fly the horse home, then I phoned the Porsche's owner and nobody was more surprised than he was when I returned his car intact. After that it was the first plane out, and a phone call to Cambridge from Heathrow, then a taxi to Knightsbridge and Sabena, and the best kind of oblivion of them all – in the arms of a woman who loves you.

17

When I was awake we either ate or made love – no matter what time it was. Jet lag makes your internal clock rev faster than a Porsche – and when I was asleep Sabena coped with the phone calls, especially the ones from the Cambridge scientist, who'd called to collect Erny's notes and things, as I'd warned her he would. After the last loving of all, which I couldn't say was the best only because they were all the best, she eased out of my arms but not too far.

'Are we going to spend the rest of our entire lives like this?' she said. 'Either sleeping or you-know-whatting? I mean I know there's a lot to be said for it, but don't you think you ought to go back to work once in a while? I mean you did tell daddy you didn't expect me to keep you.'

I yawned. I had never felt less like work in my life.

'You're absolutely right,' I said.

'That weird man from Cambridge keeps phoning,' she said.

'He isn't weird,' I said. 'He's Dr. Peabody. He's an F.R.S.'

'He's weird,' she said. 'Half the time he's gloating, and the other half he seems to be trying not to laugh.'

'He's gloating because I told him I could get him a piece of Staffordshire cheap,' I said.

'And can you?'

'Nobody can. But I can buy it dear and sell it to him cheap,' I said. 'After all, Imogen's paying.'

'Oh I do love you,' she said, and kissed me, then broke off to say, 'You'll have to do something about the press as well.'

'Such as what?'

'Such as telling them to stop phoning. Rosario's given me her notice four times.'

This would never do, so I phoned Michael Copland and

gave him the exclusive I'd promised him, which was as much of the story as I wanted anybody to know. This meant that Fleet Street would now concentrate its energies on Michael instead of me, and Rosario would stop giving notice. Then I phoned Dr. Peabody and found out why he was trying not to laugh, and then I told Sabena I had to go to Ireland, and waited for the explosion. It didn't come.

'Well of course you have,' she said. 'For God's sake hurry up and get it over with, then we can catch up on our sleeping and you-know-whatting.'

So I flew to Belfast and hung about till Dave came in on the flying horsebox he'd chartered from Malaga. By going to Belfast he'd dodged the reporters, particularly as he'd issued a statement in Spain saying he was flying to Cork to avoid publicity. So we hired a horsebox and a Volvo and towed Finn MacCool in style to Concannon House, and rehearsed what we were going to say on the way.

She was outside the door, waiting for him, and so was her father. Dave stopped in the driveway and opened up the horsebox and she stood there trying to make up her mind who she would kiss first. The only safe bet was it wouldn't be me. In the end she finished up patting both of them at once, then she insisted on our all having dinner before we, as she put it, 'got down to business'. Neither the general nor I seemed keen on the idea, and Dave wasn't keen on anything except some time alone with Imogen, but she got her way, mostly, I think, because she wanted to put off the hour of reckoning or moment of truth or whatever it was.

So once again Burke carried up my case and I bunged him another tenner because we both enjoyed it, and then we dined, which is to say, nobody ate much but we all drank a lot. Then we went back to the drawing room for brandy and port. The brandy was Grande Champagne '29, the port Dow's '45. For better or worse, this was obviously an occasion.

Dave kicked off by giving an account of The Rescue of Finn MacCool, and Imogen looked at him throughout the way a fourth-former looks at a pop-star, and then it was my turn. Because it was relevant I began with Theodore Pickel, leaving Heidi out of it. Heidi was my own particular – and very private – concern.

'Theo was why you had to go to Australia?' she said, and I nodded. 'Who put you on to him?'

'Information received,' I said. She let it go.

'But of course you knew already that he was mixed up in your affairs,' I continued.

'Did I?'

'Of course you did. He was the one who laid on the kidnapping of Finn MacCool and you knew it.'

'Suspected it, certainly. All that ridiculous Schmidt business'.

'It was why you did nothing even after we caught him trespassing at your place in Spain.'

'I didn't dare risk the horse.'

'As a matter of fact he did a bit more than that,' I said, and I told her about Teresa O'Byrne, and the attempt to kill us, the rifle ambush and the knife attack.

She looked incredulous.

'You're saying that Theo – Theodore Pickel did this?'

'Not personally,' I said. 'He hired the knife-men and the come-on girls. Probably he also hired the knife-men to kill Teresa. But the odds are he shot at us himself.'

She looked at Dave

'Is he a good shot?' Dave asked.

'Good – but not spectacular.'

'Very likely it was him then. He was paying off your agent, Mendez. Mendez drives a beige Seat. He probably borrowed it for his pop at us. Less conspicuous than his Merc.'

'You're talking about murder,' she said.

'He had a lot at stake,' I said. 'Or he thought he had. Six hundred million. So he murdered the ones who got in his way – the ones he couldn't shut up by other means. Like you.'

'Finn MacCool,' she said.

'Cross him and he'd destroy your horse. As your agent I crossed him – and he very nearly did destroy him.

'You said murders,' said the general. 'In the plural.'

'So I did,' I said. 'Erny Fluck's dead. Theodore killed him. So's his wife.' The bereaved fiancée didn't burst into tears.

'His wife,' she said. 'Why on earth did she marry him?'

I gave details.

'You should have gone to the police,' she said.

'After what I'd been up to – on your behalf? I'd have been arrested myself,' I said. That didn't worry her. 'Most likely you would, too.' That did.

'Anyway you got all his notes,' she said.

'I've done more than that – I've had them analysed,' I said.

This time she really lost her cool and started yelling. It was Dave who shut her up.

'On your behalf,' I said at last. 'Everything is on your behalf. Do you believe that?'

'Damn you. Get *on*,' she said. I took it that meant yes.

'He got at you through your father,' I said. 'He was raising a little money by claiming he had a fool proof computerised betting system. Isn't that right, Sir Robert?' I knew it was because Horry Lumley had sussed it out for me.

'Quite right,' the general said.

'Then your daughter found out.'

'I had to tell her,' the general said. 'His system wasn't as foolproof as it claimed to be. I lost rather a lot of money I didn't have.'

'So you were conned,' I told the general, then turned to his daughter. 'And so were you. You paid up.'

'What else could I do?' she said.

'Plan revenge. It's what you did do. . . . Another lot of private detectives, Mrs. Courtenay-Lithgoe?'

'Mr. Whatever-he-calls-himself – the one you met at Brown's Hotel – got them for me as well. I wanted to know where he was vulnerable,' she said. 'They told me he was a compulsive gambler. They also told me he was a genius.'

'So you bumped into him – quite literally – and he conned you all over again.'

'*What?*'

'All that stuff about low conductors – that was a con too.'

'But I had it checked. . . . So did Theo. We aren't fools, you know.'

I had my own opinion.

'He was a genius,' I said. 'You said so yourself. He was smarter than the boys you used. But I put an F.R.S. on him. It very nearly fooled him, too. But not quite.'

'Nor you either. Why didn't he fool you?'

'Because he offered me a slice of the six million he said he was after. A bribe of one and a half million quid – when I knew for a fact there was fifty grand in cash he could have used.' – I did indeed know it for a fact. It was in my bank that very minute. – 'Why offer real money if fools' gold will do?' I said. 'Believe me, Erny Fluck was a con man.'

'He cost me twenty thousand pounds,' she said.

'He cost Theodore Pickel rather more.'

'How much?'

'It's just an educated guess,' I said, 'but I think he cut you out by putting up all the development money.'

'Three hundred and fifty *thousand*?'

The news delighted her. Even the thought of it soothed away the pain of the lost twenty grand.

'So all's well that ends well,' she said.

'It isn't ended yet,' I said.

'What's left?'

'Our fees,' I said. 'Dave's and mine.'

When I told her what it would be I expected another row, but she agreed without a blink. She really did want it settled.

'There is just one more thing,' Sir Robert said.

'Leave it, daddy,' she said. 'Pour some more port or something.'

The general did indeed pour more port, but he went on talking. 'Teresa O'Byrne was murdered, you say?' I nodded. 'Why?'

'She and Gleason accepted a bribe from Pickel,' I said. But they kept something back – an old briefcase of Fluck's. She took it to Spain, then demanded extra cash for its contents – which made her a nuisance. Pickel had her killed, instead.'

'I accept that,' he said. 'I can't understand it but I accept it – But why did Pickel bribe her in the first place?'

'Leave it, daddy,' his daughter said, but he ignored her. 'Why, Mr. Hogget?'

'She was Finbar Gleason's girl. They were going to get married. The bribes were a nest egg.'

'Bribes to do what?'

'To get things for Pickel. Papers, notes, stuff like that. He was supposed to be sharing with your daughter but he wanted it all for himself. – And then of course, there was Finn MacCool.'

It was up to him to stop there, but I knew he wouldn't and I was right. 'She stole the horse'?

'Not her,' I said. 'Her boyfriend. Finbar Gleason. But you know that.'

'How could he?' Imogen said, but he made a quick, admonitory gesture with his hand, the kind he must have often used to a much younger Imogen, and she was silent.

'Yes,' he said. 'I knew that. Or rather I found out. That's why I shot him.'

He got up and went to a briefcase that lay on a sofa-table.

'By the way,' he said. 'I finished the Monte Cassino book yesterday. You'd better take charge of the manuscript, my dear.'

His hands went to the briefcase and I looked at Dave and coughed. Dave knew what he had to do, but his heart wasn't in it. All the same he got to his feet, and his right hand made a short, abrupt movement, came out holding the gun he'd hidden against such an emergency as this. He looked about as embarrassed as I've ever seen him look.

'If you don't mind, sir,' he said.

'You won't need that,' said Sir Robert and his voice was testy. 'I give you my word. Put it away.'

'Yes sir,' said Dave, and did so.

The general took a stack of typescript from the briefcase and put it on the table, then reached into the case again, came out with the Colt 38.

'You knew I had this?' he asked me.

'I thought at first it was Fluck's,' I said. 'It was hidden in the flat at Leinster Terrace.'

'Not well enough, it seems,' Sir Robert said. 'But I congratulate you on your work. Really excellent. . . . The Colt belonged to an American lieutenant I met in Rome during the war. I won it from him playing poker, then I kept it hidden here and there until it finished up in my daughter's flat in Leinster Terrace. I thought it might come in useful.' He savoured the word. 'Useful. . . . Dear God! . . . Then I found out what Finbar was up to and went to Leinster Terrace to collect it.' He turned to his daughter. 'I'd had duplicates made of your keys. You should have allowed for that. . . . I'd rather not have seen quite so much evidence of your involve-

196

ment with Fluck.'

'Daddy *please*,' said Imogen. 'There's no need for this.'

'There's every need,' he said. 'Finbar Gleason and I were both violent men. He was holding a shotgun when I – accused him. But even so – Anyway I shot him. At one point I thought I might even get away with it.'

'When the body disappeared?' I said.

'Your work, I take it?' the general said.

'No, mine,' said Dave. 'Ron had nothing to do with it. But it seemed to me we had enough trouble.'

'No doubt you meant well,' said Sir Robert, 'but then they murdered his girl, too. I didn't think of that. But I should have done.'

He came back, still holding the Colt, and finished his port, then kissed his daughter. 'Goodbye my dear,' he said. 'You're a wonderful woman.'

Already she was crying. He went to the door and turned to me.

'You're an able man, Hogget,' he said. 'Very able. You'd have done well in the 'I' Corps – ' Then he left the room.

Dave said, 'Shall I go after him?'

Still weeping, she said, 'It's too late. It was too late from the moment he shot Finbar.'

We sat for maybe five minutes before the shot came. I got up.

'I'll go,' I said, but Dave was already up and moving.

'Better leave it to me,' he said. 'It's my department.'

When he'd gone Imogen said, 'You're good friends, aren't you?'

'I think so,' I said. What she meant was 'I suppose that means I've got to be nice to you', but this was no time to take umbrage. She'd been pushed about as far as she could go.

'Look,' I said, 'you've had enough. Just tell us what you want us to do.'

'I want you to go, and David to stay,' she said. 'No offence meant, Mr. Hogget.'

'And none taken,' I said. 'But it may take a bit of time to arrange.'

It took all night, the Irish police being as nosey as all the others, but I was on the first plane out next morning. Sir

197

Robert, I'd been asked to say, had been showing signs of depression lately, for no reason. So I'd said it. Just as I'd said that I could think of no reason for him to kill himself. . . .

I got back to Knightsbridge at eleven. Sabena was having a lie-in, so I crawled in beside her.

'Nothing changes, does it?' she said. 'Not a bloody thing,' and opened her arms to me.

Later she said, 'How's Imogen?' and I told her.

'Poor Imogen,' she said.

'Poor Poppy,' I said, but she kissed me into silence.

'Not your fault,' she said, and then: 'Daddy called. He wants you to get a divorce PDQ so I can entice you into marriage. He says you're the only hope I've got. He also says that the only thing wrong with you is you want to marry me. It bothers him.'

'It doesn't bother me,' I said. 'If that was the only thing wrong with me I'd be perfect.'

*

A few days went by and I got over my jet lag, and the newspapers and the telly found other things to interest them than Dave Baxter, boy matador. That meant we had peace and quiet as well, and then came the day of the telephone calls. The first was Sir Montague asking if I'd like to have a seat on a board in an electronics surveillance firm he was buying. All very flattering, but I do my own surveillance, and it isn't by electronics. I said no, but we stayed chums. . . . Next was my sister. She'd been referred to Sabena's number by my answering service, and she was a bit shy about it, but not too shy. She wanted to meet my intended, and I wanted it too, so we made a date. I wondered what would happen when Sabena had to meet my father, because the old git would take bloody good care they would meet, but bridges can be crossed only when you come to them. . . . Next was Lady Tarleton, but she came in person. Clean, sweet smelling, no plastic bags. She'd even had her hair done.

'Try not to faint,' she said. 'A social worker found me in some doss house or other, then took me to a hospital where they scrubbed me raw. It seems Bobby's dead and left me whatever odds and ends he had, and Imogen's advanced me a few bob provided I stopped dossing. I was getting too old for it anyway.'

My guess was that Bobby hadn't left change of a quid, so it was a nice gesture on Imogen's part. Or Dave's. . . .

'I knew you'd bring us trouble,' she said. 'Not with malice. I don't mean that. Nothing deliberate. It was just – it would have been better if our paths hadn't crossed. – As if we had any choice in the matter.' Then she kissed Sabena, and then me. 'But *your* paths *had* to cross,' she said. 'Good things must happen, too.' Then she left without even a drink, and we went out to dinner. When we came back we found Heidi had left a message on the tape. From California. With a bit of luck, or maybe a lot, she'd be calling on Sabena next year.

Then we went to bed and the last call came. It was Dave. Sabena didn't make it any easier for me to talk to him. Her hands were all over me. 'What now?' she asked, when I hung up.

'Imogen's a bit better,' I said. 'He'll be coming back to London soon.'

'He's leaving her?'

'Just coming up for air,' I said. 'We fellers have to, sometimes.'

'You just try it,' she said. 'Anything else?'

'He asked about the wedding,' I said. 'Who's going to be best man.'

'Who *is* going to be best man?'

'Well Dave of course,' I said. 'Dave's best man at all my weddings.'

'I hope you told him this is positively his last appearance?' she said, and burst out laughing. 'What a swine you are. Anything else?'

'Just one thing,' I said. 'Imogen's got a new nickname for him.'

'What is it?'

'Beelzebub.'

199